SIDEWINDERS:
BLEEDING
TEXAS

SIDEWINDERS:
BLEEDING
TEXAS

William W. Johnstone
with J. A. Johnstone

PINNACLE BOOKS
Kensington Publishing Corp.
www.kensingtonbooks.com

PINNACLE BOOKS are published by

Kensington Publishing Corp.
119 West 40th Street
New York, NY 10018

PUBLISHER'S NOTE
Following the death of William W. Johnstone, the Johnstone family is working with a carefully selected writer to organize and complete Mr. Johnstone's outlines and many unfinished manuscripts to create additional novels in all of his series like The Last Gunfighter, Mountain Man, and Eagles, among others. This novel was inspired by Mr. Johnstone's superb storytelling.

All Kensington titles, imprints, and distributed lines are available at special quantity discounts for bulk purchases for sales promotions, premiums, fund-raising, educational, or institutional use. Special book excerpts or customized printings can also be created to fit specific needs. For details, write or phone the office of the Kensington special sales manager: Kensington Publishing Corp., 119 West 40th Street, New York, NY 10018, attn: Special Sales Department; phone 1-800-221-2647.

ISBN-13: 978-0-7860-3354-6
ISBN-10: 0-7860-3354-1

First printing: August 2014

10 9 8 7 6 5 4 3 2 1

Printed in the United States of America

First electronic edition: August 2014

ISBN-13: 978-0-7860-3355-3
ISBN-10: 0-7860-3355-X

CHAPTER 1

Bo Creel knew he was in trouble.

One of the worst dangers he had faced in many, many years of wandering from one end of the frontier to the other, getting into all kinds of scrapes from south of the Rio Grande to north of the Canadian border, now stood right in front of him, ready to wreak havoc in his life.

"Well, what do you think?" Lauralee Parker asked as she turned around slowly with her arms held out at her sides to let Bo get a good look at the stylish blue dress she wore.

"I think it's, uh, really nice," Bo said. "Pretty. No, make that beautiful."

That description applied to Lauralee just as much as it did to the dress.

She was a lovely woman, slender in the right places and curved in the others, with a mass of curly blond hair that tumbled around her shoulders and eyes as blue as a high mountain lake. A tiny beauty mark near her mouth just added to her allure.

Any man would be proud to have Lauralee showing off a new dress to him and asking his opinion.

The problem was, Bo was old enough to be her father, and he couldn't quite bring himself to forget that, no matter how much he might want to at times.

"You think it'll be all right to wear to the social, don't you?" she asked.

"I think it'll be just fine," Bo assured her. "Every cowboy within fifty miles of Bear Creek will be there, and they're all going to want to dance with you."

"Well, that's just too bad," Lauralee said, "because I'm only interested in dancing with one man."

The gleam in her eyes as she looked at him made it perfectly clear whom she was talking about.

Bo cleared his throat and looked down at the floor. He needed to get out of here. It was bad enough he'd allowed Lauralee to lure him up here to her bedroom on the second floor of the Southern Belle Saloon.

The blatant invitation in her gaze just made it worse.

Bo turned his black hat over in his hands and said, "You wouldn't want to, uh, disappoint all those cow-pokes. Some of them will have ridden all that way just to dance with you."

"Maybe, but I don't care. There are other ladies in Bear Creek who'll be glad to dance with them."

But none as pretty as Lauralee, Bo thought.

Not even close.

"I reckon I'd better head on back downstairs," he said. "Scratch is supposed to meet me as soon as he finishes picking up those supplies—"

"Scratch isn't going anywhere," Lauralee said as she came closer to Bo. Close enough to lay the fingertips of one elegant hand on his coat sleeve.

Bo wondered if women knew just how much of an effect it had when they touched a fella's arm like that.

He figured they did.

Lauralee went on, "If you're not downstairs when he gets here, he'll wait for you. You know as well as I do that passing some time in a saloon isn't going to be a hardship for Scratch."

That was true enough, Bo had to admit. His long-time trail partner Scratch Morton was a man who enjoyed a drink and the convivial companionship that came with it.

"So why don't you stop worrying?" Lauralee continued as she moved her hand up his arm to his shoulder.

She was close enough now that he could smell the lilac water she wore, and mixed with her own clean, natural scent, it made for a heady brew.

An insistent voice in the back of his head clamored for him to ignore the difference in their ages and go ahead and kiss her. That was what she wanted, after all.

Hell, he wanted it, too, he thought. He'd always been the more conservative, sober-sided member of the duo as he and Scratch roamed the West, a fact reflected in his parson-like garb, but that didn't mean he lacked a man's natural urges. It would be easy enough to slide a hand under that mass of blond curls, rest it on the back of Lauralee's neck, and lean down to taste those full, rosy lips . . .

"You son of a bitch! Go for your gun, or I'll drill you where you stand!"

At the sound of the angry voice coming through the partially open door from downstairs, Lauralee's hand jerked away from Bo's shoulder. He stood up straighter and muttered, "Uh-oh. Scratch must be here."

As a matter of fact, for once the trouble had nothing to do with Scratch Morton. He was still inside the general store, where he had parked the wagon he'd driven in from the Star C, the ranch owned by Bo's father, John Creel.

Scratch had volunteered to pick up the supplies on the list written by Idabelle Fisher, John Creel's cook and housekeeper. Bo had decided to ride along and keep him company.

That came as no surprise. Bo and Scratch had gone most places together, ever since they'd left Texas and gone on the drift more than three decades earlier.

Their friendship had been forged in the bloody fires of war, specifically the revolution that had freed Texas from the brutal grip of the Mexican dictator, General Antonio López de Santa Anna. They were little more than boys when they met during the Runaway Scrape and then fought side by side in the decisive Battle of San Jacinto.

Despite that, they might have grown up and gone their separate ways, although remaining friends, if not for the tragic illness that had claimed the lives of Bo's wife and children several years later.

Unable to stay where there were so many painful reminders of what might have been, Bo had taken off for the tall and uncut . . . and Scratch, with no real ties of his own to hold him down, had ridden along with him.

From time to time they had come back to Texas to visit friends and family, and this particular trip had stretched out for several months now, the longest sojourn they had spent in their hometown of Bear Creek for quite a while.

Usually by now one or both of them would have been getting restless, eager to indulge the fiddlefooted impulses that years of drifting had ingrained in them.

The fact that they hadn't was starting to concern Scratch a mite.

Had age finally caught up to them?

Were they really ready to settle down at last?

Lord, it was a worrisome possibility, he'd found himself thinking on a number of occasions.

The store clerk was sure taking his time putting Idabelle's order together. Scratch tried to control the impatience he felt building up inside him.

Bo had gone over to the Southern Belle Saloon to say hello to its owner and proprietor, Lauralee Parker, whom they had known ever since she was a little girl running around in her father's saloon. Scratch was beginning to think he should've gone with him.

Lauralee wasn't a little girl anymore, that was for sure. She was as strikingly pretty a young woman as you'd find anywhere. Surprisingly enough, she still had that crush on Bo that had started when she was just a kid.

It was like she had made up her mind when she was young that Bo Creel was the *hombre* for her, and nothing was going to change it.

Scratch found the whole thing sort of amusing, but he also felt a little sorry for his old friend. Bo was a decent, honorable man—more so than Scratch, to tell the truth—and he didn't think it was right for Lauralee to be saddled with an old codger like him. She kept throwing temptation at him, though.

"Oh my goodness. Sir? Excuse me, but could you help me?"

The woman's voice made Scratch look around. He saw her standing beside one of the shelves along the wall. She wore a dark green dress, and a jaunty hat of the same shade perched on an upswept mass of brown hair. She wasn't young, Scratch noted, but she certainly wasn't old and decrepit, either.

In fact, she was a mighty handsome woman.

"If you could give me a hand . . ." she said.

"Why, sure," Scratch said. He took off his cream-colored Stetson, revealing a full head of silvery hair. His teeth—his own teeth, not store-bought—gleamed whitely in his tanned, weathered face as he grinned at her. He held the hat over the breast of his fringed buckskin jacket and went on, "I'm Scratch Morton, ma'am, and I'm mighty pleased to make your acquaintance."

"I'm Mrs. Emmaline Ashley," she said. "Would you mind getting that down for me?"

She pointed at an enameled blue teakettle that appeared to be just out of her reach on the shelf. Scratch took it down and handed it to her, saying, "There you go, ma'am."

She had introduced herself as a missus, which changed things somewhat. When he was young, it hadn't been completely unheard of for him to get romantically entangled with a gal who had a husband, but these days he tended to steer well clear of such complications. He was too blasted old for drama.

But just because she was married didn't mean he couldn't be pleasant and polite to her. He continued to smile at her as she looked the teakettle over and nodded in satisfaction.

"Thank you, Mr. Morton," she said. "I hated to bother you."

"Oh, it was no bother," Scratch assured her.

"I would have asked my husband to reach it for me if he'd been here, the way he always did."

"He somewhere else today?" Scratch asked.

He didn't realize the finality of her statement until after the words were out of his mouth.

"I'm afraid Mr. Ashley has passed on."

"Oh! I'm mighty sorry—"

"It's all right," she told him. "It's been several years now."

"Well, I'm sorry for your loss, anyway."

"Are you married, Mr. Morton?"

"No, ma'am. I never got hitched."

"Not the marrying kind, eh?"

"It's not that I got anything against the, ah, state of matrimony," Scratch hastened to explain. "It just never has worked out that way for me, I guess you'd say."

"I understand," she said as she nodded. "Sometimes fate takes its own sweet time about these things."

"I reckon."

Emmaline Ashley held up the teakettle and said, "If I buy this, I'll want to try it out. Would you care to stop by my house for tea later this afternoon, Mr. Morton? I live only a short distance from here on Caldwell Street."

That was an intriguing invitation, Scratch thought, even though he'd never been what anybody would describe as a tea-drinking sort. Emmaline was a widow, so that meant things could go in one of two different directions.

She might be looking for a new husband to replace the one who'd passed away.

Or she might be more interested in the sort of pleasures a man could give her, without insisting on an actual marriage and all the complications that brought with it.

There was only one way to find out.

He had just opened his mouth to tell Emmaline that he would be happy to have tea with her, when the dad-blasted clerk called from behind the counter, "I've got that order all ready to load up now, Scratch."

That was a reminder he had to take the supplies back out to the Creel ranch, but he could always ride into town again after he finished that chore. And Emmaline had specifically said "later this afternoon" when she invited him for tea.

So this wasn't an obstacle that couldn't be overcome, Scratch told himself. Once again he was about to accept Emmaline's invitation when there was another interruption.

The double doors at the front of the general store were wide open, and the Southern Belle was right across the street. Scratch heard loud, angry voices coming from the saloon's bat-winged entrance, followed by a crash. Sounded like some sort of ruckus had broken out over there.

And Bo had gone to the Southern Belle, Scratch reminded himself.

He clapped his hat on his head, told Emmaline, "Wait just a minute," and rushed toward the doors.

Behind him, she exclaimed, "Well, I never!"

Regretfully, Scratch thought that was probably going to turn out to be true.

CHAPTER 2

By the time Bo reached the landing and looked down into the saloon's main room, he could feel the tension that filled the air in the place, along with the familiar smells of sawdust and beer and tobacco smoke.

A big *hombre* with rust-colored hair under his battered, thumbed-back hat stood next to the bar, stiff and obviously angry. His fingers curled as his hand hovered over the butt of the gun holstered on his hip. He was ready to hook and draw.

Bo recognized the redhead, as well as the four cowboys who stood behind him, ready to back his play. He was Pete Hendry, the foreman of the Star C ranch. The other punchers rode for Bo's father, too.

Facing them were half a dozen men, also in dusty range clothes. Some of them looked vaguely familiar to Bo, but he couldn't recall where he had seen them before.

One of those men, a lean gent with a pencil-thin mustache, said with a faintly arrogant smile quirking his lips, "Rein in that temper of yours, Hendry. We didn't come into town looking for trouble, just a friendly drink."

"You won't find anything friendly here," Hendry snapped. "There are other saloons in Bear Creek. Go have your drink there."

"The Southern Belle is the best. We have just as much right to be here as you and those Star C boys do."

"We won't have you and your Rafter F scum stinkin' up the place," Hendry responded.

Lauralee had followed Bo to the landing. He sensed her beside him and asked quietly, "Who's the fella with the mustache?"

"His name's Trace Holland," she said. "He rides for Ned Fontaine."

Bo nodded slowly. He had already figured out that much from what Hendry had just said.

Ned Fontaine was from back east somewhere. He had come into this part of Texas a while back and bought the old Winthorp ranch from Jim Winthorp's widow. Renaming the spread the Rafter F, Fontaine and his two sons, Nick and Danny, had set out to make it the biggest, most successful ranch in these parts.

That had put them on a collision course with John Creel and the Star C, and the friction between the two outfits had grown steadily worse ever since. A number of brawls had taken place here in Bear Creek when riders from the Creel and Fontaine ranches found themselves in town at the same time, and it looked like Pete Hendry was trying to start another one.

This confrontation had the potential to be worse, though, Bo sensed. As he looked at Trace Holland, he read something in the man's stance and in his eyes that set Holland apart from the other cowboys.

Bo had seen enough gunhawks to know that was what he was looking at now.

Pete Hendry was plenty tough, as well as being a good hand with both cows and men, but he was no gunfighter. There was a good chance that if he drew, Holland would kill him.

"Get back in your room," Bo told Lauralee. She didn't need to be out here if lead started flying.

She didn't take kindly to being given orders, though. She said, "This is my place, in case you've forgotten."

Then she stepped past Bo before he could stop her and started down the stairs.

"If you men are bent on killing each other, do it outside," she called down to the two groups of cowboys. "Even with sawdust on the floor, it's hard to mop up a bunch of blood."

Her intervention eased the tension some, but not by much. Hendry still looked like he was ready to slap leather as he said, "I don't mean to cause a ruckus, Miss Lauralee—"

"Then don't," she interrupted him.

Trace Holland reached up to touch the brim of his hat as he said, "Beg your pardon, Miss Parker. The boys and I just came in for a cold beer on a hot afternoon. We didn't know it was going to cause a problem."

Bo noticed that Holland used his left hand to make

that respectful gesture. The Rafter F man's right hand stayed within easy reach of his gun butt, another indication that he was accustomed to trouble.

Holland was lying, too. Bo knew that he and the men with him must have seen the Star C brand on some of the horses tied at the hitch rail outside the saloon. They had been aware before they ever came in here that they were going to encounter some of John Creel's crew.

Bo had come down the stairs after Lauralee. When he reached the bottom, he said, "Back off, Pete."

Hendry glanced at him.

"No offense, Bo, but I don't work for you. I ride for your pa and his brand. And I'm not gonna put up with any insults to John Creel or the Star C."

Holland said, "How did we insult anybody? We just came in for a drink."

Hendry's face darkened even more with anger as he said, "I heard you sittin' over there at that table and laughin'. I heard you say you weren't gonna have to put up with greasy sack outfits like the Star C for much longer."

Holland's shoulders rose and fell in an eloquent shrug.

"A man expressing an honest opinion to his friends isn't the same thing as an insult," he said. "From what I hear, the Star C's lost quite a bit of stock. That sort of thing can't go on forever without hurting a ranch."

"Damned right it can't. You wouldn't happen to know anything about all that stock we've lost, would you, Holland?"

Hendry had crossed a line with that question, and Bo knew it. So did everybody else in the room. The Star C foreman had practically accused Holland of being a rustler. That was a slap in the face that couldn't be ignored.

Holland stiffened, as if someone had just inserted a ramrod into his back. He opened his mouth to say something, but before he could, Bo stepped between him and Hendry.

"That's enough," Bo said. "Pete, take the boys and get out of here."

"I told you, you don't give me orders," Hendry snapped. "Besides, we were here first. If anybody leaves, it ought to be that bunch."

"I'm asking you," Bo said quietly. "There are innocent people in here. It's no place for a gunfight."

Hendry glared at him for a moment, then blew out an exasperated breath and muttered a curse.

"I'm doin' this as a favor to you, because I respect your old man so much," he said. "But don't try to make a habit of bossin' us around, Bo." He looked at the other Star C cowboys and jerked his head toward the batwings. "Come on. I need some fresh air anyway."

The last was said with a meaningful glower at Holland and the other Rafter F men.

With obvious reluctance, Hendry started for the door and the other men followed him. Unfortunately, their route took them fairly close to the Rafter F punchers, who moved aside a little to give them room. Bo didn't care for the two bunches being that close together, but he sort of held his breath and hoped that it would be all right.

Another few seconds would tell the story . . .

One of the Fontaine men laughed and said with a sneer, "I knew they'd turn tail and run, first chance they got."

That was the wrong thing to say, and Bo knew that as soon as he heard it.

With a furious roar, Pete Hendry whirled around and charged at the man, lowering his head like a maddened bull. He tackled the Rafter F puncher around the waist and drove him backward off his feet.

Both men came crashing down on a table where several townies had been playing poker earlier, before the trouble started. The game had been suspended while the players watched the confrontation nervously.

Now they scurried out of their chairs as Hendry and the other man landed on the table, scattering cards and money. The table legs broke under the impact with sharp cracks, and the table collapsed. Hendry and his opponent were dumped on the floor amidst the debris.

That didn't put a stop to the fight. Hendry started slugging at the Rafter F man, who had been stunned enough that he had to take a couple of blows before he regained his senses enough to fight back.

Then he began throwing punches of his own. One of them tagged Hendry on the jaw and knocked him to the side.

Bo didn't see what happened in the initial battle after that because the men from the Star C and the Rafter F had come together like two waves crashing against each other, blocking his view of Hendry and the other man. Fists flew as the brawl was on.

"Stop it, you idiots!" Lauralee shouted at them, but no one paid any attention to her.

A chair thrown by one of the combatants sailed through the air toward him. Bo grabbed her around her trim waist and swung her out of the way. The chair went over the bar and smashed into an array of whiskey bottles on the back shelf.

Bo still had his arms around her from the rescue, and Lauralee didn't seem to be in any hurry to squirm free. Instead she looked up at him, said, "Oh!" and seemed to get even closer.

Bo leaned over, taking her with him. But it was only to get them out of the way of a man who was stumbling backward after being walloped in the face. The fella hit the bar, bounced off of it, and fell facedown on the floor.

"Run and get Jonas Haltom," Bo told Lauralee, referring to Bear Creek's marshal. He pushed her toward the entrance. "I'll try to talk some sense into their heads."

"That's not going to do any good, and you know it," she said. "There's a shotgun behind the bar—"

Another out-of-control battler reeled against her. His hand went out as he tried to catch his balance.

Instead he caught the neckline of Lauralee's new dress, which ripped right down the front, ruining the dress and exposing some of her feminine charms in a thin shift.

Lauralee hadn't grown up in a saloon for nothing.

She cussed like a muleskinner, clubbed both hands together, and swung them into the man's face in a resounding blow that sent him flying away from her. Then she looked down at the wreckage of her dress, uttered another curse, and grabbed a broken chair leg to use as a club.

Bo knew she was ready to wade right into the melee, and while he admired her feistiness, he knew she might get hurt.

He grabbed her around the waist again, this time from behind, and lifted her off her feet as he swung her around toward the bar. She kept yelling as he lifted her across the hardwood and shoved her into the arms of a startled, wide-eyed bartender.

"Hang on to her, Roscoe!" Bo told the man. "Get down behind the bar!"

Since Lauralee hadn't gone to fetch the marshal, Bo would just have to try to keep her safe here in the saloon. Jonas Haltom would probably show up pretty soon anyway. Some of the townspeople who had scattered out of the Southern Belle when the fight started ought to report it to him.

In the meantime, Bo would try to settle things down. He held out both hands and started across the saloon, raising his voice to say, "Stop it! Stop this, you men!"

One of Fontaine's men lunged at him from the side, yelled, "Go to hell!" and punched him in the jaw.

Bo Creel was a peaceable man. Always had been.

But he had his limits, and he had reached them.

As the cowboy swung at him again, Bo blocked the

punch with his left forearm and buried his right fist in the man's belly. The Fontaine rider started to double over. Bo crossed with his left and caught him on the chin. The punch drove the man's head to the side and made his eyes roll up in their sockets.

Somebody else landed on Bo's back and made him stumble forward as he hammered at Bo's head. Bo reached back, caught hold of the man's hair, and hauled forward on it. The *hombre* screeched in pain and turned loose, tumbling to the floor.

He swung a leg and caught Bo in the back of the knees with it. Bo went down and landed in the sawdust. His opponent leaped at him, but Bo got his right leg up in time to plant his foot in the man's belly. He caught hold of the man's shirt, straightened his leg, and levered the fella up and over. The Fontaine man yelled as he flew through the air, a yell that was cut short as he slammed down on a table.

That one broke, too.

Bo rolled over, got his hands and knees under him, and came halfway up from the floor.

He stopped short because he found himself looking at Trace Holland a few feet away. The gunman's face twisted in a snarl, and his Colt snaked free of its holster. As the gun started up, Bo knew he couldn't draw fast enough from this awkward position to beat Holland's shot.

He was about to die here, kneeling in sawdust, blood, and spilled beer and whiskey.

CHAPTER 3

The first thing Scratch saw when he reached the saloon and slapped the batwings aside was Bo about to get shot.

Scratch reacted instantly. He didn't know who the *hombre* was who was about to ventilate his old friend, but that didn't matter.

One of Scratch's long-barreled Remington revolvers came out of its holster with blinding speed. The roar as it went off blended with the other man's shot, both reports coming so close together they sounded like one.

Scratch's shot was just a fraction of a second quicker. That shaved heartbeat of time was enough to save Bo's life. Scratch's bullet clipped the gunman's arm and knocked his aim off so that the slug from his gun smacked harmlessly into the bar. It all happened too quickly for the eye to follow.

The man's gun hand spasmed open. The Colt slipped from his fingers and thudded to the floor.

Bo scooped it up, came to his feet, and backed away as he covered the man who'd tried to kill him. He glanced at Scratch, and as their eyes met, he gave the tiniest of nods.

That was thanks and acknowledgment enough for two *hombres* who had backed each other's play for more than thirty years.

The double roar of gunfire had thrown the brakes on the ruckus. With a tendril of smoke still curling from the barrel of his Remington, Scratch looked around at the wreckage, the sprawled bodies of brawlers who'd been knocked unconscious, and the men still on their feet who had their fists cocked for punches unthrown. Some of them he recognized as men who rode for the Star C.

That meant the fellas on the other side of the fight were probably Fontaine men.

Since he and Bo had come back to Bear Creek, Scratch had been staying with his sister Dorothy and her husband, Eben, on their farm a few miles outside of town. But he had visited the Star C often enough and spent enough time with Bo to be well aware of the ongoing trouble between the two ranches. The feud was a range war in the making, and clashes like this one just aggravated the situation.

"You all right, Bo?" Scratch asked.

"Yeah, I guess," Bo replied. He was disheveled and his clothes were stained and dirty from rolling around on the floor, but he didn't seem to be wounded.

Lauralee Parker popped up from behind the bar. Her

dress was torn and hanging open rather immodestly, Scratch couldn't help but notice. She should have been trying to hold it closed, but her hands were too busy waving a shotgun around.

"Get out of my way, Bo!" she yelled. "We'll see how fast a little buckshot clears the room."

Bo reached over the bar, took hold of the shotgun's twin barrels, and pointed them toward the ceiling.

"Stop that," he said. "You set off that Greener in here and you'll puncture some innocent hides, likely including my own."

Scratch drew his left-hand Remington and waved both guns at the men who'd been battling.

"You fellas break it up," he ordered. "You boys from the Star C move over there."

He pointed to one side with a gun barrel.

Pete Hendry stepped forward. His jaw was thrust out in stubborn defiance.

"I already told Bo we don't work for him, and that goes double for you, Morton!"

The batwings creaked a little as they opened behind Scratch. A new voice demanded, "How about me, Hendry? You gonna mouth off at me?"

Marshal Jonas Haltom strode past Scratch. Like Lauralee, the lawman had a shotgun in his hands. He was a big, barrel-chested man with a gruff demeanor and not much tolerance for troublemaking cowboys.

Haltom poked the shotgun at the group of brawlers

and went on, "You heard the man. Break it up. I want Star C on one side of the room and Rafter F on the other."

The man Scratch had shot said, "I need a doctor, Marshal." He clutched his wounded arm with his other hand. Blood had run down the arm to drip off his fingers.

"I can see that, Holland. I also see your holster's empty. Drew on somebody, did you?"

Sullenly, the man didn't answer. His eyes shot daggers of hate toward Bo and Scratch, though.

Since Haltom had things under control, Scratch holstered both of his ivory-handled guns and moved over to Bo's side. Bo had let go of Lauralee's shotgun. She placed the weapon on the bar and angrily pulled together the ruined dress so that it covered her more decently.

Once the two groups of cowboys had separated from each other, Haltom drifted closer to the bar and said, "I suppose this was the usual hell-raising between those bunches, Lauralee?"

"That's right, Marshal," she said.

"Which side started it this time?" Haltom asked, then shook his head and stopped her before she could answer. "I don't suppose it matters, does it? There's no fight unless both sides go at it."

"From what I saw, they were about equally to blame," Bo said.

Pete Hendry glowered at him and said, "I'll remember you said that, Bo. I'll be sure and tell your pa and your brothers how you stuck up for the Fontaines, too!"

"I'm not sticking up for either side, and you know it, Pete."

"Tell me you'd'a done something different if some varmints started bad-mouthin' the brand you rode for!"

Bo didn't say anything, and for good reason, Scratch knew. During their wanderings, they had found themselves in more than one ruckus just like this one, fighting on behalf of the spread where they'd been working at the moment.

"I suppose the important question," Haltom said, "is whether or not you want them locked up, Lauralee."

She still looked furious, but she relented a little as she said, "I don't care so much about that. I want them to pay for the damages, though." She looked around at the broken tables and chairs and the shattered whiskey bottles. "It's not going to be cheap."

"You figure it up, and they can pass the hat," Haltom told her.

"I can't very well do any ciphering while I'm holding my clothes on!"

"You can go change," Haltom said with a shrug. "We'll be glad to wait." He glared at the two groups of cowboys. "Isn't that right?"

"What about this arm of mine?" Holland asked.

"You haven't bled to death yet. I think you can wait for a few more minutes. Now, all of you sit down."

They sat, both sides looking like they wanted to murder the other and Marshal Haltom, in no particular order.

Haltom sat down at one of the undamaged tables and

rested the shotgun on it, with the double barrels aimed roughly halfway between the two factions. He motioned Bo and Scratch into a couple of other chairs at the table.

"When I heard that all hell was breaking loose in the Southern Belle, somehow I figured I'd find the two of you right in the middle of it," he said.

"To be fair, Marshal, we didn't have anything to do with starting this one," Bo said. "In fact, I did my best to break it up before it really got started."

"And I only pulled that old smokepole of mine because Bo was about to get ventilated," Scratch added. "Who is that *hombre* I nicked, anyway?"

"His name's Trace Holland, according to Lauralee," Bo replied. "Works for the Fontaines now."

"That's right," Haltom confirmed. "He's got a reputation as a gunslick. Was mixed up in some shootings in San Antonio and Sweetwater. If he threw down on you, Creel, you're probably lucky to be alive."

"I know I am," Bo said. "Scratch deserves the credit for that."

Haltom grunted and said, "Pretty fancy shooting, creasing him on the arm like that."

"Naw, I hurried my shot," Scratch said with a grin. "I figured on blowin' his lights out."

"Good thing you didn't."

Scratch nodded solemnly and said, "I know. If I had, I'd've had to ride all the way back into town for the inquest. Never did care much for court proceedin's. They give me the fantods."

Haltom just snorted disgustedly and said to the bartender, "Roscoe, bring some beers over here."

Lauralee came back downstairs a few minutes later, dressed in a gray gown that wasn't nearly as fancy as the ruined blue one had been. She had a piece of paper in her hand that she gave to the marshal as she told him, "That ought to cover the damages."

Haltom nodded and stood up, cradling the shotgun under his left arm.

"You've got two hundred dollars to come up with, boys," he told the crews from the Star C and Rafter F. "Dig in those pockets and do it now."

Once the money had been collected—with a considerable amount of glaring and muttered cussing along the way—Haltom turned the cash over to Lauralee and then told the cowboys, "Get your horses and get out of town. I don't want to see any of you in Bear Creek for the next three or four days."

"That ain't right, Marshal," Pete Hendry protested. "We've got a right to come to town."

"And by all rights, I ought to haul the whole lot of you in front of Judge Buchanan and ask him to sentence you to a week in jail for disturbing the peace," Haltom snapped. "You still want to argue about it?"

Hendry didn't. He and all the others shuffled out, Star C going first, then Rafter F after the hoofbeats of the Creel riders had faded.

"Lauralee, I'm sure sorry about what happened," Bo said. "I'll ask my pa to have a talk with Pete and the other boys. They have to understand that this trouble can't go on."

"You know as well as I do that Holland and those other men from the Rafter F got just what they were looking for when they came in here," Lauralee said. "They wanted to start a brawl."

"She's right," Haltom put in. "Your pa has a tough, salty crew, no doubt about that, Bo, but they're basically honest cowboys. A lot of Fontaine's men—like that fella Holland—well, they've heard the owl hooting on many a dark trail, I'd say."

"It's only a matter of time until somebody gets killed," Lauralee said.

Scratch nodded toward his old friend and said, "That came mighty near to bein' Bo just now." His eyes narrowed. "You think maybe that was the reason behind all of it? The fight might've been just an excuse for Bo to get shot durin' the commotion."

"I don't think that was it," Bo said. "It looked more to me like Holland's temper just got away from him."

"Maybe so," Haltom said, "but it might not be a bad idea for the two of you to grow an extra pair of eyes in the back of your heads." Haltom got heavily to his feet. "Never can tell when somebody might try to shoot you from that direction."

CHAPTER 4

While Jim Winthorp was still alive but already battling the consumption that eventually killed him, he had allowed the ranch house where he and his wife lived to fall into disrepair.

After Jim passed on and his widow sold the spread to Ned Fontaine, the new owner made numerous repairs and improvements, even added a couple of rooms to the sprawling house. Fontaine had poured money into the newly renamed Rafter F, there was no doubt about that.

Some of that money had gone to hire men like Trace Holland, who was still muttering curses as he rode up to the ranch house later that day. The men with him veered off toward the corrals to put up their horses.

Holland swung down awkwardly from the saddle, grimacing from the pain in his arm. The bloody sleeve was cut away, and a bandage had been wrapped around the wound. Holland had stopped at Doc Perkins's office in Bear Creek and had the old medico patch up the wound.

Perkins had wanted to put the arm in a sling, but Holland had turned thumbs-down on that idea. The idea of not having the arm loose where he could use it made him uncomfortable.

"You won't be making any fast draws for a while," the doc had warned him dourly after stitching up the gash. "You'll need to let that wound heal for at least a couple of weeks before you use the arm very much."

"I'll try, Doc," Holland had said, "but I don't make any guarantees."

Indeed, if he had the chance right now to bushwhack that silver-haired son of a bitch Scratch Morton, he might take it. Sooner or later he would settle the score with Morton, and with Bo Creel, too.

The pair of big yellow curs who lived on the ranch had set up a racket when the men rode in, of course, and that had alerted the people in the house to their arrival. Holland hadn't reached the bottom of the porch steps when Ned Fontaine came out the front door and looked at him with narrowed eyes.

With his neat brush of a mustache and erect carriage, Fontaine looked like a former military man, even though he wasn't. His keen gray eyes didn't miss much, including the bandage on Holland's arm. His voice was cool and clipped as he asked, "What happened to you, Holland?"

"We had a run-in with some of the Star C bunch in town."

Holland thought he saw a flash of pleasure in Fontaine's eyes. The old man really hated the Creels. He regarded them as standing in the way of his plans to make the Rafter F the largest ranch in this part of Texas.

But then Fontaine was all business again as he said, "Were any of our men killed or seriously injured?"

Holland shook his head.

"No, I got the worst of it, I guess," he said as he lifted his injured arm slightly and winced again.

"Who did that?"

"Scratch Morton. Bo Creel's friend."

"I know who Morton is," Fontaine snapped. "Tell me what happened."

Holland did. That didn't take long. While he was telling the story, Nick Fontaine stepped out onto the porch, as well.

The elder of Ned Fontaine's two sons was a medium-sized, muscular man with glossy black hair like a raven's wing. He bossed most of the actual work that was carried out on the ranch.

He also wore a Colt in a fancy black leather holster that matched his vest. Rumor had it that Nick Fontaine was pretty fast and had killed several men in gunfights. Holland didn't know if that was true or not, but like any man who considered himself good with a gun, he had an itching to find out.

Maybe someday. For the time being, he and Nick rode for the same brand.

"You're lucky Jonas Haltom didn't throw you in jail,"

Fontaine said when Holland finished his story. "On the other hand, I'm glad you stood up to that Creel scum."

"The boys and I had to kick in quite a bit of money to help pay for the damages . . ."

Fontaine waved that away and said, "I'll pay you back. You were standing up for Rafter F, after all. See to it, Nick."

"Sure, Pa," Nick said. "Come on inside, Trace. I'll take care of that right now."

"And I'll continue with my ride," Fontaine said. He turned and called through the screen door, "Are you ready, Samantha?"

The screen opened a moment later as Samantha Fontaine emerged from the house. Ned Fontaine's only daughter, she was between the ages of her older brother, Nick, and her brother Danny, the baby of the family. She was also mistress of this house, since her mother, Ned Fontaine's wife, had passed away several years before the family came to Texas.

Holland was careful not to let his gaze linger on Samantha, but that was difficult sometimes. Now was one of those times, because she wore a man's shirt that emphasized the curves of her bosom, and on her, the denim trousers she wore looked nothing like they would have on a cowpuncher.

Samantha's long, thick hair wasn't quite as dark as her brother Nick's. Right now it was piled on top of her head and tucked under a flat-crowned brown hat held on by a taut chin strap. She was lovely enough to take a man's breath away.

Holland knew perfectly well that a gunhawk like him had no chance with a woman like Samantha Fontaine. Soiled doves in dusty trail towns were more his type.

But that didn't mean he couldn't enjoy looking at her. He just had to be discreet about it, that's all.

"Are you ready, darling?" her father asked her.

"Of course," Samantha said.

As they came down the steps, she gave Holland a nod and a faint smile. Some women in her position wouldn't have even acknowledged his existence, he thought. Samantha always did, even though she was cool and reserved about it. That was one more reason Holland admired her.

As Fontaine and Samantha walked toward the barn to get their horses, Holland couldn't help but cast a glance over his shoulder after them.

Nick noticed and said, "Stop leering at my sister's behind and get in here."

"Sorry, boss," Holland said as he climbed the step.

Nick gestured at the bandage on Holland's arm.

"How bad is it?" he asked.

"I won't be able to use a gun for a while."

Nick grunted. Holland had a pretty good idea what he was thinking.

If you can't use a gun, what good are you to me?

After a second, Nick jerked his head toward the door and said, "Come on."

The two men went in the house. Holland used his left hand to take his hat off. He asked, "Where's your brother?"

"I don't know. It's not important."

Danny Fontaine had a reputation as a hothead and a troublemaker. He was reckless and impulsive and his old man had had to bail him out of numerous scrapes.

Holland knew that Danny wasn't really the member of the Fontaine family you had to watch out for, though. That honor fell to the oldest brother. Nick was a quiet sort, most of the time, but that old saying about still waters running deep applied to him.

Holland knew that for a fact.

Nick led him into a room that served as study, library, and office for the ranch. He went behind the desk, opened a drawer, and took out a soft leather pouch that clinked when he set it on top of the desk.

"How much did you have to pay for damages in the saloon?"

Holland thought about inflating the amount, but he discarded the idea quickly. It was possible Nick might find out the truth, and Holland didn't want to risk his employer catching him in a lie.

"A hundred bucks," he said.

Nick cocked a slightly shaggy eyebrow.

"Where were you when the fight broke out?"

"The Southern Belle Saloon."

"Lauralee Parker wasn't hurt, was she?" Nick asked sharply.

Holland figured Nick was a little sweet on Lauralee. That was bound to come to nothing. She wouldn't give him the time of day, no matter how big his pa's ranch was.

"She's fine," Holland said. He didn't figure it would

serve any purpose to tell Nick about how Lauralee's dress had gotten torn.

"Good." Nick took ten gold eagles from the pouch and stacked them on the desk. "Divvy that up among the men however you need to." He hesitated, then said, "The fact that Morton creased you . . . I take it that means Bo Creel is still alive."

"Yeah," Holland said. "I was about to take the first good shot at him I could get when Morton came in and winged me."

"Maybe you shouldn't have waited for a good shot. Maybe you should have taken the first chance you got."

Holland would allow Nick Fontaine to push him only so far. His voice hardened a little as he said, "I was the one who was there. I had to use my judgment. You said for me to ride into town with the boys, stir up trouble with the Star C bunch if we could find any of them, and try to see to it that Bo Creel died during the ruckus if he happened to be there. Well, all that was working out fine right up until the end. Hell, I even had Creel cut out from the herd with Morton nowhere around . . . or so I thought." The gunman's narrow shoulders rose and fell. "It was bad luck, boss, that's all. Sometimes that happens."

"I know." Nick waved a hand at the coins. "Take the money and go on about your business."

Holland used his left hand to pick up the stack of eagles.

"I guess the whole kill-Bo-Creel-if-I-get-the-chance deal is off, huh?"

"Postponed, that's all," Nick said. "I'll figure out something else. The important thing is that one way or another, Bo Creel is a threat to my plans as long as he stays around here. If he and Morton don't pull up stakes and leave pretty soon . . . well, he'll have to die, that's all there is to it."

That was all right with Trace Holland. After what had happened today, he had his own reasons for wanting both of those damned drifters dead.

CHAPTER 5

When Bo and Scratch got back to the Star C with the wagonload of supplies, Bo's father and brothers were waiting for them. Bo could tell from the look on John Creel's craggy, deeply tanned face that his father was upset.

It wasn't hard to figure out what had gotten the old man's dander up. The Star C cowboys who'd been involved in the brawl in the Southern Belle had had plenty of time to get back to the ranch ahead of Bo and Scratch.

John Creel stood on the front porch of the ranch house with his hands tucked in the hip pockets of his jeans. He had spent eight decades on this earth, but you couldn't tell it by looking at him. His back was still straight. His eyes were keen and piercing under bushy white brows. He might not be able to spend all day in the saddle anymore, but he could still outwork a lot of younger men.

"Hear tell you had some trouble in town," he said before Bo had even dismounted.

Bo went ahead and swung down from the saddle. He handed the reins to one of his father's punchers who came up to take care of the horse.

"That's right," Bo said. "Some of Fontaine's men started a ruckus in the Southern Belle."

Riley, the second oldest brother in the family next to Bo, said, "Trace Holland tried to kill you."

"The thought crossed his mind," Bo admitted.

"This has gone far enough," Riley said. "We need to gather up all the men and guns on the place and head for the Rafter F. It's long past time we cleaned out that rat's nest."

"There was a time I'd have agreed with you, boy," John said. "Try something like that now and we'd have the Rangers down on us."

"To hell with the Rangers! They haven't done anything to stop the Fontaines from rustling our cattle, have they?"

"We haven't been able to prove Fontaine is behind that," Bo pointed out in response to his brother's angry question.

Riley just snorted disgustedly. He was a tall, lanky man with graying brown hair. Like all the Creels, he appeared to be somewhat younger than he really was. Riley was a grandfather, but you wouldn't know it to look at him.

The next brother in line was Cooper, a handsome, fair-haired man with the same muscular, broad-shouldered build as John and Bo. He was a bit of a dandy and waxed the tips of his mustache so that they curled up, but he was as hard a worker and as good a hand as any of the brothers.

Hank was the baby of the family. Stocky, with a close-cropped brown beard, he was far from a natural cowboy. He'd never been comfortable on horseback and couldn't dab a loop over a steer to save his life, but he could make sense of all the ranch's bookkeeping and was a true craftsman when it came to making and repairing saddles and tack. He turned out some fancy, hand-tooled holsters and gunbelts, as well.

"I sent a letter to Ranger headquarters in Austin asking for some help around here," Hank said now. "Haven't heard back from them, though. There aren't that many of them, Riley. I imagine they're spread pretty thin."

Cooper said, "I agree we don't need to take the law into our own hands . . . yet. There may come a time when we have to, though."

"Might be," Bo allowed. "But for now the trouble's over, and no real harm was done except to some tables and chairs and bottles of whiskey in Lauralee's saloon. She got paid back for that."

"Out of our boys' pockets," Riley said.

"And out of the pockets of the Rafter F men, too."

Riley shook his head and turned away.

Bo knew that his next-youngest brother felt some re-sentment toward him. Riley had never liked the fact that Bo had gone on the drift with Scratch instead of staying in the area to help out his family. Bo could understand that . . . but it was way too late to go back and change the past, even if such a thing had been possible.

Idabelle Fisher came out onto the porch. The tiny, gray-haired woman said, "I see you're back with those supplies I need for my kitchen."

"Yes, ma'am," Scratch said with a grin from the driver's seat of the wagon. He started to climb down. "I'll bring 'em in for you."

"No need. Cooper and Hank don't have any arms or legs broken, do you, boys?"

"No, ma'am," the brothers said in unison. They came down the steps to unload the boxes of supplies and carry them into the house.

As Hank moved past Bo, he asked quietly, "Can I talk to you in the office in a few minutes, once we get done with this chore?"

"Sure," Bo said. He wondered what his little brother wanted. From the look in Hank's eyes, he was troubled about something.

Scratch reclaimed his horse from the corral and after saddling the animal told Bo, "Reckon I'll head on back across the creek to my sister's place."

Bo nodded and said, "All right, just be careful. I don't think Trace Holland is in any shape right now to try to bushwhack you, but some of those other Fontaine men might."

"I'll keep my eyes open," Scratch promised. "I'm sorta in the habit of doin' that anyway."

Bo knew what his old friend meant. Over the years

they had spent entirely too much time with people trying to kill them.

When Scratch was gone, Bo went in the house and ambled into the little office where Hank kept up with all the ranch's paperwork. The desk was littered with documents.

Bo didn't look at them. He was smart enough to make sense of them but lacked the inclination. Over the years, the numbers that had interested him the most had been on playing cards. He was a good enough gambler to support himself and Scratch between the jobs they took.

Hank came in a few minutes later. He sat down behind the desk while Bo took the room's other ladder-back chair, turned it around, and straddled it.

"What's on your mind, Hank?" Bo asked.

"Money," Hank said. "Or the lack of same."

"How do you mean?"

"The Star C is cash-poor right now. There were some bad times a few years back. For a long time it seemed like we had either not enough rain or too much, depending on whether or not a hurricane came in."

Bo nodded in understanding. The Gulf of Mexico was only about fifty miles south, and sometimes the gigantic storms that roamed the Gulf at certain times of year dumped enormous amounts of rain inland. The resulting floods always killed some of the cattle, and other animals died from bogging down in the mud left behind. Droughts, of course, were common in Texas, with graze drying up and diminishing the herds, as well.

"The upshot is that Pa needed money to keep us

afloat," Hank went on. "He took out a loan at the bank in town."

"All right," Bo said. "That's nothing unusual for folks who make their living off the land in one way or another. Whether it's crops or cattle, sometimes a fella needs a little help."

"I know. But that note's going to come due in a couple of months."

Bo frowned and said, "Pa can't pay it off?"

"Not anywhere near all of it. In the past, Mr. Ambrose at the bank has always let Pa pay a little on the note and then extended the rest of it."

"You have any reason to think he won't do that again?"

Hank leaned back in his chair and said slowly, "No, not exactly. But the last time I was in town I ran into Ambrose, and he asked me how things were going. When I told him we were still having trouble with losing stock, he looked a mite worried. I think he might decide to cut his losses, Bo, and call in the whole amount. If he does that . . ."

"Pa won't be able to scrape up enough money," Bo finished, his voice holding a grim note now.

"I don't see how he could."

Bo said, "It'd kill Pa to lose this ranch."

"I know. It's been preying on my mind. That's why I thought I'd say something to you about it."

"No offense, Hank, but why me? You know I'd pitch in everything I have to help the old man, but it just doesn't amount to much. Scratch and I never had more than just enough to get by."

"I know, but . . . I guess it's just because you're the oldest, Bo. I was hoping you might have some idea how to handle this."

Bo shook his head and said, "I'm afraid I don't. Not right offhand, anyway. Let me think on it."

"You know, it might help if you went and talked to Gilbert Ambrose at the bank."

Bo looked pretty skeptical about that idea.

"Everybody in town was ready to string me up when we first got back," he reminded his brother. "I don't think I carry a lot of weight in Bear Creek anymore."

"Yeah, but that was all just a misunderstanding. And you and Scratch help keep the bank from being robbed. Mr. Ambrose sort of owes you."

"I guess I could talk to him," Bo said. "I don't know how much good it'll do, though."

"I'd appreciate you just trying."

"All right. I'll ride back into town tomorrow. In the meantime, do you think we ought to talk about this with Riley and Cooper?"

Hank winced at that suggestion.

"Riley would find some way to blame it all on me," he said. "And Cooper would just say that he doesn't have a head for ciphering and tell me to figure it out. As for Pa . . ."

"No, we won't tell him about it," Bo agreed without hesitation. "He already gets worked up about plenty of things, mainly that feud of his with Ned Fontaine." Bo paused. "Do you think Fontaine is behind the rustling, Hank?"

"I don't know. I couldn't track an elephant in a snowstorm. But we've had a steady trickle of losses, and it's made the ranch's financial position that much more precarious." Hank shrugged. "It sounds like something Fontaine would do, to be honest."

Bo thought so, too, and if there was any truth to the charge, one thing was certain.

Sooner or later, the showdown with the Rafter F that Riley wanted so bad would come about.

And Bo was afraid that when it did, the Texas prairie would be covered with blood.

CHAPTER 6

Ned Fontaine and his daughter rode to the top of a hill fringed with oaks and gazed across the rolling landscape in front of them. Samantha glanced across at her father and saw the look in his eyes. It was one of pride and ambition and drive. Ned Fontaine wanted to take that land with its scattered herds and transform it into the richest rangeland in all of Texas.

That was an admirable goal, Samantha thought . . . as far as it went.

This was the highest point for miles, with the best view. From up here a green line of trees was visible as it twisted across the countryside.

Those trees marked the course of Bear Creek. On the other side of the stream lay the Star C, belonging to John Creel.

If her father's ambition had stopped at the creek, Samantha would have thought it was a fine thing.

Unfortunately, Ned Fontaine had set his sights on all

that other range, and Samantha feared that ultimately his covetousness would lead to disaster.

"I wish your mother could see this, Samantha," Fontaine said without taking his eyes off the verdant sweep of countryside in front of him. "I think it would have reminded her of her home back in Ireland."

"I'm sure it would have, Pa."

"It's the devil's own shame that she didn't live to come to Texas with us."

"It is," Samantha agreed, but she knew he wasn't really paying much attention to her. He was lost in his own thoughts and memories, casting his mind back over the years.

He did that more and more these days, and that worried her. It was easy to get lost in the past, especially as a person got older. The present held less and less appeal. Reality could never quite match up to an idealized past.

People had to live in the present, though.

And some even looked to the future.

Fontaine heaved a sigh and said, "I guess we'd better be getting on back now."

"Why don't you go ahead?" Samantha suggested. "I think I might like to ride a little more."

That broke Fontaine out of his musing. He frowned at her and said, "You know I don't like you riding by yourself."

She patted the smooth wooden stock of the carbine that rested in a sheath strapped to her saddle.

"I'll be fine, Pa," she told him. "I don't expect to run

into any trouble, and if I do, I can handle it. You know I'm a good shot."

"Yes, you've got a cool head and a good eye," Fontaine admitted. "For a girl."

Samantha laughed.

"If you're trying to get an argument out of me, it's not going to work," she said.

"No, no, just telling you that sometimes you're too confident for your own good. But I'm not a stupid man. I know by now that I'd be wasting my time telling you what to do. Only . . . stay clear of the creek, all right?"

"Don't worry, I'll stay on our range," Samantha promised.

"All right." Fontaine lifted his reins. "Don't be too long."

He turned his horse and rode back toward the ranch headquarters. For a few moments, Samantha watched him go, then she eased her mount into a walk that carried her down the hill's slope toward the creek.

She hadn't exactly lied to him. He had asked her to stay away from the stream that marked the boundary between the two ranches, but she had promised only not to cross it.

Still, that rationalization was enough to make her feel a little guilty about what she was doing. She was well aware of her father's flaws but loved him anyway, and she didn't like deceiving him.

She didn't really have any choice in the matter, though.

As she neared the creek, she reined her horse to a

halt, dismounted, and went ahead on foot, leading the animal. She kept a watchful eye on the trees along the bank, alert for any sign of movement. Not seeing any, she led her mount into a particularly thick grove of trees and tied the reins to a slender sapling.

Then she waited, listening intently.

Time seemed to drag by more slowly than it really was. About a quarter of an hour had passed before Samantha heard anything other than the usual noises of small animals in the brush and the lowing of cattle in the distance.

Then she heard something large splashing through the waters of the creek.

Quietly, she drew the carbine from its sheath. There was already a round in the chamber, so she didn't have to work the weapon's lever and make any racket.

With as much stealth as she could muster, she moved through the trees and undergrowth until she could crouch behind a bush and look out at the stream. A man on horseback was crossing it about fifty yards upstream from Samantha's position. The trees along the banks cast dappled shade on the water, and that made it difficult to distinguish details about the man's face.

Samantha lifted the carbine to her shoulder and nestled her cheek against the stock. She peered over the barrel as she settled the sights on the rider, ready to blow him out of the saddle if she needed to.

* * *

Lee Creel pointed his horse toward a spot where it would be easy to climb out onto the eastern bank of Bear Creek. He appeared to ride easy in the saddle, but actually he was alert.

He was well aware that he was venturing into the realm of the enemy, and there was no way of knowing for sure what was waiting for him over there.

A slender young man in his early twenties, Lee had a shock of sandy hair under his sweat-stained, pushed-back hat. Like most men who rode this range, he carried a handgun, and while he was no shootist, he considered himself fairly good with a Colt. His father Cooper had taught him how to shoot at an early age.

It was a skill a man needed to have if he was going to survive on the frontier.

Something made Lee's nerves crawl as he rode out of the creek and up onto the bank. The skin on the back of his neck prickled. He recognized the symptoms.

He was being watched.

The important question was who was doing the watching.

He reined in, and as he did he heard something rustling in the brush. A figure carrying a carbine suddenly stepped out from behind the trees about ten yards away from him. Lee's heart jumped.

Then he hurried to meet Samantha Fontaine, and as his arms went around her, she tilted her head back and parted her lips slightly to receive his kiss.

Lord, she tasted sweet! Lee had never experienced anything like it.

Not since the last time he'd kissed her, anyway.

Samantha lowered the carbine's butt to the ground and let go of the barrel. The weapon toppled over. Luckily, it didn't go off. She lifted her arms and twined them around Lee's neck. Their bodies strained to draw even closer together.

Lee's heart was pounding fit to bust by the time he finally lifted his lips from Samantha's. His voice was a little breathless as he said, "When you stepped out from the brush with that carbine, I thought for a second I was done for. Figured you'd changed your mind about bein' in love with a no-count Creel."

"You thought I was going to shoot you?"

"Well, not really. But the idea crossed my mind for half a second."

"I could never do that," she said. "I was just being careful. I didn't show myself until I made sure it was you. I didn't want somebody else to come along and catch me out here waiting for you."

"So you planned on murderin' 'em if they did?"

She balled a fist and struck it lightly against his chest.

"You just stop your foolishness, Lee Creel. You know good and well there are outlaws and rustlers around these parts."

Yeah, and some of them were named Fontaine, he thought, but he kept that to himself. It wouldn't do any good to point out to her that he considered some of her relatives no-good.

All of her relatives, as a matter of fact. He believed there was only one good Fontaine around here—and she was in his arms at the moment.

Six months ago, the idea that he'd be hugging and kissing any Fontaine would have struck him as plumb *loco*. If anybody had made such a claim, he would have considered those fightin' words.

But that was before a rattlesnake had spooked Samantha's horse and sent it stampeding across Bear Creek onto the Creel range one day, with her in the saddle hanging on for dear life and trying unsuccessfully to bring the animal back under control.

Lee, who had been riding near the creek himself, had seen the runaway horse and gone after it without even stopping to think about who the rider might be. Samantha had been riding with her hair tucked under her hat that day, as was her habit, so Lee had figured the rider was some hapless cowpoke . . . until he'd gotten close enough to see that the figure on horseback wasn't shaped like any cowpoke he'd ever run across.

He'd grabbed the reins, of course, and brought the runaway to a halt. He could tell how nervous the young woman was by the way she kept casting glances back across the creek, as if she knew she was somewhere she shouldn't be. Lee had recognized her from seeing her with her father and brothers in town, so he'd said, "It's all right, Miss Fontaine. I won't tell anybody you're over here on this side of the creek if you don't."

"You're not going to shoot me for trespassing?"

"No . . . but I might do this."

Acting on impulse while they were both still in their saddles, he had leaned over and stolen a kiss. Samantha had gasped, slapped his face, and then laughed.

He had kissed her again before that day was over.

That was how it started, and they had been meeting out here along the creek several times a week ever since. They were careful because they both knew that her father and his grandfather would be furious if they found out. Lee's pa and his uncles wouldn't be too happy about it, either . . . except maybe for Bo. He struck Lee as pretty easygoing, and he hadn't been around when the Fontaines came to this part of the country and started causing trouble with their pushy ways, either.

Now Samantha said, "There was another fight in town today."

"I heard about it," Lee said. "That gunnie Trace Holland got shot."

"He's not—" Samantha stopped short. Lee supposed that out of family loyalty, she'd been about to claim Holland wasn't a gunman. But she knew as well as anybody else that was the truth.

Instead she said, "I wish everybody could just settle things and get along. If this turns into a range war, I . . . I don't know what's going to happen."

Lee knew. If a range war broke out, people would die. There was no getting around it. Creels and Fontaines both, more than likely.

Crazy ideas had started to percolate in his head lately.

He wished that both families could get together at a wedding.

Instead it was a lot more likely that funerals would continue to keep them apart.

He put that grim thought out of his head and cupped a hand under Samantha's chin.

"You got your dress picked out for the social?" he asked her.

That put a smile on her face. She said, "Yes, I do. It's really pretty."

"Good, because I intend to dance with the prettiest girl there."

"You mean Lauralee Parker?"

"Not hardly," he said with a grin. "I'm lookin' at the prettiest girl."

"I don't know, Lee," she said as she grew solemn. "It seems like if we were to dance together, it would be just asking for trouble."

"Town's supposed to be neutral ground, especially at something like a social."

"I know, but I'm just not sure how my brothers would react."

"Well, we'll wait and see how things go," he told her in an attempt to ease her mind.

But make no mistake about it, he thought, he *was* going to dance with Samantha Fontaine.

And anybody who didn't like it could go to hell— especially if his name was Fontaine, too!

CHAPTER 7

Riders on horseback, couples in buggies, families in wagons, all began to converge on the town of Bear Creek one evening several days later. Twice a year the town held a social that featured food, music, and dancing, and people from miles around, from Hallettsville all the way down to Victoria, attended.

The festivities were held at the Bear Creek School. The students' desks and benches were carried out to clear the floor for dancing. A group of fiddlers and guitar players set up shop where the teacher normally stood. To one side of the room was a table with a big punch bowl on it. Marshal Jonas Haltom and his deputies would take turns guarding the punch all evening to make sure no cowboy with a flask of Who-hit-John tried to spike it.

Another table held an assortment of pies and cakes baked by the ladies of the town. They would be auctioned off to raise money for the school. The mayor would probably make a speech, too.

But the dancing was what drew most people—other than the Baptists, of course. And even some of them figured the good Lord would forgive them if they backslid a little, as long as it was only twice a year.

Bo wore his usual dark trousers and long dark coat over a white shirt and string tie. Scratch had traded his buckskins for a tan suit, and he sported a string tie, as well.

"Don't we look like a couple of Kansas City dudes?" Scratch asked as they stood along one of the walls, sipping too-sweet red punch from tin cups.

"Speak for yourself," Bo said. "This is what I wear most of the time."

"Yeah, but you got your hair slicked down more than usual. I don't reckon you really needed to do that to impress Lauralee."

"I don't care whether I impress Lauralee."

"Well, I think she's tryin' to impress you. And everybody else in the place, to boot."

It was true that Lauralee Parker was attracting a lot of attention. That blue dress had been so skillfully repaired that it was impossible to tell it had ever been torn. Her blond curls were piled up in an elaborate arrangement, and her face, with a minimum of paint, glowed with a natural beauty.

The dancing hadn't started yet, so at the moment Lauralee stood talking to some of the women from the town. Not for the first time, Bo admired her ability to win folks over. In a lot of frontier settlements, a woman who ran a saloon would be a pariah. People would think she was a prostitute or worse.

That wasn't the case with Lauralee. She was accepted as a member of the community. Part of that was because she had grown up here and people had known her ever since she was a little girl. She had become such a fine adult, too, that it was impossible not to like her. If anybody in Bear Creek had trouble, Lauralee was the first one there to offer her help. She nursed people through illnesses, she fed people who might have otherwise gone hungry, she helped make sure that widows and orphans were taken care of, and she was a friend to anybody who needed one.

She wasn't perfect—Bo knew she had a temper and was stubborn as a mule—but she was about as close as anybody he had ever known.

Bo noticed Gilbert Ambrose across the room. He had promised Hank that he would talk to the banker, but he hadn't gotten around to doing that yet. This evening might not be the best time to have a business conversation, but on the other hand, Bo believed in seizing opportunities whenever and wherever they arose.

He drank the last of the punch from his cup, handed it to Scratch, and said, "Hang on to this for me, will you?"

"Where are you going?" the silver-haired Texan asked.

"I'll be back," Bo said, which wasn't really an answer.

Ambrose was talking to Judge Clarence Buchanan

and Dr. Kenneth Perkins. They were all roughly of the same age, a little older than Bo, and had been here in Bear Creek ever since the town was founded during the early days of the Republic of Texas.

"Hello, Bo," the thick-set, florid-faced judge said when Bo walked up to the little group. Doc Perkins and Ambrose muttered greetings, as well.

"Evening, fellas," Bo said. "Looking forward to the dancing?"

Buchanan made a face and said, "These bad feet of mine won't let me traipse around the floor anymore. But I'll enjoy watching the young people."

"I'm not much of a dancer, either," the spare, dour physician said.

"My wife will expect me to haul her around the floor a few times," Ambrose said with a chuckle. "You're the lucky one, Creel. You'll get to dance with Miss Parker."

Bo smiled and said, "That's more good fortune than I deserve, all right. Say, I was wondering if I could talk to you for a minute, Mr. Ambrose."

"We are talking," the banker replied. His eyes narrowed. "Or did you mean something more serious?"

"I won't take up much of your time," Bo promised.

"I didn't come here tonight to talk business," Ambrose said, frowning. "But I suppose we could have a word. If, as you say, it won't take much time."

"No, sir."

Ambrose nodded to Buchanan and Perkins and said, "If you'll excuse us, gentlemen . . ."

The judge waved a pudgy hand to signify that it was fine.

Bo and Ambrose drew off to one side, near the coat closet, and Ambrose said, "Now, what's all this about?"

"Hank mentioned that my pa had to take out a mortgage on the ranch a while back."

"I can't really discuss your father's business dealings," Ambrose said stiffly. "If you want to know anything about that, you should ask him."

Bo reined in the impatience he felt at the banker's attitude and said, "Hank handles the ranch's business these days, Mr. Ambrose, you know that, and he's the one who told me."

"That makes no difference. The ranch is in your father's name, so any discussion of the particulars of his arrangements must go through him."

"All right," Bo said, stifling a sigh of exasperation. "It doesn't matter. What I really wanted to do was let you know that you don't have to worry about the Star C. The spread is going to be just fine."

Ambrose's frown deepened as he said, "There are rumors that your family has lost a great deal of stock to rustlers."

"Every ranch has trouble with rustlers from time to time."

"But the Star C has lost more than its share, I'm told."

"I don't know that that's true," Bo said. "And even if it is, we'll get to the bottom of it."

Ambrose just grunted skeptically. He asked, "Is there anything else I can do for you, Bo?"

"I reckon not," Bo said. He had made an effort to keep his promise to Hank. He had talked to Ambrose like he'd said he would.

But as far as he could tell, he hadn't accomplished a blasted thing, and he knew it.

The Star C was still at the mercy of this soft-handed banker.

"One thing you have to remember," Ambrose said. "John Creel and I have known each other for a long, long time. We've done business for almost that long. I'm not anxious to do anything to hurt someone like that."

"I'm glad to hear you say that, Mr. Ambrose."

"Of course, there comes a time . . . No, never mind. Just remember that friendship only goes so far, too." Ambrose looked across the room as the musicians began tuning up their fiddles. "Now, if you'll excuse me, I'm sure my wife will have her heart set on dancing the first dance."

Bo nodded and said, "Sure. Thanks, Mr. Ambrose."

He watched glumly as the banker started toward a gaggle of middle-aged ladies on the other side of the room, among them Mrs. Ambrose.

Hank sidled up to him and said quietly, "I saw you talking to Mr. Ambrose, Bo. Did you do any good?"

"I don't know. I don't much think so. He makes noises like he's not eager to call in the note, but you're right, he's worried about all the stock the ranch is losing."

"We've got to put a stop to that somehow."

"You've tried, haven't you?"

"Of course we have," Hank said. "Riley and Cooper have spent days trying to track those wideloopers. But they never steal very many head at one time. It'd be easier to trail them if they made off with a big bunch. But it's not that hard to cover up the tracks of a little jag of cattle. There's no telling where they get off to."

"Bleeding the ranch to death a little bit at a time," Bo muttered.

"That's exactly what they're doing. And that's why I think there's a good chance Fontaine is behind it. The objective isn't to make a lot of money off stolen stock. It's to hurt the Star C until the damage is finally too much to recover from."

What Hank said made a lot of sense, Bo thought. But knowing there was a good chance a theory was true and proving it were two different things.

He looked around the crowded room and commented, "I figured the Fontaines would be here tonight."

"So did I," Hank said. "Maybe they don't like the rule that nobody can bring any guns in here."

That was a firm rule, too, and had been for as far back as Bo could remember. No guns at the town socials. Currently, Marshal Haltom enforced it, and he did a stringent job of it.

Usually it wasn't too difficult. Nobody in his right mind wanted any gunplay in a place where so many innocent folks were around, including a lot of women and children.

Scratch drifted up and extended a freshly filled cup of punch to Bo.

"You fellas look mighty solemn," he said. "You're supposed to forget about your troubles tonight."

"I'll give it a try," Bo said.

They walked over to a corner of the room that had been taken over by the Creel family. John sat there on one of the benches that had been pushed up against the wall, with Idabelle Fisher beside him. All the Creel sons, daughters-in-law, grandchildren, and great-grandchildren made for a formidable brood. Everybody seemed to be having a good time drinking punch and visiting with friends who came by.

Everybody except for his nephew Lee, Bo noted. Cooper's oldest boy stood rather tensely as he watched the door with an expectant look on his face. He was waiting for somebody, Bo thought. A girl, more than likely. Lee was in his early twenties, the prime age for a young *hombre* to start looking for a wife.

Two things happened then, at just about the same time. The fiddlers and guitars broke into a sprightly tune, resulting in a flood of dancers into the center of the room.

And several newcomers came through the schoolhouse's open doors, causing an angry stirring among the Creels.

The Fontaines had arrived.

CHAPTER 8

Ned Fontaine entered first, as befitted the patriarch of the clan. He stepped in, paused and looked around the big room with a hawk-like gaze, then extended a hand back through the open double doors.

A very attractive, dark-haired young woman took Fontaine's hand and allowed him to lead her into the school. That was Samantha Fontaine, the old man's daughter, Bo knew. She had been pointed out to him a few times here in town.

Close behind Samantha came her two brothers, Nick and Danny. The older, more solemn brother, Nick, looked uncomfortable in a gray suit, as if he didn't like being dressed up or having this many people around him.

Danny, on the other hand, was in his element. A blond, sharp-featured young man, he wore a flashy brown tweed suit and had a cocky grin on his narrow face. Danny was always looking to start a fight or steal a kiss from a pretty girl. He had been in plenty of trouble in the past but had always skated out of it due to his father's money and influence.

Right behind the Fontaine brothers were several men who rode for the Rafter F, including Trace Holland. The gunman's right arm wasn't in a sling, but he held it a little stiffly, Bo noted. That bullet crease had to still be bothering him some.

Scratch watched the newcomers just as intently as Bo did. He said quietly, "You reckon they got any hide-out guns on 'em?"

"I doubt it," Bo said. "Marshal Haltom has deputies posted outside the door to pat down all the men who come in. Anyway, I don't reckon Ned Fontaine would allow it. He knows that folks here in town have tried to stay neutral when it comes to the trouble between him and Pa. If Fontaine or his men were to try to stir up a ruckus at one of these socials, though, the people would turn on him."

Scratch grunted and said, "Reckon you're right. That don't mean I trust the varmint."

"No," Bo allowed, "me, neither."

The Fontaines' entrance into the school had had a ripple effect. The fiddle players had slowed their sawing with their bows and then stopped. The guitar players quit picking. The Creels and their men who had come into town with them bristled like a pack of dogs that has just spotted a rival pack. The Fontaine riders did likewise. The crowd parted slowly and opened a lane between the two factions.

Likely no one really believed powdersmoke was about to roll, but just on the off chance that it was, nobody wanted to be in the line of fire.

John Creel stood up from the bench where he'd been sitting and stepped forward so that he was at the front of his group. Bo could tell that his father and Ned Fontaine were looking directly at each other. Each man had his face set in a hard, expressionless mask.

Then, as if some unfathomable signal had passed between them, both men nodded. Each moved his head only a fraction of an inch, but it was enough.

The truce was declared.

With a screech of strings, one of the fiddlers started to play again. The rest of the musicians followed suit, and a spritely tune soon filled the schoolhouse. The couples on the floor began to dance again.

"Looks like war's been averted," Scratch said. "For now."

"Yeah," Bo agreed. "I hope it lasts."

Samantha Fontaine danced the first dance with her father, then had a dance with each of her brothers. Lee watched her as she twirled around the floor with them. In the yellow dress that she wore, she had never looked prettier, he thought.

He tried not to stare. In fact, he danced with several of the girls from town and from some of the smaller ranches in the area. Some of them were mighty nice, too, and sent unmistakable indications of interest in his direction.

But none of them were Samantha.

He was careful not to stare. Danny Fontaine was a known hothead. If he saw a Creel staring at his sister, he was liable to lose his temper and start a fight over it.

Lee didn't want that. He was determined to dance with Samantha tonight, but he was going to pick his moment. If everyone was going to see the two of them in each other's arms, everything had to be right.

Lee hoped he could stand to wait that long. Samantha was so beautiful that the temptation was mighty fierce . . .

As the evening progressed, a couple of squeezebox players joined the fiddlers and guitar pickers. Given the number of settlers in the area who had German ancestry, it was inevitable that they'd play a few polkas. Lee thought he might be able to switch off with somebody and claim Samantha for a dance during one of those numbers, but it didn't work out that way.

But a square dance was coming up. That was even more inevitable than the polkas. And one of the main features of a square dance was that the dancers had to change partners while it was going on.

Lee was going to make sure he was in the right place in the dance's intricate pattern.

He was starting to think the right moment was never going to arrive, but then one of the fiddle players, an old man with a short white beard, began to call out the opening moves of a square dance. Everybody here knew what to do, of course, and moved eagerly into position. Those who weren't dancing began to clap out the rhythm. All grudges were forgotten in the joy and excitement that gripped the room.

The caller's words, like those of an auctioneer, spewed out almost too swiftly to understand. But people knew what to do, and they whirled and twirled around the floor, feet stomping and shuffling, big grins on their faces as they dosey-doed. Breath came fast, and the air in the room heated up some.

During the evening, some of the men slipped outside to smoke and take nips from flasks and tell bawdy stories. The music of the square dance drew them back in, though, and the schoolroom was packed. There wasn't much room for a misstep.

When one came, it was at the worst possible time for Lee. He figured that in another ten seconds or so, they'd be switching partners again, and this time it would be Samantha who wound up in his arms.

But no, that was when Danny Fontaine had to go and bump into Lee's older brother, Jason. The impact was hard enough to stagger both men for a second.

And Danny, being Danny, had to yell, "Hey, watch where you're goin', you damned clumsy Creel!"

That outburst made an apprehensive hush fall over the room. Jason, who sported a thin mustache and a goatee that made him look a little like a Confederate cavalry commander during the Late Unpleasantness, responded into the tense silence, "It was you who bumped into me, Fontaine."

"That's a damned dirty lie!" Danny blazed back at him.

Jason reacted to that insult the way any man would. He balled his hands into fists and took a step toward Danny.

Before any punches could be thrown, though, Marshal Haltom got between them. The burly lawman held up both hands and said, "There's not gonna be any fighting in here, and you boys know it. That's against the rules."

"No man calls me a liar and gets away with it," Jason said.

"You got any scores to settle, you do it outside," Haltom snapped.

Danny sneered and said, "Fine by me." He turned and stalked toward the door, stripping off his suit coat as he went. It was an undeniable challenge that couldn't go unanswered.

Jason stomped along behind him, yanking his tie and shirt collar loose in preparation for battle.

Lee was left standing there with Samantha only a few feet away from him, almost within arm's reach.

But he wasn't fated to reach her, because the crowd began to flow between them as an exodus started. If Danny Fontaine and Jason Creel were going to fight, people wanted to get a good look at the combat.

Samantha's eyes met Lee's just before the view

between them was blocked. Their gazes held mutual disappointment.

Then the press of people around them carried them toward the doors, too.

Bo said to his brothers, "Should we try to stop this?"

"Stop it, hell," Cooper said. "My boy's not gonna stand for what that little Fontaine coyote said to him. If he did, I'd kick his behind myself."

"Could be this is a trick of some sort?"

"No, it's not," Riley said. "You saw it with your own eyes, Bo. This is just Danny Fontaine being the hot-headed fool he always is."

Riley was probably right about that, Bo thought.

The Creel brothers, along with Scratch, emerged from the schoolhouse. A large group of men surrounded an open area under the trees where the kids played during their recess. The women all stayed inside, since it wouldn't be fitting and proper for them to witness a fight like this . . . but that didn't stop them from peeking avidly out the windows.

Several men had found lanterns and lit them, and the light from them washed over the area where Danny Fontaine and Jason Creel faced each other.

Both young men were in shirtsleeves now. Danny rolled his sleeves up, and Jason followed suit. Danny lifted his fists in a boxer's stance and moved them back and forth slightly in front of his face.

Somewhat awkwardly, Jason did the same thing. As

soon as his arms came up, though, Danny dropped his and charged, ducking under Jason's arms to tackle him around the waist.

The unexpected collision knocked Jason off his feet. He crashed down on his back with Danny on top of him. Danny began hammering punches at Jason's head, while at the same time trying to dig his knees into Jason's groin and belly.

Jason grabbed Danny by the head. He was a little bigger and stronger than his opponent. He flung Danny off of him and rolled away. Jason tried to get to his feet first, but Danny was too quick for him. He swung his legs up and kicked like a mule. The heels of Danny's boots thudded into Jason's chest and knocked him sprawling again.

This time Danny sprang up and tried kicking and stomping the other man. He landed a couple of kicks to Jason's ribs that must have been painful, but when he tried to bring his heel down in the middle of Jason's face, Jason was able to grab Danny's foot and wrench it savagely. Danny yelped in pain and toppled as Jason twisted his leg.

The onlookers shouted encouragement to the two brawlers as the fight continued. In the garish lantern light, the blood that began to well from Danny's nose after Jason landed a wild punch looked even redder than it really was. Danny gouged at Jason's eyes and missed, but his fingernails left ragged scratches down Jason's cheeks that oozed crimson.

Bo looked around and saw his father and Ned Fontaine standing on opposite sides of the circle around the fighters. They were glaring at each other as much or more than they were watching the clash.

It was almost like they were the ones who were really battling here tonight, Bo thought. The two younger men were just surrogates, stand-ins for this festering conflict between two old-timers.

Eventually, Jason's superior size and strength began to prevail, although not until he and Danny had battered each other bloody and nearly senseless. Danny must have sensed that he was on the verge of losing, because he threw everything he had into one final, reckless rush.

Jason met him with a solid, well-thrown punch that landed cleanly on Danny's jaw and stretched him out on the ground. Danny tried to push himself up again, then groaned and fell back. All the fight went out of him. He lay there gasping for breath as his chest heaved. He seemed to be only semiconscious.

Men thronged around Jason to slap him on the back and congratulate him. Bodies bumped and pushed all around Bo. He had gotten separated from Scratch in the crowd, as well as from his brothers.

He was looking around for them when something struck him from behind. He felt as much as heard cloth rip, and then he felt the unmistakable touch of cold steel as it slid along his ribs.

CHAPTER 9

The icy touch of the blade turned hot as it sliced into Bo's skin.

But he was already twisting away from the knife and throwing an elbow up and around behind him. Bone struck bone, and he knew he had caught his opponent in the head.

By the time he got turned around, though, someone grabbed his arm and demanded, "Whoa there, Bo! What are you doin'?"

He saw the familiar round face of Orin Moody, one of Bear Creek's storekeepers. Moody wouldn't have tried to knife him. Bo was certain of that. His assailant must have ducked behind the merchant when he realized that his thrust had failed to kill his intended victim.

"Orin, did you see who was just standing here behind me?"

"You mean the fella you hit with your elbow? I saw him, but I didn't get a good look at him."

"You don't know who it was?"

Moody shook his head and said, "Nope, afraid not. He had his hat pulled down so I couldn't see much of his face, and I wasn't really payin' attention, you know. I was watchin' all those fellas slappin' your nephew on the back. Heck of a fight, wasn't it?"

"Yeah," Bo said. "A heck of a fight."

He knew that finding the man who'd attacked him was hopeless now. There had to be more than a hundred men out here. The would-be killer could blend into the crowd and be completely safe.

Bo's left side stung. He put a hand to it, felt the tear in his coat where the knife had gone through. Under it, he touched the warm wetness of blood. He was pretty sure that he wasn't hurt badly, but the wound would need to be cleaned up.

Scratch appeared at his side and asked with a worried frown, "Bo, are you all right?"

"What do you mean?"

"I can tell something's got you shook. You don't ride with a fella as long as I have with you and not be able to tell when something's wrong."

"Somebody just came within a couple of inches of putting a knife in my heart," Bo said, quietly enough that only his friend would hear in the continuing commotion.

Scratch's eyes widened in surprise.

"Good Lord!" he exclaimed. "I'll go find Doc Perkins—"

"I don't think the wound is that bad. Find Lauralee instead." Bo smiled grimly. "If you don't get her before the dancing starts again, those *hombres* in there will never let her leave."

Scratch hurried off and returned a few minutes later with Lauralee, who had draped a white lace shawl around her shoulders.

"Scratch says you're hurt," she said anxiously to Bo.

"It doesn't amount to much," he assured her, "but I thought maybe we could go back to your place and patch it up."

"That's a good idea. Come on."

The three of them started to walk away from the school. As they passed Lee Creel, the young man asked, "Where are you goin', Uncle Bo? The dance ain't over."

"Just getting some air," Bo said. "Maybe we'll be back later."

Lee shrugged. He seemed to have something else on his mind. Probably that young woman he'd been waiting for earlier.

Bo, Scratch, and Lauralee crossed the bridge over Bear Creek and went to the Southern Belle, which was open but not doing much business on this night of the semi-annual town social. The saloon would be busy later, though. With so many people in town, a lot of them would want a drink after the social was over.

Roscoe the bartender greeted them by saying, "Didn't expect to see you back this early, Miss Lauralee."

"The social wasn't as exciting as usual," she said dryly. She took Bo and Scratch through a door at the end of the bar and into her office. Once the door was closed, she told Bo, "Get that coat and shirt off."

Bo complied with the order, revealing a thin gash that stretched for several inches along his ribs. The wound had bled quite a bit, but it wasn't deep. The would-be killer's aim had been off.

That made Bo wonder if the man had struck it with the wrong hand. Trace Holland was right-handed, but his right arm would be too stiff for him to use it to stab someone. Trying it left-handed could have been responsible for making him miss.

That was pure speculation, though, Bo cautioned himself. He had no proof Holland had tried to kill him again.

Lauralee used a rag soaked in whiskey to clean the blood away from the wound. Bo's jaw tightened at the stuff's fiery bite, but he didn't make a sound.

"I don't think it'll need any stitches," Lauralee announced after she had studied the injury. "I'll just clean it up a little better and then bandage it."

"I'm obliged to you," Bo told her. He trusted Lauralee's judgment. She had helped out Doc Perkins enough in the past that she was probably better qualified to practice medicine than some of the pill-pushers on the frontier.

Scratch tilted his hat back and asked, "Which one of those Fontaine skunks you reckon did this, Bo?"

"What makes you so sure it was a Fontaine man?"

Scratch snorted.

"Does anybody else around Bear Creek have a reason for wantin' you dead?" he asked.

"Well . . . to be honest, I can't think of anybody," Bo

admitted. "It sort of crossed my mind that Trace Holland might have made another try for me. He's a better gunman than he is a knife artist, though."

"Lucky for you . . . and lucky for him, too."

Bo raised an eyebrow quizzically.

"If he'd killed you, then I'd have had to kill him," Scratch explained.

For two *hombres* who had been trail partners as long as these two, that made perfect sense.

Samantha could tell that her father was angry because of how thin-lipped his mouth was when he rejoined her in the schoolhouse. He always looked like that when he was trying to hold in hot words.

"Is Danny all right?" she asked him.

Fontaine snorted disgustedly.

"Better than he deserves, the arrogant young pup," he said. "I told him I didn't want any trouble here tonight. I specifically told him to watch his step around that Creel bunch."

Samantha had been hoping to catch a moment alone with one particular member of "that Creel bunch" in the aftermath of the fight, but that hadn't worked out. Lee was in the middle of his relatives, where she couldn't very well approach him.

Fontaine's expression softened a bit as he went on, "Still, I suppose Daniel didn't have much choice. I didn't raise him to back down from trouble when he's in the right."

That was the problem, Samantha thought. Danny was always in the right as far as their father was concerned, especially if there were any Creels involved. Ned Fontaine let his dislike of the family color all of his opinions.

"Anyway," Fontaine continued with a curt gesture, "the boy's going to be bruised and sore, and his pride is certainly wounded, but other than that he's fine. Some of the men dumped a bucket of water over his head, and he came around right away. I told them to get him cleaned up and take him back out to the ranch."

"Are we leaving, too?" Samantha asked, trying to keep the despair out of her voice.

"Yes, I think so. We don't really belong here with these ruffians."

Samantha sighed, causing her father to frown.

"What's the matter?" he asked. "Did you want to stay?"

"I don't see other people very often . . ."

She couldn't explain to her father that she'd been hoping to dance with Lee Creel tonight. He had promised that they would.

Of course, she was logical enough to know that it was probably better if they didn't. That would be just asking for more trouble, and there had already been enough of that tonight, thanks to Danny.

She summoned up a smile and went on, "But that's all right. We can go. It *is* awfully warm in here."

Fontaine grunted agreement and took her arm to lead her out of the schoolhouse.

Samantha glanced around and asked, "Where's Nick? I don't see him."

"I don't know. He can come back in his own good time."

Samantha started to ask why it was all right for Nick to stay at the dance but she had to leave. She bit back the words before they came out, knowing they would just annoy her father. Anyway, the answer was obvious.

Nick could do whatever he wanted because he was male, and because their father trusted him.

After all, Nick practically ran the ranch these days, didn't he?

A few yards away from where Nick Fontaine stood under an oak tree, two of the Rafter F punchers were helping a still-groggy Danny Fontaine into his saddle. Once he was on the horse, Danny swayed back and forth so perilously that one of the men had to grab his arm to steady him.

As Nick leaned against the rough-barked trunk, he dragged deeply on the cigarette he had rolled. As the coal on the end of the coffin nail flared up, its orange glow cast faint shadows over the harsh planes of his face.

"It'd serve him right if he fell off and broke his fool neck," Nick said. "Try to keep him from doing that, though."

"Sure, boss," one of the men said. "We'll ride on either side of him so he can't topple clean off. Mulligan, I'll hang on to him while you fetch our horses."

The other cowboy hurried off to do that.

A dark shape sidled up to Nick in the shadows under the tree. The newcomer started to say something, but Nick lifted a hand to stop him for the moment. The two men stood there until Danny and his minders had ridden off.

Then Nick said in a low, angry voice, "That's twice you've missed, Trace. You reckon you deserve a third try?"

"I don't see how Creel's not dead," Trace Holland replied, equally quietly. "He must've shifted a little just as I went to put the knife in his back."

"Or else your aim was off. Either way, Creel's alive. Was he at least hurt bad enough to lay him up for a while?"

Holland hesitated, then answered, "The way he walked off under his own power with Morton and that saloon gal, it didn't really look like it."

Nick blew smoke out his nose and stood there stiffly for a few seconds before he muttered, "I'm tired of this."

"I'll get Bo Creel, boss, I swear it—"

"I'm not talking about your feeble attempts to kill Bo Creel. I'm talking about this whole damned dance we've been doing with his family for the past year. I'm tired of trying to ease them out of the way. It's time to take more direct action."

Holland's lean form practically trembled with anticipation as he said, "Are you talkin' about a raid on the Star C? Because if you are, I can get enough good men together to wipe that bunch off the face of the earth. If we bring in Palmer's bunch alone—"

"Don't be a damned fool," Nick snapped. "That might have worked ten years ago, but if we tried something like that now we'd have the Rangers down on our necks. We've kept things quiet enough so far that we haven't drawn their attention, and I'd just as soon keep it that way."

"Then what do you mean?"

Nick flicked the butt of the quirley away from him in the darkness and said, "We're going to let the law do all the hard work for us."

CHAPTER 10

After Lauralee patched up the wound in Bo's side, Scratch stayed close to his old friend as they returned to the schoolhouse for the rest of the social. If anybody else made an attempt on Bo's life, Scratch intended to be there to stop it.

Now that the fight was over, the dancing continued. Bo wasn't really up to it, but he insisted that Scratch and Lauralee get out there on the floor.

Scratch knew Lauralee wouldn't have any trouble finding dance partners, but he took her in his arms and led off in the waltz the musicians were playing. He said, "Since we're spinnin' around, we can take turns keepin' an eye on Bo."

"Do you think he needs someone to keep an eye on him?"

"He's come too blasted close to gettin' killed a couple of times lately. I don't see any of the Fontaine bunch around anymore, but I ain't takin' no chances. If I see anything that looks fishy, I'm gonna take a hand in a hurry."

"Yes, I agree with you," Lauralee said. "He won't like having people watching out for him, though. He always thinks he can take care of himself."

"And most of the time he can. I got a bad feelin' about the things goin' on around here these days, though."

"I can't argue with that. The Fontaines are really on the prod. Of course, Danny always is."

Scratch grunted. He and Bo had had a run-in with Danny Fontaine the same day they'd returned to Bear Creek several months earlier, and things hadn't really changed since then.

Somebody tapped on Scratch's shoulder. He looked around to see one of Bo's nephews standing there with a grin on his face. Scratch couldn't recall the kid's name right offhand. There were too many of them.

"I'm cuttin' in," the youngster said.

Scratch thought about telling the kid to go climb a stump, then thought better of it. Could be that Lauralee would enjoy dancing with somebody closer to her own age.

"All right," he said as he stepped back. "As long as the lady don't object, that is."

"That's fine," Lauralee said with a smile. Her new partner took hold of her hands, and they spun away in the crowd of dancers.

Scratch figured he would go and sit with Bo, but as he turned he found his path blocked by an attractive, yet formidable, barrier.

"You never came and had tea with me, Mr. Morton," Mrs. Emmaline Ashley said with an accusing frown. "I thought we had agreed on that."

"Well, I, uh, that is . . ."

This was a different sort of threat than the ones Scratch was accustomed to facing, and he didn't quite know what to do.

When in doubt, he told himself, fall back on the truth.

"After what happened, I mean with me rushin' outta the store like that, I didn't figure you still wanted to have tea with me, ma'am," he said.

"Don't you think you should have let me make that decision?"

"Well, I reckon maybe I should have."

"Never assume you know what a woman wants, Mr. Morton. There's a good chance you'll be wrong."

"Oh yes, ma'am, I figured that out a long time ago."

She raised an eyebrow at that, and Scratch thought maybe he should've kept his mouth shut, but Mrs. Ashley said, "If you're really repentant, you can make it up to me by dancing with me. At least, that will be a start."

"Yes, ma'am. I think I can do that."

Scratch took her in his arms.

Emmaline—she insisted that he call her that—proved to be a fine dancer.

"I know I'm not as young and gorgeous as Lauralee Parker, of course, but I hope you enjoy dancing with me,

Scratch," she said. "Is she a particular ladyfriend of yours?"

"What, you mean Lauralee? Shoot, no. I mean, she's a lady and she's a good friend, no doubt about that, but I've known her ever since she was a scabby-kneed little kid runnin' around Bear Creek."

"So has your friend Mr. Creel, but that hasn't stopped him from taking an interest in her."

"What Bo does is his own business." When nobody was trying to kill him, that is, Scratch corrected himself mentally. "I'd say the interest is more the other way around, though."

"Really? Miss Parker has been pursuing a man old enough to be her father?"

"The feelin's in a person's heart don't have to make sense to anybody but the one feelin' 'em, I reckon."

Emmaline laughed and said, "Why, Scratch, that's positively profound."

"Better'n profane."

Somehow while they were dancing and talking, she had managed to get closer to him. In fact, he was holding her pretty doggoned close now, and the music had slowed down so that he could feel her soft warmth moving with him.

"Scratch . . ." she said softly.

"Yes, ma'am?" he asked, his voice sounding a mite huskier than he expected it to.

"What *is* your real name? Surely your mother didn't name you . . . Scratch."

"It's been so long since anybody called me anything else, I sort of disremember," he lied.

"I'm acquainted with your sister, you know. I could always ask her."

"Maybe you should do that," he told her, knowing good and well that she wouldn't get anything out of Dorothy. "Then if she tells you, you can tell me and we'll both know!"

Emmaline laughed and moved even closer, close enough to rest her head on his chest.

Scratch resisted the temptation to reach up and tug at his shirt collar. Maybe it would be a good idea if this dance went ahead and got itself over with, he thought.

After a while, the musicians played "Goodnight, Ladies," and folks started to drift toward the doors. Some of the families had long wagon rides ahead of them before they got home. The kids would sleep in the back, the wives would doze against their husbands' shoulders, and the men would try not to nod off over the reins as they kept their teams moving.

Most of the cowboys would head for the saloons to get drunk and then sleep it off before making miserable, hungover rides back to their home ranches in the morning.

Bo had tried to convince Lauralee to dance the final dance with Scratch, but she had refused to budge from where she was sitting by his side.

Instead Scratch was out on the floor with a nice-looking woman Lauralee identified as Mrs. Emmaline Ashley, a widow who lived here in Bear Creek. Bo had noticed them dancing several times earlier.

"Looks like Mrs. Ashley has her cap set for ol' Scratch," Bo commented with a smile.

"She's nice enough, I suppose," Lauralee said. "She's wasting her time, though, if she's looking for another husband. The chances of Scratch ever settling down are pretty slim."

Bo had to chuckle at that. He said, "I reckon you're right."

"How about you, Bo? You ever give any thought to putting down roots again?"

His smile went away as he said, "That didn't work out too well the first time."

Lauralee knew his history, knew about the family he had lost so many years ago when he was a young man. She said quietly, "Just because something bad happened once, that doesn't mean it will again."

"Doesn't mean it won't," Bo said without looking at her.

"No, I suppose not." She paused for a moment, then said, "Whenever you find something worthwhile in life that comes with an iron-clad guarantee, you be sure and tell me about it, Bo. Because I've never run across anything like that, myself."

He knew he had annoyed her, which was a damned shame. But there wasn't anything he could do about it. She was a young, vital woman who deserved a home and a family and happiness. She didn't need to get herself tied down to an old codger like him who couldn't give her any of those things.

Someday, if he was lucky, she would realize that he was just trying to look out for her, the same way he always had.

As people began to leave, Scratch came over and said, "I, uh, told Miz Ashley I'd walk her home. She sort of insisted. But I can tell her I got to ride back out to the Star C with you if you want, Bo."

"I don't want that," Bo said without hesitation. "You go ahead and see the lady to her door, Scratch. I'll be fine. I'll walk Lauralee back to the Southern Belle and then head for the ranch myself."

"You'll do no such thing," Lauralee said. "Your family is getting ready to leave now, Bo. You go with them. I can get back to the saloon just fine on my own."

He frowned and said, "I don't much like that idea."

"I can take care of myself, you know," Lauralee insisted. She slipped a hand in a pocket of the blue dress and brought it out with a two-shot derringer lying on the palm, holding the weapon discreetly so that nobody except Bo and Scratch could see it.

Scratch grinned.

"There's a rule against bringin' guns to a social," he said.

"Yes, well, for some reason Jonas's deputies didn't search me when I came in."

"I would've liked to see 'em try," Scratch said with a chuckle.

To Bo, Lauralee said, "So you can see you don't have

to worry about me. You go on with your pa and the rest of the family. Whoever tried to kill you earlier wouldn't dare make another attempt while you're with them."

"Probably not," Bo admitted. "All right, if you're sure."

She leaned over and brushed her lips against his cheek.

"I'm sure."

They joined the flow of people out of the schoolhouse and went their separate ways. As Bo joined his family, Riley suggested, "Maybe you better ride in the wagon, Bo, seeing as you got stabbed and all. Sitting a saddle might not be good for that wound."

"I can ride just fine," Bo said, aware that he was being stubborn but not in the mood to do anything about it.

"Suit yourself," Riley said with a shrug. "You open up that cut again, it's Lauralee you'll have to answer to, not me."

He had a point. Bo didn't want to undo Lauralee's work in patching up the wound. He said grudgingly, "I reckon I can tie my horse on behind Hank's wagon, if that's all right with him."

"You know it is," Hank said.

A few minutes later the large group, split about equally between wagons and horseback, started out of Bear Creek, heading south toward the Star C. Hank's wife was riding in the back of their wagon with some of the grandkids already asleep around her and in her lap, so Bo rode on the seat next to his youngest brother.

Bo saw a faint flicker of lightning, far in the distance,

which was nothing unusual. Little squalls moved in frequently from the Gulf.

Hank saw it, too, and commented quietly, "Looks like a storm comin'. You think it'll get here or die out before it does, Bo?"

"No telling," Bo said. "I reckon it'll do whatever it wants."

Events around here seemed to be the same way, he thought grimly. If trouble was moving in, they had about as much chance of stopping it as they did that distant thunderstorm . . .

CHAPTER 11

Gilbert Ambrose was pleasantly tired when he and his wife got back to their house after the social. It had been a good evening. Ambrose had danced not only with his wife but with several attractive, much younger women, the wives of men who had borrowed money from the bank. If his hands had strayed a bit while they were dancing—just a bit, you know, nothing too improper—none of the women said anything about it.

As was fitting since he was the banker, Ambrose's house was one of the biggest and nicest in Bear Creek. It had two stories and was set in a grove of trees.

When they went in, Judith paused at the bottom of the stairs with a hand on the banister and said, "Are you coming right up to bed, Gilbert?"

He knew the socials sometimes left her feeling amorous, one of the exceedingly rare occasions when that miracle took place. He could tell from her tone of voice that was true tonight.

Unfortunately, Ambrose didn't return the feeling

anymore, so as he loosened his tie, he said, "No, I don't think so, my dear. I need to look over a few documents in my study, and I thought I'd have a little brandy while I'm doing that."

"I could keep you company . . ." she suggested.

"No, no, that's not necessary," Ambrose said firmly. "I know you're tired. You go on up and get some rest. Don't try to stay awake for me. I may be a while."

Judith sighed and said, "Very well. Good night, Gilbert. It . . . it was a lovely evening."

"Indeed it was," he agreed.

He waited until she had ascended to the second floor, then went along the hallway from the foyer to the door of his study. They had left a lamp turned low in the parlor before they went out, and its soft glow lighted his way.

The study was dark, though, when Ambrose opened the door. The curtains were snug over the windows, so no light from the moon and stars came in from outside.

The gloom didn't matter. Gilbert Ambrose had lived in this house for years and knew every inch of it. Unerringly, he walked across the room to the desk, lifted the chimney on the lamp that sat there, and took a match from a box of them on the desk. He struck it, held the flame to the wick, and lowered the chimney. Yellow light filled the room.

As it did, it revealed the man standing in a corner with a gun in his hand.

Ambrose dropped the smoking match he had just

shook out and gasped in shock and fear. His first thought was of robbery.

"I—I don't have much money here in the house," he stammered. "But you can take what I have. Just don't hurt me or my wife."

He hoped the thief wouldn't force him to go down to the bank and open the safe. Ambrose knew he would give in and do that to save his life, but it would ruin him.

Then the man with the gun moved closer, so that his features under his pulled-down hat brim weren't so shadowy, and Ambrose felt another shock. He knew this man pointing a Colt at him.

"Take it easy, Ambrose," Nick Fontaine said. "I'm not here to rob you, and I don't want to hurt you."

Ambrose's eyes blinked rapidly in astonishment. He said, "Then . . . then why . . ."

Nick slid the gun into a holster under his coat.

"I didn't want you letting out a yell when you first saw me," he explained. "There's no need to alarm your wife. Is she the only other person in the house?"

Ambrose swallowed hard and nodded.

"That's right. What's this all about, Nick?"

He was still frightened, but he was starting to get a little angry, too.

Nick didn't answer directly. Instead he said, "There's no need for Mrs. Ambrose to know I've been here. When you hear what I have to say, I have a hunch you'll agree with me."

Ambrose was definitely angry, now that it was obvious Nick didn't intend to murder him where he stood.

With his jaw jutting out a little, he demanded, "Just what is it you have to say?"

"I thought we'd have a little talk about you and Dulcie Lamont."

This time the shock Ambrose felt was great enough he had to put a hand down on the desk to steady himself.

"How . . . how did you know . . ."

He couldn't bring himself to go on.

A sardonic smile didn't do anything to lessen the harshness of Nick Fontaine's face. The younger man said, "How did I know you'd been paying visits to her place north of town? I keep an eye on things everywhere around here, Ambrose. Anyway, did you really think you could get away with it forever? You figured the town banker, a pillar of the community, as they say, could go see a whore once or twice a week and nobody would notice?"

That was exactly what Ambrose had thought, or to be more precise, he hadn't really given the question much thought. He'd been too caught up in what he was doing. Too enamored of the excitement he'd felt at being with a younger, attractive woman again . . .

Defensively, he said, "She's not . . . Dulcie isn't . . . what you said. She's simply an unfortunate woman who's had a run of bad luck since her, ah, husband passed away."

"A run of bad luck, and a long line of gentleman callers—including you."

"I—I was merely counseling the young woman—"

Nick's laugh interrupted Ambrose's faltering excuse at a rationalization.

"Yeah, I'll bet you counseled her real good. Like I said, once or twice a week."

Ambrose sighed and gestured at the chair behind the desk as he asked, "May I sit down?"

"Sure, go ahead."

Ambrose settled into the chair and sighed again.

"What is it you want from me, Nick?"

"Why, I just want you to do your job, Mr. Ambrose. You run the bank. You decide when it's all right to extend a note—or call it in and demand payment in full."

Ambrose's watery eyes widened slightly. He was smart enough to see right away what Nick was getting at, but at the same time he was puzzled by the demand.

"You're talking about the mortgage I hold on the Star C, aren't you?"

Nick grinned and shrugged.

"How did you know about that?" Ambrose asked. "Such business arrangements are supposed to be private."

"There are other people who work in that bank besides you," Nick pointed out. "Some of them see paperwork that maybe they're not supposed to. And some of 'em talk in a saloon when it's late and they've had too much to drink and they're holding bad cards in a poker game." Nick shook his head. "It really doesn't matter how I found out, does it? I know about the money John Creel owes you, and I know about your visits to Dulcie

Lamont's house. Seems pretty clear to me what needs to happen next."

"You want me to call in Creel's note," Ambrose said in a hollow voice.

"It's coming due, isn't it? You've got every right in the world to call it in, especially if it looks like Creel won't be able to pay. In fact, I'd say it's your duty as an honest banker to do just that. You *are* an honest banker, aren't you, Mr. Ambrose?"

"There's never been a hint of scandal about my business!" Ambrose said, angry again now.

"All the more reason you don't want anybody finding out about you and Dulcie. Has the bank *loaned* her any money?"

Ambrose looked down at the desk without saying anything. He couldn't meet Nick's eyes. That was all the answer the other man needed, anyway.

After a moment, Ambrose said, "If I . . . if I call in John Creel's note . . . ?"

"Then your wife won't find out about your little whore, and neither will your friends here in town. Nobody will have any reason to suspect you've done anything improper. You'll be the same fine, upstanding citizen you've always been."

The unwelcome visitor's mocking tone made Ambrose's face flush hotly. He wanted to stand up and give Nick Fontaine a good sound thrashing.

Of course, that was impossible. He couldn't risk angering the man. And Nick was a lot younger and in better shape. Not to mention the cruelty that lurked in his eyes and around his mouth. Ambrose knew that if he threw a punch, Nick would hurt him.

"All right," he said in a half whisper. "I'll do whatever you say."

"I knew you'd see it my way," Nick said with a self-satisfied smirk. "Just remember, you're not doing anything illegal. Hell, the way the Star C has been losing stock, you might have called in that loan anyway. Pretty soon that spread's not going to be worth what Creel owes on it."

Something occurred to Ambrose and made him lift his head. He asked, "Have you had anything to do with that?"

"Creel's rustler trouble, you mean?" Nick's eyes narrowed. "I'm going to forget you just asked me that, Mr. Ambrose. I'd advise you to do the same."

The cold menace that Ambrose saw on Nick's face now made a fresh jolt of fear go through him.

"Of—of course," he stammered. "I didn't mean anything by it. I don't know what got into me."

Nick nodded, but his features remained set in hard lines.

"Since we understand each other, I'll show myself out," he said. A humorless chuckle came from his lips. "I showed myself in, after all."

He stepped out into the hall. Ambrose stayed where he was behind the desk while he listened to Nick Fontaine's quiet footsteps receding. The front door opened and closed.

Ambrose hoped Judith hadn't heard that upstairs. He

didn't want to have to explain what was going on to her. There was no way he *could* explain. If she found out the truth, she would never forgive him. She would hate him for the rest of her life. Despite his lack of any deep feeling for her, he didn't want that. He didn't want to hurt her.

Feeling twenty years older than he had when they got home, he pushed himself to his feet and stumbled to the sideboard where several glasses and a decanter of brandy stood. He splashed liquor in one of the glasses, lifted it to his mouth with a trembling hand.

The brandy's warmth going down braced him a little. He poured another drink and gulped it down, as well.

Nick Fontaine's behavior was outrageous, unforgivable. Breaking into a man's home in the middle of the night! Threatening him. Blackmailing him.

On the other hand, Nick had told the truth when he said he wasn't asking Ambrose to do anything illegal. There was every chance in the world that he would have called in John Creel's note anyway. Yes, of course there was. He was a banker, after all. He had certain responsibilities. He could do what Nick wanted, and no one would ever suspect that any pressure had been involved.

It was just good business, that was all.

Ambrose started to pour yet another drink, but then he stopped himself. He put the cork back in the neck of the decanter.

One thing was certain, he told himself. He had to stop seeing Dulcie Lamont. He couldn't open himself up to anything like this ever happening again. But he would miss their times together, no doubt about that. A man needed a bit of comfort now and then, no matter who he was.

Gilbert Ambrose blew out the lamp in the study and trudged toward the staircase.

God, he hoped Judith was sound asleep when he got upstairs!

CHAPTER 12

A week had passed since the dance in town. The knife wound in Bo's side was still tender, but it was healing nicely. Idabelle Fisher, who'd had experience herself at patching up an assortment of gun and knife wounds, changed the dressing on it every day and assured Bo he was going to be fine except for a scar.

"It's not like that's the only one of those I've got," he told her with a smile.

Idabelle snorted at that comment.

"You're not telling me anything I don't already know, Bo Creel! You men make a habit of getting yourself shot up and cut up. You're all so eager to fight, I don't see how civilization has a chance."

"Some say civilization is overrated," Bo pointed out. "Sooner or later the barbarians are going to come out on top no matter what we do."

"Well, we can at least try to postpone that day for a while."

"Yes, ma'am," Bo agreed.

One day during that week, a Star C puncher rode in to report that a couple dozen cattle were missing from one of the pastures. Bo rode out there with his father to have a look, along with Riley and Cooper and Scratch, who happened to be there at the time.

"You're probably the best tracker among us, Scratch," John Creel said when they reached the pasture. "See if you can follow the sign, if you don't mind."

"That's just what I was plannin' to do, Mr. Creel," Scratch said. He roamed back and forth around the countryside for a quarter of an hour before he found the tracks the stolen cows had made as they were being driven off.

The trail led west, toward a region of thickly wooded knobs and gullies. Bo knew it was going to be difficult to follow the rustlers, and sure enough, they had gone only a few miles before Scratch reined in and said, "Looks like they split up. There were enough of the varmints that each man took two or three cows apiece. Reckon they've got it set up to rendezvous somewhere later."

"Can't you follow any of the trails?" Riley asked.

"All we need to do is track one of the rustlers," Cooper added. "He'll lead us to the others."

Scratch shrugged and said, "We can give it a try, but I got a hunch these fellas know what they're doin'. They've been gettin' away with it for a while, after all."

The search proved to be futile. The group from the Star C took one trail, then another and another, only to have them all peter out. As Scratch had indicated, the rustlers were skillful.

Finally, late in the day, the men headed back to the ranch with an air of discouragement hanging over them. Two dozen cattle wouldn't make or break the Star C . . . but losing that many every few weeks over time added up to considerable shrinking of the herd.

John Creel cussed the Fontaines all the way back. It was true that the stolen cattle had been driven west, in the opposite direction from the Rafter F, but that didn't mean anything. The rustlers could still be working for Ned Fontaine.

Fontaine didn't want to blot the brands and add the cows to his own herd, Bo thought. He just wanted to hurt the Star C.

It was a couple of days later that Gilbert Ambrose arrived at the ranch driving a buggy. A fine black horse pulled the vehicle, which had brass trim. Had to expect the town banker to travel in style, Bo thought from where he was sitting on the porch, playing dominoes with Scratch.

"Gentlemen," Ambrose greeted them with a nod. He climbed down from the buggy and tied the horse's reins to the hitching post in front of the porch. "Are your father and brothers here, Bo?"

"Pa and Hank are," Bo said as he stood up. "Riley and Cooper are out on the range somewhere. You need to talk to them, too?"

Ambrose shook his head.

"No, that's all right. John and Hank handle all the business for the ranch. I just need to speak with them."

Ambrose paused at the bottom of the steps, as if asking permission to come any farther.

"Come on and have a seat," Bo told him. "I'll tell Idabelle to fetch some lemonade while I go get Pa and Hank."

"I can do that," Scratch offered. "Why don't you keep Mr. Ambrose company, Bo?"

"All right."

Bo thought Ambrose looked uncomfortable. When the banker reached the porch, he took out a bandanna and mopped his forehead. The day was warm, but not hot enough to make Ambrose sweat like that.

Bo waved Ambrose into one of the rockers, then said, "Unless you'd rather go inside and talk in the office . . . ?"

"No, this is fine," Ambrose replied with a shake of his head as he put away the bandanna and sat down. "I . . . I like the fresh air."

"So do I."

John Creel pushed the screen door open and stepped out onto the porch. Hank was close behind him.

"Hello, Gil," John said. "What brings you out here?"

Bo figured he already knew the answer to his father's question—and none of them were going to like it.

Ambrose hesitated before saying, "I need to talk a little business, John."

"I understand Idabelle is bringing some lemonade.

Let's wait for that. Always easier to talk business when you don't have a dry throat."

"I, uh, I suppose so."

The four men sat on the porch making small talk while they waited. Nobody had asked Bo to leave, so he stayed. As the minutes dragged past, Ambrose looked more and more uncomfortable.

Idabelle emerged from the house carrying a tray with a pitcher of lemonade and four glasses on it. She set it on the domino table, gave the visitor a slightly chilly, "Hello, Mr. Ambrose," and went back inside after filling the glasses.

John Creel took a long drink of the cool liquid, then licked his lips and said, "All right, Gil, what's this all about?"

"I . . . I think you know, John," Ambrose said.

"The money I owe the bank." John nodded. "I've got some set aside to pay on it."

"The, uh, note is due in full soon. I don't suppose you have enough to . . . pay all of it?"

The old rancher's voice was flat and hard as he said, "You know I don't, Gil. The Star C has had more than its share of trouble lately. But you know I'm good for it. You know that in the long run the bank'll get every penny I owe, and every bit of the interest, too."

"Perhaps, but you've been granted several extensions already. I have responsibilities, John—"

"To who?" Creel interrupted. "You own the bank. You don't have any stockholders you have to worry about."

"No, but I do have other customers, and they're all

counting on the bank remaining solvent," Ambrose said. "If it were to go under, it would hurt a lot of people in town. Nearly everyone, in one way or another, I'd venture to say."

Hank said, "Mr. Ambrose, you don't expect us to believe that the money we owe is enough to threaten the bank. I know it's quite a bit, but you can grant us another extension. We'll pay a little on the principal—"

Ambrose shook his head and said, "I'm sorry, Hank. I just can't." He looked at John Creel and added, "I really am sorry, John. It's just business, that's all."

"A pretty sorry business, if you ask me," John growled. "We been friends for how long?"

"Long enough that this makes me sick to my stomach," Ambrose said, and Bo actually believed that. The banker looked like he was genuinely in pain. "But that doesn't make any difference. I'm calling in the note in full on its due date, and if you can't pay it off, I have no choice but to declare the loan in default and start foreclosure proceedings on the Star C."

"By God, you can't do that!"

Bo would have expected such an angry response from his father, but it was mild-mannered Hank who was on his feet, hands clenched into fists as he glared at Gilbert Ambrose.

"You won't get your hands on this ranch!" Hank went on.

John Creel lifted a hand to motion his son back.

"Sit down, Hank," John said. "Gil's an old friend. We're not gonna lose our tempers with him."

Ambrose mopped his face with the bandanna again and said, "I appreciate you remembering that, John."

"I'm makin' an effort to, anyway," John said. "Six weeks."

"Until the note is due? Yes, that's right."

"And if I pay it off, we're square."

"Of course."

"Well, then, I'll see you in your office in six weeks with the money," John said. "Until then, this is still my land, and I'll thank you to get off it."

Ambrose winced as the sharp words lashed at him.

"I wish you could understand just how much I regret this," he said as he stood up.

"Oh, I understand. I just don't care."

With a hangdog look on his face, Ambrose climbed wearily into his buggy and drove off. Once the banker was gone, Hank said, "Pa, you know we can't pay off that note."

John Creel sighed and said, "We've got some figurin' to do, all right. Ride out and find your brothers, Hank. Bring 'em back here. Maybe if we put our heads together, we can think of something. If we can't come up with the money, we'll have to stall Ambrose somehow."

Bo said, "He didn't have the look of a man who's going to be stalled, Pa." Bo paused. "In fact, he looked like a man who'd been backed into a corner."

"Maybe so, but that don't change anything."

"Why don't you let Scratch and me bring in Riley and Cooper?" Bo suggested. "That way you and Hank can go ahead and get started going over the books."

Scratch had stepped out onto the porch, and he nodded in agreement with that idea.

"All right," John Creel said with a wave of his gnarled hand. "I appreciate the help, Bo. This ain't really your problem."

"The hell it's not. I may not have been around here as much as I should have been over the years, but I'm still a Creel."

A few minutes later, he and Scratch had saddled their horses and headed out to find Bo's other two brothers. As they rode, Bo said to his old friend, "I reckon you heard what Ambrose had to say."

"Sure," Scratch replied. "I didn't want to butt in on your family's business, but I was eavesdroppin' inside the door."

Bo chuckled and said, "I figured as much."

"You think there's any way your pa can come up with the money he needs?"

"Actually, that's why I suggested the two of us go look for Riley and Cooper," Bo said. "I wanted a chance to talk to you. I've got an idea that might let us do just that."

CHAPTER 13

It took a while for Bo and Scratch to find Bo's brothers, since they were checking the stock on different parts of the ranch. But they were back at the Star C headquarters with Riley and Cooper well before nightfall.

Both men wanted to know what was going on, but Bo didn't go into the details of Gilbert Ambrose's visit.

"It'll be better if you wait so we can hash it all out together," he told them.

"It can't be anything good," Riley said with a gloomy look.

"Yeah, a banker doesn't come to see you unless he's got something bad to tell you," Cooper added.

They picked up several other riders on their way in: Lee, Davy, and Jason Creel, all equally curious about why they were gathering at the home ranch. Bo knew his nephews were all solid young men, but the discussion that was coming would be between him, his brothers, and their father.

Earlier, he had sketched out his plan to Scratch, who had agreed that it might work.

"One thing you can count on," the silver-haired Texan had said. "I'm comin' along."

"I don't want you feeling like you have to," Bo had said. "This is a family problem—"

"And if you don't think the two of us are the same as family after all these years, then you ain't been payin' attention, Bo Creel," Scratch had declared in a voice that allowed no argument. "Besides . . . I got another reason I figure it might be a good idea for me to get outta Bear Creek for a spell."

That statement had put a grin on Bo's face as he said, "That reason wouldn't be a certain brown-haired widow, would it?"

Scratch had winced at the question.

"Emmaline's nice as she can be, and she sure ain't hard to look at, but her mind is workin' in ways that've got me plumb spooked."

"Marrying ways?"

"You remember how I walked her home, the night of the social?"

"Sure, I remember."

"Well, turns out that when I got her back to her house, she expected me to come in and, uh, keep her company for a while. I got away with just a good-night kiss on the front porch—that time—but you know how a good-lookin' woman has always been able to wrap me around her little finger, Bo."

"That's true," Bo had said with a solemn nod.

"Anyway, I've spent some time with Emmaline since then and she seems to think we're courtin' or somethin', and she's one o' them women who figures that courtin' leads straight as a string to marryin', and you know I ain't never been the marryin' type. So if there's a good reason for the two of us to get outta these parts for a while, I ain't exactly gonna argue. If I can lend a hand to you and your family, even better."

"We'll see," Bo had said. "Chances are, we're going to need all the help we can get."

Now, as the group reached the main ranch house, Scratch lifted a hand in farewell and said, "I'll see you later, Bo. Let me know what you fellas decide to do."

Riley snorted and said to Bo, "You can tell your old pard what's going on, but you keep your own brothers in the dark?"

"You won't be in the dark much longer," Bo said. "Come on."

The brothers dismounted and went in the house while the younger men took care of putting up the horses. Idabelle met them inside and said, "Your father's in the study with Hank. And he's in as dark a mood as I've seen from him in a long time, so be careful."

They found John Creel sitting behind the desk, his rugged features even more lined than usual by the strain of the dilemma facing him. Hank waved his brothers into chairs and said, "I suppose Bo's told you what happened earlier this afternoon."

"We know Gilbert Ambrose was here," Riley said. "Bo wouldn't explain any more than that."

Cooper said, "I reckon we can make a pretty good guess, though. He's callin' in the note, isn't he? The whole thing?"

Hank nodded.

"Pa and I have been going over the books, seeing just how much money we can come up with—"

"It won't be enough," Riley said flatly. "We all know that, Hank. You don't have to go into the details."

"Actually, he does," Bo said. "How much money would it take to pay off the note, Hank?"

"Well . . ." The youngest Creel brother scratched at his beard. "I figure twelve thousand dollars would do it."

"Twelve thousand—" Riley seemed to choke on the amount. When he could speak again, he went on, "Might as well be a million. We'd have just as much chance of comin' up with it."

Bo leaned forward in his chair and said, "That's not strictly true. How many head of cattle are out there on Star C range?"

"Somewhere between fifteen hundred and two thousand, I'd say," Riley replied. "And I know what you're thinking, Bo. It's the wrong time of year to start a drive. Anyway, it'd take months to get a herd to the railhead and get back with the money to pay off that note."

"I wasn't talking about going to the railhead," Bo said. "They still ship cattle out of Rockport, don't they?"

John Creel leaned forward and brought a fist crashing down on the desk.

"I'll be damned if I sell my cows to a bunch of hide-and-tallow men!" he declared.

Bo shook his head and said, "It's not like that anymore, Pa. I'm not talking about selling the herd to a rendering plant. They ship beef down there on the coast now."

"And they pay half what the buyers at the railhead pay for animals they can take back to Chicago," Cooper pointed out.

"That's true," Bo admitted. "But they pay enough that if we took a good-sized herd to Rockport, that would pay off the note."

John Creel's frown deepened. He said, "When you consider what we got sunk in those animals, we'd be takin' a loss."

"So you'd lose a little now to do away with the threat of that note at the bank," Bo said. "It's a poor trade, sure, but I don't know what else we can do."

With a look of growing hope, Hank said, "Bo's right. We're cash poor, but we've got the stock. We have to make use of it however we can."

"You're sayin' we'll strip the range," Riley argued. "That'll ruin the ranch, too, won't it? What the hell good is a cattle spread without cattle?"

"You'll still have the land. And you won't have to strip the range. We'll leave a few hundred head to start building the herd again." Bo shrugged. "It's risky, I won't deny that. But it's also the only way I know of to come up with that twelve thousand dollars."

Cooper rubbed his chin and frowned in thought before saying, "Might work, Pa. Rockport's a little less'n a hundred miles away, and it'd be a fairly easy drive. We'd have to cross the Guadalupe River, Coleto Creek, and the San Antonio River, but those are the only streams of any size. We ought to be able to put a pretty good herd together in a couple of weeks, then it'll take two more weeks to get 'em to the coast and get back here with the money. That gives us some leeway on when the note's due."

Riley shook his head stubbornly.

"I don't like it," he declared. "We'll be throwin' away money in the long run. If we can take 'em to the railhead next year—"

"We won't have them to take to the railhead next year," Hank interrupted. "The bank will take the herd and everything else. We'll be busted if we don't do this." He paused, then added, "You just don't like the idea because Bo came up with it."

Riley surged up out of his chair and put his face in Hank's.

"Don't you talk to me like that, little brother," he said through clenched teeth. "I can still whip you—"

"We need to be working together instead of fighting amongst ourselves," Bo said.

Riley rounded on him and stuck out his jaw belligerently.

"You think you can come waltzin' back in here after all these years and start tellin' us what to do!" he accused. "Damn it, Bo, you turned your back on this family a long time ago. Don't start acting like you care about it now!"

John Creel growled, "Stop it, the both of you. You can whale the tar outta each other like you did when you were kids if you want, but it won't change a blasted thing." He sat back and sighed. "I'm mighty sure Ned Fontaine's got somethin' to do with this. Somehow he put pressure on Gil Ambrose to call in that note."

Bo thought his father was probably right about that, but it didn't change anything. He said, "We'll deal with the Fontaines after we take care of this problem."

"Well, I vote no on making a drive to Rockport," Riley said.

"It ain't a votin' matter," John Creel said in a flinty voice. "Not as long as I'm on this side of the ground it ain't. I don't mind listenin' to what you fellas have to say, but I'm the one who'll make the decision."

None of the others argued with that.

John looked at Hank and said, "You really think we can raise enough this way to pay off Ambrose?"

"Yes, sir, I do. We can use the money we'd saved up to pay on the principal to outfit a drive. I'd have to know exactly how many cows we're taking down there, and I'm not sure what price the buyers are paying right now, but . . . it ought to be enough."

"Ought to be," Riley repeated mockingly.

John ignored him and turned to Bo.

"You reckon we can pull off the drive itself in the time we've got?"

"With a week or two to spare," Bo said. "Of course, it's good to have that extra time, because things always go wrong unexpectedly."

Riley said, "What if a hurricane comes in and blows the whole place away, like it did with Indianola a few years ago?"

"I recall a cyclone nearly gettin' our herd a few years ago when we were making a drive up the trail to the north," Cooper said. "Weather's always a wild card in Texas."

"That's true," John muttered.

He looked down at the desk for a long, silent moment before he heaved himself to his feet and gazed around at his sons.

"All right," he said. "Start the roundup. We're takin' a herd to the coast."

Riley looked like he wanted to argue some more, but he swallowed whatever he was going to say and nodded.

"You're the boss, Pa," he said instead.

"Damn right I am. And whatever it takes to save this ranch . . . that's what we're gonna do."

CHAPTER 14

The workday was always long and hard on a ranch, stretching from dawn to dusk, from can to can't.

For the next two weeks on the Star C, that was more true than ever.

Scratch came over to join in the roundup. He and Bo had worked plenty of similar gathers during their years of drifting. Whether it was Texas, Montana, or anywhere in between, the work of pushing the cattle out of the brush, driving them to a central location, branding the ones that needed branding, and keeping them from scattering again was pretty much the same. Long hours in the saddle fighting dust and tedium. A man couldn't afford to get bored, because that might cause him to let his guard down, and then some proddy old bull would be just waiting to stick a horn in him or knock his horse down and bust his leg.

One thing that worried Bo was the possibility that Ned Fontaine might get wind of what was going on. If John Creel was right about Fontaine having something to do with Gilbert Ambrose threatening to call in the note, then Fontaine had a vested interest in keeping the Creels from paying it off.

Bo didn't know how far Fontaine would go to stop the drive from being successful, but given the probability that he was behind the rustling, it seemed likely he wouldn't worry too much about staying on the right side of the law. So Bo suggested to his father that they set up a regular patrol along the western bank of Bear Creek, to make sure no one from the Rafter F snuck over and witnessed the roundup.

That was why Lee Creel found himself riding slowly along the creek one day a week or so into the gather. He would have rather been working the range, but his uncle Bo thought this was an important job, too, and everybody was taking a turn at it. In fact, Uncle Hank was on guard duty nearly all the time, since he wasn't much good when it came to the other chores involved in getting ready for the drive.

Lee hadn't seen Samantha in more than a week. With all the activity on the ranch, there just hadn't been a chance for him to slip off and meet with her. Since he had missed several of their regular rendezvous, he figured she was mad at him by now. She probably wasn't even coming to the creek to watch for him anymore. He'd be lucky if she didn't hate him.

Despite feeling that way, he kept an eye on the far bank anyway. That was his job, wasn't it, watching out for Fontaines who weren't where they were supposed to be?

He wasn't really expecting to see anything, so he stiffened in the saddle as he caught a flash of color in the brush on the far side of the stream. He reined his horse to a halt, straightened in his stirrups, and peered across the creek.

The brush parted, and a vision stepped out.

Samantha wore a red blouse over a black, divided riding skirt. Her hat, also black, hung on her back from its chin strap. Instead of being tucked up, today her long dark hair was in braids that dangled on the front of her shoulders.

As he looked at her, Lee felt like his heart was trying to punch its way out of his chest.

He figured the other fellas riding the boundary line right now were at least half a mile away. Without thinking too much about what he was doing, he turned his horse, heeled the animal into motion, and found a spot where the bank was gentle enough to get down to the creek. The stream was shallow here, so the horse didn't even have to swim as it forded to the other side with water splashing around its hocks.

Lee swung out of the saddle and jumped onto the other bank as soon as he was close enough. Samantha had come to meet him. He took her in his arms, brought his mouth down on hers as she tilted her head back.

The kiss packed a whole week's worth of frustration and longing. Lee felt the impact all the way to his core.

Judging by the way she moaned deep in her throat and pressed her body to his, so did Samantha.

Finally, Lee lifted his head and said, "Whew. I reckon you must've missed me as much as I missed you."

"Don't get a swelled head," Samantha said with a musical little laugh. "I can get along without you perfectly well, Lee Creel."

He knew that wasn't true, but he didn't say so. Instead he said, "Well, I can't get along without you." He couldn't contain the sigh that came up inside him. "Problem is, I reckon I'm gonna have to, at least for a while."

That statement made Samantha's forehead crease in a frown.

"What are you talking about?" she asked. "Why can't you be here?"

"I, uh, got some place I have to go," Lee answered awkwardly. When he'd made his previous comment, he had spoken from the heart and hadn't considered the implications of it. Of course Samantha would want to know why they couldn't continue meeting.

But how much could he tell her? The reason he was out here patrolling along the creek, after all, was to make sure the Fontaines didn't find out about the planned cattle drive to the coast.

Samantha wasn't like the rest of her family, though. She didn't want to see any harm come to the Creels. She wanted to have peace between the families so that she and Lee could be together without having to sneak around.

Lee knew that none of his brothers, cousins, uncles,

father, and especially his grandfather would agree with him, but he trusted Samantha Fontaine.

"I don't understand," she said. "Where are you going?"

"We've got a roundup goin' on. We're takin' a herd down to Rockport, on the Gulf Coast."

Samantha's eyes widened in surprise. She said, "I never heard of anybody doing that."

"From what my pa and my uncles have said, folks used to do it all the time right after the war, before somebody got the idea of takin' the cattle north through Indian Territory to the railroad in Kansas. Back then they mostly used the hides and then rendered the carcasses down for tallow, but they shipped beeves to New Orleans and on around Florida to the East Coast, too. The buyers down there don't pay as much as they do at the railhead, but we ain't got time to take a herd north."

"But why is it so pressing that your family has to sell some cattle right now?"

Since he'd already told her as much as he had, Lee figured he might as well go whole-hog.

"Because Mr. Ambrose at the bank is threatenin' to call in a note on the Star C in a little more than a month, and if my grandpa can't pay it, he'll lose the ranch."

"That's terrible!"

Lee nodded and said, "Yeah, but it's legal. So we're doin' the only thing we can to raise the money Grandpa needs."

"And you have to go along?"

"Can't very well stay behind," Lee said, bristling

slightly. "It's my family we're talkin' about. I got to help out any way I can."

"Of course," she said quickly. "You're a decent, honorable man, Lee. I wouldn't expect any less of you, and I didn't mean to sound like I did. It's just . . ." She sighed. "I'm going to miss you so bad!"

"I feel the same way. But maybe we can get together another time or two before I have to leave. And then it'll only be a couple of weeks before I'm back. It ain't like we're goin' all the way to Kansas. Just down to Rockport and back."

She kissed him and whispered, "You'll be careful, won't you?"

"Sure," he told her as he nuzzled his cheek against hers. "You don't have to worry about me."

"And you don't have to worry about me. I won't say anything to any of my family about this."

He was glad she'd brought that up without him having to say anything about it.

"I never thought you would," he said, although the possibility had indeed crossed his mind.

But you had to trust somebody in this world, and for better or worse, he trusted Samantha Fontaine.

Today was paying some dividends that he had never expected, Trace Holland thought as he sat his horse in the shadow of a live oak thicket and watched Samantha Fontaine riding back toward the headquarters of the Rafter F.

All he had planned to do when he followed her was keep an eye on her, maybe catch a moment or two alone with her if circumstances arose so that he could do so without alarming her.

Far, far back in his mind lurked the idea that he might risk getting a kiss or even more from her. If he did that, likely it would have to be by force, and that would mean he'd have to move on immediately. His job at the Rafter F would be over.

But there were always other places where a man who was good with a gun could make a living. Now that his wounded arm was just about healed, Holland knew he could draw and fire again as swiftly and accurately as he always had.

His main worry was Nick Fontaine. If he assaulted Samantha, her brothers probably would try to track him down and kill him. He wasn't worried about Danny. Holland knew he could take care of the kid without much trouble.

Nick Fontaine was a different story. He could be dangerous.

But all of those thoughts had evaporated instantly when he saw Samantha kissing one of the Creel boys. Lee, Holland thought it was.

That lying little slut, always acting so prim and proper, and all along she'd been sneaking off to spark one of the enemy!

That would be enough to interest Nick right there, but when Holland had crept closer, using all the stealth of a natural-born owlhoot to slide soundlessly through the brush, he had discovered something even better. He had hoped to catch a glimpse of Samantha with her clothes off, but instead he had overheard Lee Creel telling her about how the Star C was getting ready to drive a herd to the coast and sell it in Rockport.

There was only one reason they'd be doing that, Holland knew. They were desperate to raise money. He wasn't sure why that would be the case, but every instinct he possessed told him it had to have something to do with Nick's scheming against them. Nick didn't share all of his plans with his henchmen, but Holland knew his speculation made sense.

Samantha and the Creel boy hadn't done anything except kiss and talk. Considering what they'd talked about, Holland couldn't be disappointed about that. He'd waited, well-hidden in the brush, until they parted reluctantly. Creel went back across the creek. Samantha headed home.

Holland was eager to get back to the Rafter F headquarters himself. He wanted to talk to Nick Fontaine. He was already figuring out exactly what he wanted to tell his boss. There was no real need to muddle the situation by bringing Samantha into it, he decided.

Once he passed along what he'd learned today, he thought with a self-satisfied smirk, there was no question who would be Nick's second-in-command among the hired guns.

And that was the thing about being second in line.

One of these days you could move up to first . . . even if it took a knife in the back or a bullet in the dark.

CHAPTER 15

Sulphurous curses leaped from Nick Fontaine's mouth as he slammed a fist down on the table, making the coins in the pot and the cards in the discard pile jump a little.

"Are you sure about this, Trace?" he demanded.

"Heard it with my own ears," Trace Holland replied.

Nick's eyes narrowed.

"What were you doing over on Star C range?" he asked.

Holland's narrow shoulders rose and fell in a shrug. He said, "It's been a while since any of us went across the creek. I thought I'd mosey over there and see if I could find out what those Creels have been up to." He chuckled. "I found out more than I'd bargained for."

"You're lucky you didn't get your hide ventilated, Trace," said one of the men who'd been playing poker in the bunkhouse with Nick. "Those Creels see a Rafter F man over there, they're liable to shoot first and not bother with any questions."

"I know. That's why I was careful."

Nick picked up the glass of whiskey at his elbow and threw back the liquor that was left in it. As he thumped the empty glass back down on the table, he said, "So you heard a couple of the Creel boys talking about driving a herd to the coast, did you?"

"That's right. One of 'em was Lee Creel, and I can't recall the other one's name. But the roundup's going on now, Nick. A few more days and they'll be ready to start the drive." Holland paused, then added, "Wonder why they're doin' such a thing."

Nick scowled. He knew that Holland was angling for information. The gunman didn't really need to know any more than he did right now, though. Nick's arrangement with Gilbert Ambrose was between just the two of them, and he figured it was safer if they kept it that way.

He threw in his cards, no longer caring about the game, and stood up.

"I appreciate you telling me about this, Trace," he said. "Next time, though, let me know before you go wandering off across the creek. If it comes down to a shooting war with the Creels, I want to be the one to pick the time and place."

"Sure, boss," Holland said. Nick could tell he was disappointed that he hadn't learned more about what was going on, but that was just too damned bad.

And Trace Holland was maybe just a little too ambitious, Nick mused. It might be a good idea to keep an eye on the *hombre*. Ambition in a man who wasn't as smart as he thought he was could be a dangerous thing.

"Good game," he told the men he'd been playing cards with. He left the bunkhouse and headed for the main house.

Samantha came out of the barn, and her course intercepted his. He could tell from her outfit that she'd been riding, which she did way too much as far as Nick was concerned. Samantha didn't seem to understand just how much trouble a gal could get into when she went riding alone, even on her father's ranch.

"You look upset about something," she said as she fell in step beside him.

"No, I'm fine," he told her. "Just have some ranch business on my mind, that's all."

"You can tell me about it if you want to," she offered.

He started to snort in disbelief but stopped himself before the noise came out. Talk over ranch business and his plans for the Star C with a woman, even if she was his sister? Not damned likely.

"That's all right," he said instead. "It's nothing I can't take care of."

"I have a stake in this ranch, too, you know," she reminded him.

He let that pass. She *didn't* have a stake in the Rafter F. When it came time for their father to hand over the reins, *he* would be the one taking control. Not Samantha, and sure as hell not Danny. Neither of them seemed to be aware of it, but for all practical purposes, Nick was already running things around here.

He had already started to think of the Rafter F as his spread.

And he would do anything to see that it grew and succeeded.

He stopped and turned around.

"I thought you were going inside," Samantha called after him as he headed for the barn.

"I thought of something I need to check on," he said over his shoulder without slowing down. "Tell Pa I'll be back later."

Nick went into the barn and saddled one of his string of horses. He kept a sheathed Winchester in the tack room, and he strapped it onto the saddle. While he was doing that, one of the wranglers came in and asked if he needed a hand. Nick shook his head and said no.

The job he was about to do had to be carried out alone.

Bo and Scratch were taking their turn at the branding fire when John Creel rode up, tall and ramrod-straight on a black horse.

Bo was in shirtsleeves, because branding was hot, dirty work. He thumbed his hat back, wiped sweat from his forehead, and said, "You don't have to be out here, Pa. Everything's going along just fine."

"I've been out here every day since we started this fandango, haven't I?" John asked.

"Well, yeah, but that's my point. You're going to wear yourself out. You know you're not—"

Bo stopped short without finishing his sentence.

His father leaned forward in the saddle, eyes flashing.

"Not what?" John Creel demanded. "Not as young as I used to be? Is that what you were about to say?"

Scratch grinned and said, "Shoot, Mr. Creel, ain't none of us as young as we used to be. Most mornin's when I get up, I feel like I'm a hundred years old."

"Well, I'm twenty years closer to it than you are, boy," John snapped.

Scratch looked at Bo and said, "That's why I like comin' over here. It's the only place where anybody ever calls me 'boy' anymore."

"Neither of us have been boys in a long time," said Bo.

"Hell, you don't know what it's like to be old," his father said. "You just wait. Your time's comin'."

"If nobody shoots us first," Scratch said.

"Yeah, there's always a chance of that," John Creel agreed. "How many head have been brought in today?"

"Somewhere around forty, I'd say," Bo replied.

"Slowin' down, ain't it?" John asked with a frown.

"We knew it would. The longer a roundup goes on, the harder it is to find all the places where those stubborn old mossyhorns are hiding. Most of the ones that are left are way back in the brush."

"Anybody had a look in those gullies over by Caddo Knob?"

Bo shook his head and said, "I don't know. Scratch

and I haven't been over there. Maybe some of the others have."

John Creel lifted the reins and turned his mount's head.

"I'll go see for myself," he said.

"Be careful," Bo told him. "That's rough country over there."

John snorted disgustedly.

"You figure I don't know that? I'd been all over every foot of this country while you were still in short britches, boy."

"Now there's something I don't reckon I've ever seen," Scratch said. "Bo Creel in short britches."

"Better stir up that branding fire," Bo said. "It's fixing to get cold."

Grinning again, Scratch did as his old friend suggested while John Creel rode off.

The work continued, and Bo didn't think much more about his father's visit. One thing nagged at his brain, however. He knew that his father intended to come along on the drive to the coast, and he wasn't sure that was a good idea.

It was true that John Creel was a lot spryer than most men his age. He could still work as hard as punchers who were forty or fifty years younger than him . . . but only for short periods of time. John didn't possess the stamina he'd once had.

And if there was one thing a man needed on a cattle drive, it was stamina. All the long hours in a saddle required it.

Bo had started to think that the job was going to be too much for his pa. John Creel had always ramrodded his own drives, but this was different. They would have to push the herd pretty hard to reach Rockport in time to sell the cattle and get back with the money to pay off the bank loan. Bo didn't think it would be worth it to save the Star C if his father collapsed because of the trip, his health ruined—or worse.

Of course, John Creel probably wouldn't see it that way. The Star C meant more to him than life itself. And after all the years of running things, he didn't want to relinquish the reins. That was understandable.

Riley could trail boss the cattle drive, though. He'd been the old man's *segundo* on dozens of harder drives than this one would be. Bo was confident that his brother could get the herd to Rockport.

"What're you woolgatherin' about?" Scratch asked.

Bo was about to pass it off as nothing, but before he could say anything, a distant sound drifted to his ears and caused him to lift his head.

"Did you hear that?"

"Yeah," Scratch said, apparently unconcerned. "Sounded like a shot."

Hearing a gunshot out here on the range was nothing unusual. Sometimes a man came across a rattlesnake and blew the fanged varmint's head off. Or he might see a coyote loping across the range and take a shot at it. It wasn't even uncommon to encounter a javelina, one of the vicious wild pigs that haunted the chaparral country.

to the southwest. Sometimes one of those tuskers strayed this far.

But something about this shot bothered Bo. After a moment, he realized what it was.

The sound had come from the direction of Caddo Knob . . . and that was where John Creel had been headed when he rode away from the branding fire a while earlier.

That fact sunk in on Scratch at the same time. The silver-haired Texan frowned and said, "That's the way your pa went. But there could be lots of other explanations for that shot, Bo. Likely it didn't have a thing to do with John."

"I know that," Bo said.

"But you ain't gonna be satisfied until you see for yourself, are you?"

"I wouldn't mind making sure he's all right."

"Well, don't think I'm gonna argue with you." Scratch tossed the branding iron he was holding into the edge of the fire and started tugging off the thick leather gloves he wore. "Let's go have a look at Caddo Knob."

CHAPTER 16

Rising several hundred feet from the plains and rolling hills around it, Caddo Knob was covered with brush and was rockier than most of the landscape around it. Whatever geologic upheaval in ages past had caused it to jut up from the Texas earth had torn numerous gullies in the surrounding countryside, as well. Erosion had deepened those gullies, and over time they had grown thick with brush.

Some of the Star C cattle, especially the older, wilier steers, liked to work their way back into that brush where they would be left alone for the most part. Finding them was a chore, and chousing them out was an even bigger one.

Despite the fact that the day wasn't overly warm, Lee Creel's faded blue shirt had grown dark with sweat. The batwing chaps he wore protected his legs, but the brush had torn his shirtsleeves and raked the flesh under them, leaving red welts.

Lee wasn't sure what had possessed him to ride over

here into this hellhole by himself. He wasn't trying to impress anybody by taking on one of the harder tasks. It was just a job that needed done, that was all.

He was tired, though, and hadn't done much good. He had four cows and a couple of calves he had pushed into a temporary brush corral, and that was all he had to show for several hours of work.

When he heard a horse approaching, he was more than happy to accept it as a reason to take a break. He pushed out of the thicket where he had been searching and rode into the open on the edge of one of the gullies.

This particular gully wasn't deep, maybe ten feet, and about twice that wide. Its banks dropped off sharply, though.

A familiar figure rode up to the other side. Lee lifted a hand in greeting and called, "Howdy, Grandpa."

John Creel reined in and nodded curtly.

"Lee," he said. "You out here by yourself?"

"Yes, sir."

"Bring one of the other boys with you next time," John Creel advised. "Too many things can happen to a fella when he's ridin' the range alone, and most of 'em are bad."

"Yes, sir. Usually I work with Jason or Davy, but they're off somewhere else today."

"Well, the two of us can ride together for a while. How's that sound to you?"

Lee smiled and said, "Why, I'd like that mighty fine."

As far back as he could remember, his grandfather had been a stern, forbidding figure, not the sort of warm, friendly grandpa some fellas had while they were growing up. Lee knew that John Creel was a true pioneer, one of the first ranchers in this part of Texas. Almost a legendary figure. He had plenty of respect for his grandfather, but they had never been particularly close.

Because of that, he welcomed the opportunity to spend a little time with the older man, just the two of them.

"Havin' much luck?" John Creel asked.

"Not today. Half a dozen head."

"Every half dozen is that many more," John said with a nod. "Where's the closest place a man can get across this gully?"

Lee pointed to the right and said, "There's a spot where the banks are washed out, about a quarter mile that way."

"Let's ride down there, then. You want to cross over, or should I?"

"Why, it don't make any difference to me, sir."

"You're the one who's been workin' this part of the country today," John said gruffly. "You know better than I do where we ought to head next."

"Well, in that case, I ain't really finished over here, so if you want to join me . . ."

"That's more like it," John Creel said, nodding again. "When it's your decision to make, go ahead and make it, by God." He turned his horse. "I'll meet you there."

Because of the pathways in the brush he had to

follow as he rode along the gully, Lee soon lost sight of his grandfather. The old man had asked where he could cross the gully, but Lee figured John Creel already knew. He'd heard his grandfather boast many times that he knew every foot of the Star C as well as he knew his own face in the shaving mirror.

Lee reached the crossing first and reined in to wait. He could still hear John's horse moving through the brush on the other side of the gully. He took his hat off, sleeved sweat from his brow, and heard something else.

It wasn't much, just a little crackling of branches, but it was enough to tell Lee that somebody—or something— was over there on the other side of the gully. His first thought was that some cagey old steer was lurking in the brush. Those mossyhorns would sometimes attack a rider if they got the chance.

His grandfather came into view. Lee opened his mouth and was about to call out a warning when he saw something that froze the words in his throat for a second.

A rifle barrel had poked through a gap in the brush, unmistakable in its blued-steel menace.

And it was pointing right at John Creel.

"Grandpa, look out!" Lee yelled as his hand flashed toward the butt of the revolver holstered on his hip.

John reacted as quickly as a younger man would have. He yanked back hard on the reins, and his horse reared a little just as the rifle cracked. The animal screamed and jumped.

At the same time, Lee's Colt boomed as he triggered

a pair of shots. The bullets tore through the brush near the spot where Lee had seen the rifle barrel, which disappeared abruptly.

He hoped he had hit the bushwhacking snake.

John Creel's rearing, mortally wounded horse fell backward and to the side. John kicked his feet out of the stirrups and tried to leap clear, but he was too late.

The black's weight came crashing down on him.

On the other side of the gully, the rifle blasted again. Lee heard the slug's high-pitched whine as it passed close to his head. He dived out of the saddle, hit the ground running, and fired twice more as he dashed for the cover of the nearest tree.

He reached it unharmed and made himself as small as he could as he crouched behind it. He reached behind him to the loops in his shell belt for fresh rounds to replace the ones he had fired.

From where he was, he could see his grandfather's horse lying motionless on the gully's other bank, but he couldn't see John Creel. The horse's body blocked Lee's view of the old man.

"Grandpa!" Lee shouted. "Grandpa, are you all right?"

There was no answer. Fury and fear rose up inside Lee.

Fury at whoever had ambushed his grandfather.

Fear that the old man might be dead.

The hidden rifleman hadn't fired again. Lee risked sticking his gun hand and part of his head past the tree trunk. He squeezed off three fast shots, spacing them along the other bank in the vicinity of the bushwhacker's hiding place. The man didn't return the fire.

But as the echoes of the shots began to die away, Lee heard something else—the swift rataplan of hoofbeats receding into the distance.

The rifleman had fled.

But Lee waited a few minutes before moving anyway, just to be sure. The delay gnawed at his guts. He wanted to get over there and find out how badly his grandfather was hurt. John Creel hadn't made a sound since he and the horse had gone down.

Lee was almost certain that the bushwhacker's first shot had struck the black horse and killed it. More than likely, that hadn't been the hidden gunman's intention, but if the falling horse had crushed the life out of John Creel, that accomplished the purpose. Dead was dead, either way.

Lee reloaded again, so he'd have a full wheel in the Colt, and then when he couldn't stand it anymore he darted out from behind the tree and ran to the place where the bank was caved in. He bounded down the slope, sliding a little but quickly catching his balance. Weaving around bushes, he ran across the gully and charged up the broken-down bank on the other side.

Nobody took a shot at him, which convinced him more than ever that the would-be killer was gone.

Lee raced along the bank. He could see his grandfather now, lying there without moving, the horse's carcass pinning down his legs. Lee holstered his gun and dropped to his knees beside John Creel.

"Grandpa!" he said. "Grandpa, can you hear me?"

He thought the old man was breathing. He rested a hand on John's chest until he was sure of it. His grandfather's eyes remained closed, however. He must have hit his head when he fell, Lee decided, and knocked himself unconscious.

More hoofbeats sounded, but this time they were coming closer on this side of the gully. Lee moved his hand to the butt of his gun, then heaved a sigh of relief when his uncle Bo and Scratch Morton galloped into sight.

The two older men were out of their saddles before their horses even stopped moving. Bo said, "Scratch, take a look around," as he knelt on John Creel's other side.

Scratch already had his ivory-handled Remingtons in his hands. He nodded and hurried along the bank, alert for any sign of danger.

"The varmint who did this is gone," Lee said. "He rode off a few minutes ago."

"Are you sure about that?" Bo asked. "Maybe he doubled back and is trying to trick you."

The same possibility had occurred to Lee, but he'd been too worried about his grandfather to check it out. So it was a good thing Scratch was doing that.

"What happened?" Bo went on. "We heard a shot and were about to head in this direction, but before we could get mounted up it sounded like a war had broken out over here."

"That's about what it felt like," Lee admitted. Quickly, he told Bo how someone had taken a shot at his grandfather from the brush, only to miss and kill the horse instead because of John Creel's quick reaction to Lee's warning.

"I reckon you saved his life," Bo said.

"Maybe, maybe not. He acts like he don't want to wake up."

As if to contradict Lee's statement, John Creel abruptly let out a groan. His eyelids flickered open under the shaggy white brows.

"What . . . what in hell . . ."

Bo leaned over him and said, "Take it easy, Pa. You've been hurt."

"Am I shot?"

"I don't think so, but a horse fell on you."

John groaned again and said, "It feels like it, too."

Scratch came back and reported, "I found hoofprints and some empty cartridges. Looks like the fella's long gone, Bo."

"All right. Now, Pa, we've got to get this carcass off of you."

"I'll get my rope," Scratch said.

They tied the rope to the saddle on the dead horse, then threw it over a tree branch and tied it to both of the saddles on Bo and Scratch's mounts. Scratch led the horses away, which lifted the dead animal's weight from the lower half of John Creel's body.

Bo and Lee were ready. They grasped John's arms and pulled him clear.

That movement was enough to make John let out a high-pitched yell of pain.

"My leg!" he gasped.

"I see it," Bo said. "I'm sorry to tell you this, Pa, but that right leg of yours is busted."

"The drive—"

Bo shook his head and said, "You won't be going on a cattle drive any time soon."

CHAPTER 17

Not even John Creel was stubborn enough to argue with a broken leg.

In fact, he didn't say much of anything as Bo did a rough job of splinting the injured limb to keep the damage from getting worse until they could get some medical help.

While that was going on, Riley, Cooper, Davy, Jason, and several more of the Creel cousins who'd been working the gather showed up, drawn by the shots they had heard earlier. Bo sent some of the young men back to the ranch headquarters for the wagon.

"Put a lot of blankets in the back to make a nice thick pallet," he told them. "Then get as close as you can with it. We'll make a stretcher and carry him out to meet you."

Bo noticed Riley frowning a little and figured his little brother didn't like the way he had taken charge, but he wasn't going to worry about such a thing right now.

Taking care of their father was more important than anything else.

They cut down some saplings and used them along with a lariat and a saddle blanket to rig a crude stretcher. Then several of them gathered around and lifted John Creel onto it. John grunted once, but that was the only time he gave any sign of the pain he had to be feeling.

Four of the cousins, two on each side, lifted the stretcher and carried it away from Caddo Knob.

"Be careful," Riley told them. "Don't jolt him around, and for God's sake, don't drop him."

Lee, who was one of the stretcher bearers, said, "Don't worry, we'll take it mighty easy with him."

John Creel finally spoke up, growling, "I ain't a damn porcelain doll, you know."

Bo and Scratch stood with Riley and Cooper and watched as the younger men proceeded cautiously away from the gully. Quietly, Bo said, "Coop, I reckon your boy Lee saved Pa's life." He explained how Lee had ruined the ambush attempt.

"Has anybody tried to track the son of a bitch who did this?" Riley asked.

Scratch said, "I looked around enough to know that he took off toward the creek."

"Toward the Rafter F, you mean."

Scratch shrugged.

"That's the way he started. Can't speak as to where he finished up."

"You know good and well the Fontaines are to blame

for this." Riley looked around at the others. "We all know that, as sure as we're standing here."

"I don't doubt it," Bo admitted. "But proving it could be a problem." He scraped a thumbnail along his jawline as he frowned in thought. "Scratch, let's have a look at those hoofprints you found."

Scratch led the others to the tracks. Bo hunkered on his heels and studied them, as did Riley and Cooper. After a few minutes, they had committed to memory all the nicks and other little oddities in the marks the horseshoes had left, and they would recognize the tracks if they saw them again.

Scratch held out his hand with the empty shell casings lying in his palm and said, "They're .44 rounds. Bushwhacker probably had a Winchester. Which don't tell us a blasted thing. There's only about a million of 'em in Texas."

"What we ought to do is get everybody together and ride over to the Rafter F," Riley said. "Go in there with our guns out and make the bastards tell us the truth."

"Go in there and get a bunch of people killed, that's what you mean," Bo said. "Scratch and I have been mixed up in a few range wars in our time, and I've never seen one yet where innocent folks didn't get hurt."

"Nobody on the Rafter F is innocent."

"Now, Riley, that's not true and you know it," Cooper said. "Some of the hands working for Fontaine used to ride for us. They're just honest cowboys. They're not gunslingers. And what about Ned Fontaine's daughter,

Samantha? She didn't have any part in this or any of our other troubles."

"How can you be so sure of that? You don't know it for a fact. As for those punchers, they're just a bunch of traitors as far as I'm concerned."

Cooper blew out an exasperated breath and shook his head.

"There's just no arguin' with you, is there?" he said. "Never has been. You're as hardheaded as an old mule."

Riley clenched his fists and took a step toward his brother as he scowled darkly.

Bo moved between them and said, "Pa's been hurt. We can stand around here and butt heads like old billy goats, or we can go see how he's doing."

"You fellas go on," Scratch said. "I'll trail this *hombre* and see if I can find out where he went."

Riley looked like he wanted to argue some more, but after a moment he nodded and said, "All right, I reckon we'd better get back to the house. We should've told one of the boys to ride into town and fetch Doc Perkins."

"I think they're smart enough to figure that out on their own," Bo said. He added with a faint smile, "They're Creels, after all."

"I'm not sure that means much anymore," Riley said ominously.

Nick Fontaine was mad enough to chew nails by the time he got back to the Rafter F headquarters.

Part of the anger was directed at himself. He had

acted impulsively when he took his rifle and headed across Bear Creek to find and kill John Creel. He knew that. It had been a reckless, foolish move.

But it had almost paid off. He had come damned close to ventilating the old pelican. He'd had a good shot at one of Creel's grandsons, too. If he had managed to kill both of them, it might have been enough to make that stubborn bunch give up.

Probably not, though, he mused as he rode into the barn and swung down from his saddle. John Creel's sons were as bullheaded as the old man.

But if all of them were to die . . .

"Where have you been, Nick?"

The question made him look around. His father had just walked into the barn.

"Just out on the range checking a few things," Nick answered easily. When the family had first come to Texas, Ned Fontaine had been determined to learn the cattle industry from the inside out, but of late his interest in the ranch's workings had lagged. These days, Nick did pretty much whatever he wanted, without his father questioning him or giving him orders.

That was the way Nick liked it.

Fontaine nodded and asked, "Everything all right?"

"Yeah, sure." For a second, Nick considered telling him about the cattle drive the Creels were putting together. But there was no real point in it, he decided. He would have to deal with that threat himself, with no help from his father. The old man waffled too much these days. If he knew some of the things Nick had done—

No point in thinking about that, Nick told himself. He would keep his father in the dark until it was too late to do anything except seize control of the ruined Star C ranch.

Fontaine rubbed his chin and went on, "You haven't seen Danny, have you?"

"Danny?" The question actually took Nick a little by surprise. He shook his head and went on, "No, not since breakfast this morning. Is something wrong?"

"No, I don't think so. I hope not. He's probably gone into town."

Nick thought there was a good chance his father was right. Danny had a hard time staying away from whiskey and whores and poker games for very long.

That was fine with Nick, too. Being a full-time wastrel kept Danny out of the way.

"It's just that I'm a little worried about the boy," Fontaine went on. "He's not around much, and he does hardly any work. That's not fair to you, Nick."

"I don't mind, Pa, you know that."

"Of course, but still, you shouldn't have to bear all the load yourself. There'll come a time when you two boys will have to take over here. When I'm gone, half of this ranch will belong to Danny. He needs to stop shirking his responsibilities."

Nick's jaw clenched. His father had said things like that before, about splitting the ranch between his two sons, and Nick didn't like it. Danny could still live here if he wanted to, and Nick would even see to it that he had enough money to continue with his decadent ways, but he sure as hell didn't deserve half of the Rafter F.

That would be even more true once Nick had doubled the size of the spread by taking over the Star C.

The old man didn't say anything about Samantha, which came as no surprise to Nick. She was expected to marry somebody and go live with her husband. If she didn't, then Nick would see to it that she was taken care of, like Danny, but she was no real threat to his plans.

"Danny's still sowing his wild oats, Pa, you know that. But I'll have a talk with him and tell him he needs to straighten up a mite. Maybe I'll try to find him one particular chore around here that it can be his job to take care of."

Ned Fontaine nodded and said, "That's an excellent idea, Nick. Thank you. I knew that if I talked to you, you'd come up with an idea. You always know what to do."

"I try," Nick said.

He knew one thing that needed to be done. He ought to pull the shoes off his horse, put a new pair on, and bury the old ones. He didn't think anybody would be able to track him here—he had ridden into the creek and followed it for several miles before coming out on the eastern bank—but just in case someone did, he didn't want any incriminating evidence linking him to the attempt on John Creel's life.

He could get started on that as soon as his father got

out of here. He put a worried frown on his face and said, "You look a little gray, Pa. Are you all right?"

"Well, I am feeling a bit peaked, now that you mention it," Fontaine said.

"Why don't you go on back in the house and take it easy? It won't be long now until supper."

"All right." Fontaine started to turn away, then paused and said, "I don't know what I'd do without you, Nick."

"Well, you won't ever have to find out," Nick said. "I plan to be around here for a long, long time."

On *his* ranch.

CHAPTER 18

Dr. Kenneth Perkins's examination confirmed what anybody with eyes could see: John Creel's leg was broken about halfway between the knee and ankle.

"Will I walk again, Doc?" John asked as he looked up from the bed where Perkins had just finished setting his leg.

He had slugged down a considerable amount of whiskey to help dull the pain, having refused any of the doctor's potions that would have put him under. So he was a little bleary-eyed but seemed to be coherent, Bo thought.

"Whether or not you walk again is going to depend entirely on how stubborn you are," Perkins said as he started to roll down the shirtsleeves he had rolled up earlier.

"Then I reckon you know the answer," John said. "I'm the stubbornest *hombre* you ever saw. I'll be up and around again before—"

The doctor held up a hand to stop him in mid-declaration.

"You misunderstand me, John," he said. "What you were about to say is exactly what I'm talking about. If you insist on getting up before that leg has had time to heal properly, there's a good chance you *won't* ever walk again."

"You see?" Idabelle Fisher said from where she hovered over the head of the bed and reached down to wipe some of the sweat from John's face with a towel. "I've been trying to tell you for years that being so mule-headed isn't always a good thing."

John glared at her, then at the doctor.

"You're tellin' me I'm stuck in this bed?"

"For the next several weeks, at least," Perkins said. "And even then, you'll only be able to get up for short periods of time. You'll need a lot of help."

"He'll get whatever he needs," Idabelle promised quietly.

"Great jumpin' Jehoshaphat!" John said. "I've got a herd of cattle to get to the coast!"

"We'll do that," Bo said. "There are plenty of us, Pa. You've got a big family, remember?"

"Yeah, yeah," the old man muttered. He narrowed his eyes at the doctor and went on, "You sure there ain't no way you can prop me up on a pair of crutches—"

"No," Perkins said flatly. "I'm sorry, John, but you're not going anywhere."

John's head sagged back against the pillows propped

up behind him. He lifted a gnarled hand and waved it at the door.

"Get out, the whole bunch of you. Leave an old man alone in his misery, why don't you?"

Idabelle patted his shoulder and said, "All right, but we'll be close by if you need anything."

"A new leg, that's all I need." As everyone started to file out of the bedroom, John added, "Thanks, Doc."

"Just doing my job," Perkins said crisply. His tone softened slightly as he went on, "You listen to Idabelle and let her take care of you, and I'm sure you'll be all right, John. Old bones don't knit as well as young ones, but you *are* the stubbornest man I know, and sometimes that comes in handy."

"Damn straight," John said. He raised himself a little on one elbow. "Bo, you and Riley hold on a minute." He glanced at Idabelle. "It's all right if I talk with my sons, ain't it?"

"Just don't wear yourself out," she told him. "You've been through an ordeal. You need your rest."

"Yeah, sure."

When he and Riley were the only ones left in the room with their father, Bo asked, "What is it you want to talk to us about, Pa?"

"You know damn good and well what I want to talk about. That cattle drive."

Riley said, "We'll take the blasted cows to Rockport—"

"I know that. I'm countin' on you boys to get 'em there and get back here with that money. But somebody's got to ramrod the drive."

"I've taken plenty of herds to Kansas—" Riley began.

"Bo's in charge," his father interrupted.

Bo and Riley said, "What?" at the same time.

"Bo's the trail boss on this drive. You'll be *segundo*, Riley, just like you were with me all them other times."

Riley's face was dark with anger. He said, "That whiskey you guzzled down must be muddling your brain, Pa. This can't be about Bo bein' older than me. That doesn't count. Not when he left home forty years ago and hasn't hardly been back since!"

"I figured Riley would be in charge, too, Pa," Bo said.

His brother glared at him.

"Sure you did. What did you say to Pa before I got there, out by Caddo Knob? You've been tryin' to take over ever since you got back, like you had some sort of right to run things around here!"

"If you think I have any interest in running anything, you don't know me very well, little brother. I've spent the past forty years like you said, riding away from responsibility."

John Creel said, "You boys settle down. You ain't kids anymore, and this squabblin' don't serve any purpose. My mind is made up. Bo's runnin' the drive. If you can't go along with that, Riley, I reckon you don't have to."

"You mean—"

"I mean you can stay here."

"The hell with that! If you think I'm gonna let Bo hog all the credit—"

From the doorway, Idabelle said, "Land's sake, what's all the yelling going on in here? I left this poor injured man in here to rest, not to be harangued by a couple of *loco* cowboys. Now, shoo! Go on and let your father get some sleep."

"Might as well not waste your time arguin' with her, boys," John Creel said with a chuckle. "It won't get you anywhere. It never has when I do it."

With his jaw tight from anger, Riley said, "All right, we'll go." He pointed a finger at Bo. "But this ain't over."

"It is as far as I'm concerned," Idabelle said. "Git!"

They got.

Scratch rode in about suppertime to report that he had followed the bushwhacker's tracks to Bear Creek.

"But I wasn't able to pick up the trail on the other side," the silver-haired Texan told Bo and the other Creel brothers. "The fella didn't want anybody followin' him, and he put some effort into it."

"But the tracks led to the creek," Riley said. "That means it had to be the Fontaines or one of their hired guns."

"There's a lot of Texas east of Bear Creek," Bo pointed out. "The bushwhacker could have cut through Rafter F range and gone on somewhere else."

"You don't really believe that."

Bo shrugged and admitted, "No, I don't. But we'd have to find those same shoes on a Rafter F horse to prove anything, and I doubt if Fontaine is going to let us look."

Hank said, "He wouldn't have any choice if it was the law asking to have that look."

"Jonas Haltom's just the town marshal," Cooper said. "He doesn't have any jurisdiction out here. We might persuade the sheriff up in Hallettsville to send a deputy down here, though."

"I can't believe the whole lot of you," Riley said. "When Pa settled the Star C, there was no law anywhere in these parts except what a man carried in his holster."

"Things were simpler then," Bo agreed, "but times have changed, whether we like it or not."

"So what do you think we should do, Bo?" Riley asked with a challenging tone in his voice. "Just forget that somebody tried to kill Pa and was responsible for that broken leg of his?"

"We're not going to forget about it," Bo said, and now a grim note had come into his voice. "But we can't afford to let this distract us from saving the Star C. And that means getting those cattle to Rockport, so that's our first goal."

Riley didn't say anything for a moment, but then he nodded.

"You're right. But when we get back . . ."

"When we get back, we'll find out who took that shot at Pa," Bo said. "And once we do . . . we'll make that *hombre* wish he'd never been born."

* * *

The roundup continued for several more days before Bo tallied the herd and decided they had enough stock to make the drive. He and Hank sat on the fence of a wooden chute and watched as riders pushed the cattle past them. Bo and Hank each had a length of rope with knots tied in it to help them keep count. The ropes slid through their fingers with practiced ease as they tallied the stock.

"That's fifteen hundred," Hank announced first.

"I make it fourteen ninety-eight," Bo said. "Close enough."

He took his hat off and waved it over his head, signaling to the others that they didn't need to drive any more cows through the chute.

They didn't know exactly how many head they needed to take to Rockport because they wouldn't know for sure what the buyers were paying until they got there. But fifteen hundred would be more than enough, Bo thought. The number gave them a good cushion.

The rest of the animals that had been rounded up would be turned back out onto the range to grow fatter and wait until next time. They had been given a reprieve, Bo mused from his perch on the fence, but it was strictly a matter of the luck of the draw.

All too often, it seemed to work the same way with people. There was no way to fathom the workings of fate.

A similar thought went through Lee Creel's head later that day as he waited for Samantha in a grove of trees near the creek. The last time they were together, they had arranged to meet today because Lee worried that it might be their last chance. He knew the end of the roundup was fast approaching.

Sure enough, earlier this afternoon Uncle Bo had said they had enough stock gathered to start the drive to the coast.

Fate would determine whether or not Samantha would be able to sneak off from her home and meet Lee here today, just as fate had charted the course of the rest of their relationship. What else could you call it? Had he just happened to be in the right place at the right time when Samantha's horse ran away from her? Or had some other mysterious force been at work that day?

Lee figured that had to be the answer. It couldn't be just pure luck that had brought a Fontaine and a Creel together and allowed them to discover the feelings they had for each other.

He heard a horse's hooves splashing through the creek and eased his mount forward as he peered anxiously through the trees. His heart gave a little jump as he spotted Samantha riding toward him. He started to move out into the open to meet her, then reined in the impulse.

It was better to wait and let her ride into the trees. If anybody was spying on them, the growth would obscure the view, anyway.

"Lee," she called softly as she steered her horse into the grove.

"Here," he replied.

A moment later they were off their horses and in each other's arms, and for a while there wasn't much talking going on.

Eventually, though, Samantha said, "Something's bothering you. I can tell."

"Yeah," Lee said with a sigh. "We've finished the roundup. We'll be startin' for the coast soon, maybe as early as tomorrow."

"Well, we . . . we knew this day was coming," she said, and he could tell that she was trying to put a brave face on. "And it's not like you're going to be gone forever or anything. You said it would only be a couple of weeks."

"Thereabouts," he agreed. "Even so, it's gonna be a *long* two weeks if I don't see you the whole time."

"I'll be here when you get back," Samantha promised. "And maybe . . . maybe once your grandfather's ranch is safe again, he and my father can start getting along better."

Lee smiled down into her face as he held her.

"You really think so?"

"You never know," she said. "Father's changed some. He's not as loud and angry as he used to be. Sometimes he seems so unlike himself that I . . . I almost worry about him." Her voice steadied. "It would be good for everyone if there was peace between the Rafter F and the Star C."

"You won't get any arguments from me on that score. I don't know if we'll ever see it happen, though. Even if your pa decides to live and let live, there are still your brothers. No offense, but Danny's got a hell-raisin' streak in him."

Samantha sighed and said, "I know. I keep hoping he'll grow up, but so far . . . I just try to be as good an influence on them as I can. On *all* of them."

"Well, you keep it up," Lee said. "Maybe it'll do some good. Can't hurt to try. In the meantime, I think we got some more sayin' good-bye to do."

"I think you're right."

It got quiet again in the grove of trees.

CHAPTER 19

Samantha had been in there a long time, Trace Holland thought as he lowered the field glasses he had trained on the oak trees across the creek. Obviously, the Creel kid had been waiting for her among the trees.

Holland had been following Samantha every time she rode out on the Rafter F range, ever since he'd discovered that she was carrying on with Lee Creel. Sometimes they met on one side of the creek, sometimes on the other. There didn't seem to be any rhyme or reason to it, but he supposed it made sense to them.

As much sense as anything could make to a couple of youngsters all stirred up with passion.

Nick Fontaine didn't know that Holland had been spying on his sister. That might not have set well with him.

But he did know that Holland was keeping an eye on the Star C. Sometimes Holland even risked crossing the creek, knowing that he might have to shoot his way out if he were discovered. He wanted to be sure what the Creels were up to before he reported back to Nick.

They were going ahead with the preparations for the cattle drive, no doubt about that. They had a good-sized herd bedded down a couple of miles south of the Star C ranch house. They even had a chuck wagon out there, a sure sign that the drive would be getting underway soon.

The country was buzzing with talk about the attempt on old John Creel's life. Doc Perkins had brought word back to town about it, after he'd been summoned out to the Star C to patch up the injured rancher.

Holland didn't know for sure who the bushwhacker had been, but he would have bet a new hat that it was Nick, giving in to his anger and striking out at his enemy.

Holland didn't really care one way or the other who had taken that shot at Creel and wound up being responsible for the old man's broken leg. What was important was that John Creel's injury hadn't stopped the rest of his family from carrying on with their plans. They were taking that stock to Rockport.

And Nick was going to do something to stop them. Holland felt that in his gut.

He wanted to be part of it. He had a score to settle with Bo Creel and that pard of his, Scratch Morton.

In the distance, Samantha emerged from the trees and rode toward the creek. Holland put the field glasses on her again in time to see her wipe at her eyes with the back of a hand with a riding glove on it.

She was crying, he thought. She was upset about something.

The most reasonable explanation was that Lee Creel had just told her he was leaving with the rest of the bunch, heading for the coast on that cattle drive.

Nick would want to know that.

Holland stowed the field glasses away in his saddle-bags and turned his horse to ride down the gentle, grass-covered slope behind him. This little rise wasn't very big, but it was enough to shield him from Samantha's view.

He headed for the ranch house, figuring that there was no need to keep an eye on the young woman any-more.

When he got there, he found Nick at one of the corrals, watching a bronc rider busting a big sorrel with a bad attitude. While the other punchers who lined the corral fence were calling encouragement to the rider on top of the bucking, sunfishing horse, Holland sidled up beside Nick and said quietly, "Got some news, boss."

Nick looked around, then jerked his head toward the barn.

"Come on," he said. "We'll talk in there."

The two men went into the shade of the barn. Nick, who wasn't wearing a hat or a gun today, tucked his hands into the back pockets of his jeans and gave Holland a level stare.

"What is it?" he asked.

"Just what we were afraid of," Holland said. "I think there's a good chance the Creels are pulling out for the coast with that herd tomorrow. The next day, at the latest."

Nick cursed bitterly.

"They're going ahead with it, are they?" he said.

"I think so."

Holland didn't explain how he had reached that conclusion, and Nick didn't ask. Holland was perfectly content to leave things that way.

Nick stood there frowning darkly for a long moment, then said, "Put your saddle on a fresh horse, and saddle that paint of mine while you're at it."

"Where are we goin'?" Holland asked with a frown of his own.

"It's time I paid a visit to Judd Palmer."

The two men rode east from the ranch a short time later. The farther they went in that direction, the thicker the growth of mesquites and twisted live oaks became. By the time they left Rafter F range and crossed the stage road from Hallettsville to Matagorda, they were in country that was a lot rougher going than its generally flat appearance seemed to indicate. A man had to know the trails, or it would be easy to get lost in these tangled thickets that stretched all the way to the Colorado River.

"I appreciate you bringing me with you, Nick," Holland said as they rode. "I've never met Palmer. Always thought he'd be a good man to ride with."

"As long as you don't cross him," Nick said. "He's not in the habit of giving a man a second chance."

Palmer was good at what he did, though, Nick reflected. The man was wanted in several states and territories in the Southwest for murder, train robbery, bank holdups, and assorted other mayhem. When he wasn't being a desperado, he was a gun for hire, and he headed up an equally salty crew.

They had been perfectly happy to try their hand at rustling—for the right price, of course. Nick's war of attrition against the Creels meant that there wasn't a lot of profit from the stolen cattle, so Nick had had to pay Judd Palmer and his men handsomely for their efforts.

That had put a strain on the Rafter F's finances, but nobody knew that except Nick. There was a time when his father had kept a close eye on the books, but not any longer. Money didn't seem to interest Ned Fontaine all that much.

Money meant plenty to Danny, but as long as it kept flowing to him so he could indulge his vices, he didn't care about anything else. And Samantha wasn't privy to that information. Only Nick knew how much he had sunk into ruining the Creels.

It would all be worthwhile, he told himself, when the Star C was his, too, and his range stretched for miles and miles along both sides of Bear Creek.

Nick smelled a faint odor of smoke and knew he and Holland were getting close to their destination. As if to confirm that, a moment later a man stepped out into the trail from the concealment of the brush and leveled a rifle at them.

Holland's hand started instinctively toward the butt of his gun, but Nick motioned for him to stop.

"Take it easy," he said. "I was expecting this."

"Might've warned a fella," Holland muttered.

The sentry lowered his rifle and said, "I recognize you now, Fontaine. Might be a good idea to sing out next time you come callin'."

"I was just about to do that," Nick said. "I need to talk to Judd."

The hard-faced man gestured with the rifle barrel.

"You know the way," he said.

Nick and Holland rode past him and followed the winding trail another five hundred yards before they came out into a large clearing where several low, rough cabins sat. Off to one side was a brush corral with about two dozen horses in it.

A number of men were lounging around the little camp as well as a couple of slatternly women. The man who stalked forward to meet the two visitors looked like somebody had hacked his face out of a tree stump with a dull ax. Wiry dark hair curled under his pushed-back hat, and he sported a narrow mustache under a large nose that had been broken several times in the past.

"Hello, Judd," Nick said.

"Fontaine," the outlaw chief greeted him curtly. Palmer's dark eyes narrowed as he looked at Holland. "Who's this?"

"Trace Holland."

Palmer nodded slowly and said, "Reckon I've heard of you, Holland."

"And I've heard of you, Palmer," Holland said. "Good to finally cross trails with you."

"Huh. We'll see." Palmer turned his attention back to Nick. He didn't invite the visitors to get down from their horses. "What're you doin' here? You ready for us to make off with another jag o' Star C stock?"

Nick shook his head and said, "No, that's over and done with."

"Good! When I threw in with you, I didn't know that penny-ante stuff was gonna go on for so long. The boys have been gettin' a mite restless, and so have I."

The boys, as Palmer called them, were as vicious-looking a bunch of cutthroats as could be found anywhere in Texas. Nick knew that with a nod of Palmer's head, he and Holland would be dead, and there wouldn't be a damned thing they could do about it.

But killing them wouldn't make any money for Palmer, and he was a man who didn't do anything without a payoff being involved. Right now, his best hope for a big payoff lay with Nick.

"The Creels have been rounding up their stock the past couple of weeks," Nick said.

Palmer frowned and said, "Kind of late in the season for that, ain't it? They plan on startin' to the railhead with a herd?"

Nick shook his head.

"No. They're making a drive down to Rockport, on the Gulf Coast."

Palmer threw back his head and let out a harsh laugh.

"Hell, they'll lose money at that!"

"John Creel needs cash," Nick said. "I need him flat broke."

A look of understanding appeared in Palmer's eyes. He nodded again and said, "So you don't want that herd gettin' to where it's goin'."

"I don't care if the herd gets there. I just want it to be in your hands when it does. Do you know any place on the coast where you can dispose of it?"

"I know people on the wrong side of the law anywhere you go in Texas," Palmer said, and Nick didn't doubt that for a second. "You want us to steal that whole herd."

"That's right, and you can keep whatever you get for selling it."

"How about the bunch takin' it down there?"

Nick shook his head and said flatly, "I don't care what happens to them. The less trouble they can give any of us, the better."

"That makes it mighty plain."

Nick nodded toward Holland and went on, "One more thing. I want Trace to go with you."

Holland looked a little surprised by that, and not completely comfortable with the idea, either.

Evidently Palmer felt the same way. His eyes narrowed as he asked, "What's the matter? All of a sudden you don't trust me, Fontaine?"

"That's not it at all. Trace is a good man to have on your side. You must know that, or you wouldn't have heard of him—which you admitted that you had."

Palmer rubbed his darkly stubbled chin and said speculatively, "Yeah, that's true."

"And he's got a personal grudge against a couple of the men who'll be with that herd," Nick said.

Holland spoke up, saying, "You want me to make sure Bo Creel and Scratch Morton don't come back alive, is that it, boss?"

"That's it," Nick said. "Those two worry me more than any of the others. How about it, Trace?"

Holland inclined his head toward Palmer and said, "Judd's calling the shots."

That put a grin on Palmer's face. He said, "Damn right I am. And I reckon I'd be glad to have you come along, Holland. Light and set, and we'll talk about how we'll make sure those varmints you're after wind up dead."

CHAPTER 20

Samantha had taken her time getting back to the ranch after her bittersweet farewell with Lee in the live oaks. She hadn't been able to stop herself from crying, and she didn't want to ride in with swollen, red-rimmed eyes. That would only lead to questions she didn't want to answer.

Once she felt like she could control her emotions enough to stop weeping, she dried her eyes, waited a little longer, and then headed back to the Rafter F headquarters.

She was approaching her home when she spotted two figures in the distance, riding away from the ranch toward the east. Samantha's eyes were keen, and she recognized the horsebackers as her brother Nick and Trace Holland.

Holland was a gunman, even though he made a pretense of being just another ranch hand. Samantha knew that and didn't like having him and the other men like him around, but that wasn't really any of her business, she had always told herself. She knew that when her father died, he would leave the Rafter F to Nick and Danny, so she didn't have a say in anything.

That knowledge grated on her. What her father planned to do wasn't fair. But she had learned to accept it.

It wasn't unusual to see Nick and Holland together, but there was something furtive about the way they were riding off together. Samantha couldn't put her finger on what it was. Maybe just some instinct that caused a concerned frown to appear on her face.

Nick was the one who had hired Holland, she recalled. Not only that, but he had also brought in the other gunmen. Their father had gone along with it, saying that they had to be prepared for trouble with the Creels. Samantha didn't think that was what Nick was doing, though.

Nick was getting ready to go to war.

That thought had been lurking in her mind for quite a while now, and it had bothered her even more since she'd fallen in love with Lee Creel. If a range war broke out between the Rafter F and the Star C, a lot of people would be hurt, and there was a good chance Lee would be one of them.

She didn't know if she could stand it if anything happened to him. It was amazing what a big part of her life he had become in such a relatively short period of time.

Maybe it was all the worrying she had been doing, plus the loss she felt at knowing she wouldn't see Lee for a couple of weeks, that made her suspicious about seeing Nick and Holland riding off together. Whatever the reason, she reacted without thinking about what she was doing.

She turned her horse and followed them.

Samantha stayed well back where it would be harder for them to spot her, but they didn't seem to be paying much attention to what was behind them. They rode for a long time, leaving Rafter F range and continuing into an area where Samantha had never been before. It was flat, brushy country, and the thick growth made it hard for her horse to get through.

Hanging back so she wouldn't be discovered turned out to be a mistake. After a while Samantha realized she couldn't see or hear her brother and Holland anymore. As she reined her horse to a stop, a feeling of despair filled her.

She was lost.

Her heart pounded in her chest, much as it did when she was in Lee's arms, but this reaction was caused by fear, not passion. She was miles away from home, and the narrow trails that ran through the brush twisted around so much she wasn't even sure anymore which direction the ranch was.

"Don't panic, Samantha," she told herself aloud. "You can figure this out."

She peered up at the sky. Knowing that the hour was fairly late in the day, she was aware that the sun was in the west. Once she had established that direction, her nervousness eased. All she had to do was ride toward the sun, and sooner or later she would be back on the Rafter F.

Of course, that meant giving up on finding out what Nick and Holland were up to, but that was a lost cause, anyway. She had no idea where they had gone.

Samantha turned her horse and got moving again. She could tell the animal was weary and she wished she could let it rest, but the last thing she wanted to do was get caught out here far from home when night fell. She had already been gone so long that her father might be getting worried about her.

She wondered if she could ask Nick where he'd been going with Trace Holland. She decided against it. He probably wouldn't tell her, and she didn't want him thinking that she had been spying on him—even though she had.

The sun was almost down by the time she rode into the ranch yard. Her father stood on the porch, evidently waiting for her, and she could tell he was angry by the stiff way he carried himself when he came down the steps and walked toward her as she rode the horse into the barn.

"Where have you been, Samantha?" he demanded. "It's not like you to be gone all afternoon."

She dismounted and handed the reins to the wrangler who had come to take care of the horse.

"I was riding and I lost track of time," she said. "I'm sorry. It won't happen again."

Ned Fontaine grunted.

"I was worried that something had happened to

you," he said. "With those Creels just across the creek, there's no telling what they might do."

"No, I suppose not," Samantha agreed.

Actually, she thought that she would be safe no matter which of the Creels she might encounter. They were probably all as decent and honorable as Lee. Otherwise he wouldn't have turned out the way he had.

She couldn't say that to her father, though. He already seemed to be feeling poorly these days. If he found out she'd been allowing one of the Creels to court her, he might drop dead from apoplexy.

"Well, come on inside," Fontaine said. "Danny's ridden to town, and Nick doesn't seem to be around anywhere, either, so it'll just be the two of us for dinner. I swear, none of you youngsters stay home anymore."

"Don't worry, Father," she said as she linked arms with him and they walked toward the house. "I'm not going anywhere."

Not for a while, she added to herself. Not until Lee got back from the coast. And then . . .

Well, sooner or later her father would have to be told, she thought. Because she had made up her mind that she was going to marry Lee Creel.

With that thought filling her head, she forgot all about the mysterious trip her brother Nick had made with one of his hired gunmen.

The long table in the dining room of the Star C ranch house was full this morning. Idabelle Fisher had been up since long before dawn, cooking a big breakfast for the crew on the day they would start the drive to the coast.

Nearly everyone here was a relative, either by blood or marriage. The Creels hired a few hands, but most of them, along with Hank, would be staying here to take care of the ranch while the others were gone.

Saving the Star C was going to be more of a family affair than anything else.

The table was piled high with platters of pancakes, biscuits, fried eggs, bacon, steaks, and hash brown potatoes. Pots of coffee and pitchers of cream and buttermilk were scattered around so everybody could help themselves.

Idabelle brought in a fresh pot of coffee to replace one that was empty. As she used a thick piece of leather to set it down, she said, "That old man is bellowing like a wounded bull. He wants to be down here with you boys so bad he can hardly stand it."

"You're not letting him get up, are you?" Bo asked.

Idabelle sniffed.

"Do you think I've lost my senses?" she said. "Of course I'm not. The doctor's orders were perfectly clear."

"You'd better keep a close eye on him," Cooper advised. "He's so stubborn, he's liable to try something when he thinks nobody's looking."

"That's why I've got one of his granddaughters watching him all the time. Sadie's up there with him now."

That satisfied Bo. He knew that no one could be

trusted to take care of his father more than Idabelle. She was devoted to John Creel and had been for many years. Actually, he was surprised that the two of them had never gotten married after losing their spouses, but he supposed one marriage apiece had been enough for them.

The sun was barely up when breakfast was finished. The men drank the last of the coffee, thanked Idabelle for the meal, and went outside. Their horses were saddled and waiting for them.

Hank stood on the porch and said, "I wish I could go with you fellas."

"No, you don't," Cooper said with a chuckle. "You never have cared for cowboyin', Hank, and you know it. The last thing in the world you want to do is sit a saddle for twelve or fourteen hours a day."

"You're not really any good at it, either," Riley added bluntly.

"I can't really argue with that," Hank admitted with a sheepish grin. "I'll do my best to take care of the ranch while you're gone, though."

"And all of us will sleep a mite easier knowing that you're here, too," Bo told him.

Before Bo, Riley, and Cooper could mount up, Idabelle came out onto the porch and told them, "Sadie just came downstairs and said that your father wants to see you before you leave. He's threatening to climb out of bed if you don't go up there. That stubborn old goat."

Bo chuckled and said, "We weren't going to leave

without saying good-bye. Guess we might as well go take care of that now."

"You're the boss," Riley said.

Bo looked at him, a look that Riley returned with a challenging stare.

Bo hoped that Riley wasn't going to be a total jackass all the way to the coast about him being put in charge. It sure as blazes hadn't been his idea, and Riley ought to know that.

But saying anything now wouldn't serve any purpose. Bo went back inside, and the others followed him.

John Creel was propped up in bed with his heavily splinted and bandaged leg stretched out straight in front of him. A tray with an empty coffee cup and the remains of his breakfast sat on the little table beside the bed.

"So you're pullin' out for the coast today, are you?" he greeted his sons.

"That's right," Bo said.

"You know I wish I was goin' with you. It ain't fittin' that somebody else has to save this ranch for me."

"It's our ranch, too," Riley said. "Besides, it wasn't your idea for some no-good gunman working for the Fontaines to take a shot at you and make your horse fall on you."

"No, I reckon not, but I still don't feel right about it."

Bo said, "How many times have you taken care of the rest of us, Pa? We couldn't repay you for everything you've done for us with a dozen cattle drives."

"You boys don't owe me a damned thing," John said

gruffly. He thrust out his hand. "Now shake, and then get movin'. You're burnin' daylight out there."

They shook hands with the old man. Bo didn't know about his brothers, but he felt a definite tightness in his chest as he gripped his father's gnarled hand.

They put that emotional farewell behind them as they rode out to the bed ground where some of the hands were holding the herd. Scratch met them there, having ridden over early that morning from his sister's place.

"Did you say your good-byes to the Widow Ashley?" Bo asked his old friend, trying not to grin as he did so.

"Yeah, and she wasn't too happy about me leavin'," Scratch replied. "She told me if I went off and got myself killed in a stampede or something, she wasn't ever gonna forgive me." The silver-haired Texan sighed. "I swear, Bo, I don't know how I keep on gettin' myself in these messes."

"You can't say no to a pretty woman. That's how."

"Well, that's true, I reckon." Scratch chuckled. "Especially one who don't say no to me."

From the driver's seat of the chuck wagon, an old man with a white spade beard and a bald pate under a battered cavalry hat with the brim turned up in front called to Bo, "Are we ever gonna get started on this here cattle drive, or do you intend to lollygag around here all day?"

"Sorry, Mr. Hammersmith," Bo said. "We're fixing to pull out right now."

Alonzo Hammersmith, who made his living as a chuck wagon cook for hire and had gone along on several of the Star C cattle drives in the past, nodded and lifted his reins.

"I'll get on out ahead, then," he said. He got the team of mules moving, and the chuck wagon swayed slightly on its springs as it rolled toward the southwest.

"We were lucky to get that old pelican to sign on with us," Cooper commented as he watched the chuck wagon dwindle into the distance. "We wouldn't have if all the regular drives hadn't already been over this year."

"Yeah, there's not many people *loco* enough to start driving cattle this late," Riley said.

Bo ignored that barbed comment and said, "Let's get the crew spread out and start pushing those cows. Like Pa said, we're burning daylight!"

CHAPTER 21

The route was an easy one, mostly grassy plains with a few rolling hills and only three streams to cross. Those streams—the Guadalupe River, the San Antonio River, and Coleto Creek—had fairly tall and steep banks, however, so the herd would have to zigzag some in order to find good fords at which the cattle could cross.

Riley and Cooper knew this area fairly well, but they had never tried to drive a herd through here before.

Bo had memories of these parts, but they were quite a few years old. So he was perfectly willing to defer to his brothers' judgment about which way they should go.

For that reason, he put Riley and Cooper up front to lead the herd, while he and Scratch rode on the right flank. There were three pairs of flankers on each side, all of them Creel boys in their twenties except for Bo and Scratch. Several of John Creel's grandsons in their late teens rode drag, and a couple more wrangled the remuda.

They kept moving at a decent pace, but nobody got

in too much of a hurry. Even a short drive could run some pounds off the cattle if they moved too fast, and that could affect the price they would get for the herd in Rockport.

After going to this much trouble, the last thing Bo wanted to do was come up short in the amount of money they needed to pay off the bank note and save the Star C.

By midday they had covered about five miles, Bo figured. The men didn't stop for lunch, only to switch their saddles to fresh horses. They had canvas sacks tied to their saddles with sandwiches in them made from biscuits and thick slices of roast beef in them that Idabelle had prepared.

That so-called greasy sack lunch would serve as their midday meal. Calling a ranch a greasy sack outfit was usually a derogatory term, but there was nothing to be ashamed of where Idabelle's cooking was concerned.

Since it had been a couple of hours after dawn when they started, if they made ten miles today that would be a good day's drive. Bo would be satisfied with that. He figured to make eleven or twelve miles most days.

From time to time they had to veer around an area where farmers had come in and strung barbed-wire fences. There weren't many of the fences so far, but Bo knew that was what the future of Texas looked like. Here, the same as most other places in the West, the open range days were fading.

The same thought had occurred to Scratch. As he rode beside Bo while they were making one of those detours around a homestead, he said, "I remember a time when you could ride from one end of Texas to the other and never have to worry about a dang fence."

"So do I," Bo said. "It doesn't really seem like all that long ago, does it?"

Scratch grinned and said, "When you get to be our age, the years go by so fast nothin' seems like it was all that long ago."

Bo agreed with his old friend about that. All he had to do was cast his mind back to the days when he'd been a young married man with a growing family.

The years fell away, and it seemed like only yesterday that he was there with his wife and kids, setting out on a life that should have been long and uneventful and happy . . .

Instead he had spent forty years on the drift, stumbling into one shooting scrape after another, and as much as he loved Scratch like a brother, if he could somehow go back and change the course of his life so that tragedy never claimed those dearest to him, he would do it in a heartbeat.

Such thoughts were pointless, of course, and he knew it. A man couldn't help but indulge himself in a bittersweet daydream now and then, however. Bo recalled the cabin he had built on a little rise overlooking Bear Creek. Plain as day he could see it, the door open, his wife standing there looking pretty as she waved to him in welcome, a couple of small forms beside her clutching her skirts . . .

Bo knew they were waiting for him. One of these

days he would see them again. He would ride up to that cabin and swing down from the saddle and take them in his arms and they would all go in for supper and he would be home, home at last . . .

The crack of a gunshot shattered that reverie. Bo's head jerked up as he peered toward the front of the herd. The shot had come from up there where Riley and Cooper were.

"What in blazes!" Scratch exclaimed.

Bo dug his heels into his horse's flanks. The animal leaped into a run. Scratch galloped beside him. Bo yelled over his shoulder to the other flankers, "Keep 'em bunched!"

They rode beside the herd until the leaders came into view. Bo's brothers sat out in front of the herd on their horses. Both of them appeared to be all right, and that was a relief, thought Bo.

Blocking the way were half a dozen men on horseback. Each man carried either a rifle or a shotgun. They wore overalls and wide-brimmed straw hats. Bo could tell instantly that they were farmers.

"What's going on here?" he asked his brothers as he and Scratch drew their horses to a halt.

Before either Riley or Cooper could answer, one of the men blocking the way asked in a loud, angry voice, "Are you the boss of this outfit?"

"I am," Bo said. He didn't even glance in Riley's direction. At the moment, he didn't care how Riley was taking him being in charge.

"Then you might as well turn them cows around and

take 'em back where you come from," the man said. He was thin and rawboned, with a lantern-jawed face and iron-gray hair under his hat. "You ain't bringin' 'em through this way."

"We're driving them to market down on the coast."

The man shook his head stubbornly.

"Not through here, you ain't," he declared.

"Look, if you've got farms and fences up ahead, we'll respect them," Bo said. "We'll go around. That's what we've been doing so far. We don't want to ruin anybody's crops."

"You can't get through," the man said. "We've got fields all along the Guadalupe in the bottomland. You'll have to go down to Victoria and take the old San Antonio Road."

Riley said, "That's twenty miles or more out of the way!"

"That ain't our problem," the spokesman for the farmers said.

Something occurred to Bo. He said, "Our chuck wagon would have come along here earlier. Where's our cook?"

The farmer took his left hand off the Winchester he held and jerked a thumb over his shoulder.

"Some of our fellas got him back yonder a ways, under a shade tree. He tried to argue with us, too."

Riley said, "By God, he'd better be all right."

"He's fine," the farmer snapped. "We just got a couple o' boys keepin' an eye on him so he can't cause no trouble. You turn around and we'll send him to catch up with you."

"We can't turn around," Riley said. "It'll take too long."

His horse took a nervous step forward.

The farmer lifted his rifle and said, "We fired one warnin' shot already. That's all you're gettin'!"

Bo didn't want to hurt or kill any of these men who were just trying to protect their homes and livelihoods.

But if the farmers opened fire, he and his brothers and Scratch wouldn't have any choice but to defend themselves.

One of the other farmers suddenly yelled, "If you won't turn those beasts, we'll turn 'em ourselves!"

He kicked his horse into a run, raced past Bo and the others before they could stop him, and galloped straight at the herd, shouting and firing his rifle into the air.

Bo yanked his horse around and called, "Stop it, you crazy fool!" but it was too late.

Spooked by the shots and the rider charging toward him, the old bull leading the herd lowered his head and broke into a run. The steers behind him followed, bellowing in their panic, and that reaction spread like lightning through the herd.

In less than a handful of heartbeats, the cattle stampeded straight ahead, a rolling tide of hide, hooves, and horns.

The farmer who had so foolishly set them off brought his horse to a skidding halt and tried to turn the animal.

The horse's legs went out from under it and as it fell the farmer was thrown from the saddle. Yelling stridently in terror, he flew through the air and crashed to the ground directly in the path of the stampede.

The other farmers fled blindly, trying to get out of the way of the cattle at all costs. None of them made a move to help their companion.

Bo and Scratch did, though. Bo yelled to his brothers, "Try to head 'em off!" then raced toward the fallen man, who hadn't moved since he landed. Bo figured the fall had knocked him senseless.

Scratch galloped alongside. Over the thunder of hooves, Bo called to his friend, "Veer off! I can get him!"

"Where you're goin', I'm goin'!" Scratch responded.

Bo wasn't surprised by that. They had sided each other during times of trouble, backed each other's play so many times, that it was entirely second nature by now.

The leading edge of the stampede was only a hundred yards away when Bo and Scratch reached the unconscious man. Scratch swung down from the saddle, got his hands under the man's arms, and heaved him upright. Bo grabbed him and hauled the limp form onto the back of his horse. The farmer's horse had already gotten up and raced off, evidently unhurt by the fall.

Scratch vaulted onto his mount. Bo had turned around and was racing away from the stampede. The cattle were only about twenty yards behind Scratch as he galloped after his old friend.

Since Bo's horse was carrying double, it didn't take long for Scratch to catch up. He could have gone on past, but instead he slowed his horse to keep even with Bo. Neither of them could reach the edges of the stampede, so their only hope for survival was to stay in front of it.

Bo looked around and didn't see Riley or Cooper or any of the belligerent farmers. He and Scratch and the man they had rescued were the only ones caught in front of the runaway herd. That was good, anyway.

By now the others would be riding hard beside the leaders, trying to force them to veer to the side. That was really the only way to stop a stampede, by turning the leaders until they were running in a circle. Once that happened, eventually the cattle would start milling around and the stampede would peter out.

The trick was to stay ahead of the runaways until that happened. Bo didn't know if that was going to be possible or not. He was mounted on a good horse, but it was carrying double. Already the animal was starting to falter a little.

From the corner of his eye, Bo saw unexpected movement. A rider darted around the front of the stampede and angled toward them, riding with incredible speed. It was a daring, even foolhardy move. Bo didn't recognize the paint horse or the slender rider in a brown Stetson, but the *hombre* was risking his life by getting in front of the herd.

The gap between them gradually narrowed. As it did, the farmer woke up and panicked. Bo had to tighten his grip on the man to keep the fool from falling off and being trampled.

It would have served him right, Bo thought. The farmer had started the stampede and put them all in deadly danger. But despite that, they would do what they could to save his life.

The other rider pulled alongside Bo and shouted, "Let me take him! I'm lighter! My horse can carry him better!"

Even with all the racket in the air, Bo recognized that voice. The recognition hit him like a punch in the gut. He exclaimed, "Lauralee!"

She leaned forward in the saddle and grinned recklessly at him, just about the last person in the world Bo would have expected to see in a situation like this.

CHAPTER 22

"Let me take him!" Lauralee yelled again, pointing at the farmer riding in front of him.

Bo didn't know where she had gotten the paint, but the horse was a big, strong-looking animal and obviously had some speed and stamina. Lauralee weighed only a little more than half what Bo did. Without a doubt, their chances would be better overall if the farmer was riding with her.

"Do it, mister!" Bo shouted at the man. "You've got to switch horses!"

The farmer turned a wall-eyed, terrified look at him and yelped, "I can't!"

"Then I'll dump you off and you can find out if you can outrun those beeves on foot! I'll get my horse as close to Lauralee's as I can. All you got to do is jump over and grab on!"

"Just be careful how you grab!" Lauralee told him.

The farmer grabbed the horse's mane and clung to it for dear life as he moaned, "I can't! I can't!"

"Oh hell," Bo muttered, indulging in a rare curse. Sheer terror had paralyzed the man, and nothing Bo could say would break through that fear's grip. "Stay here, then. I'll do it!"

He and Lauralee brought their horses closer together. Lauralee was to Bo's left. Scratch moved closer on the right. Bo reached over and handed the reins of his horse to his old friend.

"Hold her steady!"

It was an awesome spectacle, the three horses galloping at full speed so close together that a man could barely fit a hand between them, with the herd of runaway cattle crowding them from behind. Bo kicked his feet free of the stirrups, told the farmer, "All you have to do is hang on right where you are!"

He let go of the farmer and lunged out of the saddle. He threw himself as hard as he could onto the back of Lauralee's horse and wrapped his arms around her. For a harrowing second his legs hung in midair, but then he was able to heave his left leg over the horse's back and haul himself upright just behind the cantle of Lauralee's saddle.

"Got it?" she called over her shoulder to him.

"Got it!"

"Then let's get out of here!"

She urged her horse to greater speed. Scratch did likewise, and since he was leading Bo's horse, that animal had no choice but to call on its reserves of strength, too.

The gap between the riders and the stampede widened slightly.

Bo looked back and saw the leaders curving away to the right. Through roiling clouds of dust he spotted riders on the left flank pushing them in that direction.

"Veer left!" he told Lauralee. That would take them away from the direction the herd was turning.

With Lauralee and Scratch heading one way and the herd going the other, it was only a matter of minutes before the riders were out of danger. They slowed and stopped. The gallant horses stood there with their muscles trembling, their sides heaving, and their sleek hides covered with the foam of sweat.

Now that they weren't about to be trampled to death, Bo realized just how tightly he was holding Lauralee and how close together their bodies were pressed. He felt the soft warmth of her breasts against his arm.

Embarrassed, he let go of her.

If she minded how he'd been holding her, she gave no sign of it.

"Powder River and let 'er buck!" Scratch exclaimed as they watched the gradually slowing herd. "I wish I could've seen that instead of bein' right in the middle of it. It must've been like somethin' out of one of those dang Wild West Shows!"

Bo slid down from the back of Lauralee's horse and was glad to get his feet on the ground again. She dismounted, too, and asked him, "Are you all right?"

He nodded and said, "Thanks to you, I am." He paused, then added, "What are you doing here?"

"Saving your bacon, from the looks of it," she said with a grin. He could tell from the lines of strain on her face, though, that she realized how close they had all come to dying.

"I was sure mighty glad to see you, Lauralee," Scratch said from the back of his horse. "I never seen an angel in a Bible storybook that looked like you, but it sure seemed like you was sent from heaven when you came gallopin' up beside us!"

Scratch was right. In boots, jeans, a man's shirt, and the brown Stetson with her curly blond hair tucked underneath it, Lauralee didn't look like a biblical angel. Throw in the deviltry that usually lurked in her eyes and she sure didn't, thought Bo.

But she had saved them, and it was pretty miraculous the way she had done it, too.

None of which answered the question he had asked her.

"You didn't tell me why you're here," he said to her.

"Because I want to be," she answered with a defiant tone in her voice. "Everybody in town knew that you were driving that herd to the coast. Some of us can make a pretty good guess why, too. The Star C needs cash. I knew you Creels would be too proud to accept a loan from me, but I figured I could come along and help you with the drive."

"You don't have enough cash to take care of my pa's problem," Bo said.

"How do you know how much I have? The Southern Belle is mine free and clear, and it's the most successful saloon in Bear Creek!"

She had a point there. And knowing how smart she was, maybe she really had managed her money well enough to have twelve thousand dollars on hand, Bo mused.

But it didn't matter. She was right about the Creel pride. Not only that, but taking a loan from her to pay off the bank would still leave the ranch in debt. Putting an end to that situation was what this cattle drive was all about.

"Since when did you become a cowgirl?" Scratch asked. "I never knew you could ride like that!"

"I don't spend all my time in a saloon. I've been riding ever since I was a little girl. I'm a fair hand with a rope, too." She touched the butt of the Colt holstered on her hip. "And with this, when I need to be."

Scratch grinned and said, "Dadgum, girl, you're just full of surprises!"

Lauralee gave Bo a challenging look and said, "All anybody had to do was ask, if they really wanted to get to know me better."

Bo didn't know what to say to that, so he turned to the farmer they had rescued from the stampede. The man was still on Bo's horse, slumped forward over the animal's neck, holding on tightly as he let out an occasional moan.

"You can let go now, mister," Bo said. "You're safe."

The man was in his mid-twenties, Bo estimated, with

a rumpled thatch of dark hair and a beard. His eyes were still so wide that they seemed about ready to pop out of their sockets as he turned his head to look at Bo.

"You . . . you saved me," he said.

"We didn't want to see a man get trampled," Bo said.

"Even a damned fool," Scratch added.

"I . . . I don't know what to say . . . Thank you. You risked your lives for me, and I . . . None of this would have happened if I hadn't—"

"You're right about that," Bo snapped. He pointed. "Here come your friends."

The other five farmers rode hurriedly toward them. As the men reined in, the one who had been the spokesman earlier called anxiously, "Samuel, are you all right?"

"Yes, Asa, I am." The young farmer nodded toward Bo, Scratch, and Lauralee and added, "Thanks to these people."

Gruffly, the farmer called Asa said, "I reckon we owe you folks a debt of gratitude—"

"Darn right you do," Scratch interrupted him. "If we hadn't gotten him out of there, you wouldn't even recognize this young fella as human after those cows got through tromping over him."

Asa's face hardened. He said, "I know that, but you still can't—"

"Don't waste your time blustering, mister," Bo said. "It's all moot now, anyway."

"It's all . . . what?"

"Whether you want to let our herd go across your

land or not, it doesn't matter now. Those cows have slowed down, but they're not going to stop completely until they get to the Guadalupe River. And that's your doing, not ours."

"You mean it's my doing," Samuel said with a hang-dog look. "If I hadn't lost my head and acted so crazy . . ."

Asa looked like he still wanted to argue, but he turned and looked for a moment at the dust cloud trailing off to the southwest before he sighed.

"You're right," he said. "The damage has already been done. And since we owe you for saving Samuel's life . . . Well, there's nothing more to be said, is there?"

"Not really," Bo agreed. "But for what it's worth, I'm sorry if any of your crops were ruined. Once a herd starts running away like that, there's only so much you can do to stop them."

Samuel climbed up behind one of his friends, and the farmers all rode off to find his horse. Bo and Lauralee mounted their horses and joined Scratch in riding after the herd.

"I think you should head back to Bear Creek," Bo said.

"You'd better be talking to Scratch," Lauralee said, "because I'm not going anywhere except to the coast with you."

"Who's going to take care of the Southern Belle while you're gone?"

"Roscoe can handle that job just fine, and you know it," she said.

"Cattle drives can be pretty dangerous," Bo pointed out.

"I know," Lauralee said with a smile. "I believe I proved that I can take care of myself a little while ago."

Scratch said, "Looked to me like you sort of took care of Bo, too. I ain't sure any of us would've made it out of there if it wasn't for you, gal."

"Thank you, Scratch," Lauralee said as Bo cast a brief glare at the silver-haired Texan. "It's nice to know that somebody appreciates what I've done."

"I appreciate you," Bo said. "I just don't want you to get hurt."

"And again, I can take care of myself."

"I'll just be wasting my time if I keep on arguing with you, won't I?"

"I'd say so," Lauralee replied. "And I can think of better ways for you to spend it."

Bo didn't figure it would be a good idea to ask her specifically what ways she was talking about.

Knowing Lauralee, she just might tell him.

CHAPTER 23

Not long after that, they spotted Riley and Cooper riding toward them in the distance. Bo was greatly relieved to see his brothers. He had figured they were smart enough to stay out of the way of the stampede, but accidents could always happen.

"Lauralee Parker!" Riley exclaimed when the two groups of riders met up and reined in. "What in blazes are you doing way out here?"

"People keep asking me that," Lauralee said. "No 'howdy, nice to see you' or anything."

"Howdy, Miss Parker," Cooper said with a twinkle in his eyes. "It's mighty nice to see you, as always."

Lauralee laughed.

"And you're a charmer, as always, Mr. Creel," she told him.

"What happened to that blasted farmer?" Riley asked. "Did he get trampled?"

"He's all right," Bo said. He explained how they had managed to get Samuel—and themselves—safely out of the way of the stampede. "If Lauralee hadn't come along, though, we probably wouldn't have made it."

"I think that gives me the right to be part of this drive, doesn't it?" she said.

Riley frowned, took his hat off, and raked his fingers through his hair.

"Never heard of takin' a woman along on a cattle drive before," he said stiffly as he put the hat back on. "I'm grateful for the help you gave us, Miss Parker, but—"

"But I need to turn around and go back to Bear Creek and run my saloon like a good little girl, is that it?"

Riley's nostrils flared as he took a deep breath.

"Didn't say that. I'm just not sure it's a good idea for you to be out here with us."

"Then you and Bo are in agreement on that."

Riley glanced at Bo, who figured his brother was a little surprised that they agreed on anything these days.

"I already told her to go home," Bo said.

"And she told him to go climb a stump, pretty much," Scratch added with a grin.

Cooper said, "Are you sure you want to spend a couple of weeks around a bunch of cussin', spittin' cowboys, Miss Lauralee?"

"Who do you think make up most of the customers in my saloon?" she asked.

That prompted Cooper to shrug, chuckle, and say, "She's got a point there, boys."

Bo said, "You can come along, Lauralee, but if you do, you have to remember one thing."

"What's that?"

"You'll be just another hand on this drive, which means you'll follow my orders as trail boss, and Riley's, as well, since he's the *segundo*."

Lauralee looked like the idea of taking orders didn't sit all that well with her, but she said, "All right. I can do that."

Bo wasn't sure if she could or not, but he supposed they could at least give it a try. It wasn't like they were headed out into the middle of nowhere. There were a number of little towns they would be passing nearby where they could leave Lauralee and pick her up on the way back if they had to.

With that settled, the five of them rode after the herd. Bo asked, "Was anybody hurt during that stampede?"

"Good luck was with us," Riley said. "All the boys did their jobs just fine. Nobody got thrown or gored or anything else."

"May have to find a creek where some of the younger ones who hadn't been through a stampede before can wash out their longhandles, though," Cooper said. "Beggin' your pardon for being so crude, Miss Lauralee."

"That's all right," Lauralee told him. "I was raised in a saloon, remember? You probably never ran into a girl like me before."

"That's the truth," Bo muttered, but when Lauralee

asked him what he'd said, he told her he had just been clearing his throat.

Bo's prediction that the cattle would stop when they reached the Guadalupe River proved to be accurate. Along the way they had broken down some fences and trampled through several fields of cotton and one of sorghum.

Bo hated to see the damage to the fences and crops, but there was nothing he and his brothers could do about it. They hadn't started the stampede. If those farmers had been willing to work with them, they could have avoided most of this trouble.

When they got to the river, they found the herd gathered on its eastern bank, held there by Lee, Jason, Davy, and the rest of the Creel grandsons. Alonzo Hammersmith and the chuck wagon were with them, the old cook having been released by his captors.

Lee rode out to meet Bo and the others and waved a hand toward the stream.

"Bank's too steep to take 'em across here," he reported. "A couple of the boys went lookin' for a ford."

"Upstream or down?" Riley asked. "I remember a place a mile or two downstream where we ought to be able to get the cattle across."

"Actually, one went one way and one went the other," Lee said. "We figured one of 'em was bound to find a place."

Bo nodded and said, "That was good thinking. For

now, we'll let the cattle rest and graze a mite after running like that." He glanced at the sun. "It's late enough in the day we might want to wait until morning to make the crossing."

Riley gave a grudging nod of agreement.

Most of the younger Creels were looking curiously at Lauralee. They all knew who she was, even the younger ones who weren't allowed in the Southern Belle yet.

"You boys know Miss Parker," Bo went on. "She helped Scratch and me rescue that hotheaded farmer who started the stampede." He paused, then added with obvious reluctance, "She's going along on the drive with us. I expect all of you to treat her with absolute respect at all times."

"If you don't," Riley said, "you'll get your ears boxed— if you're lucky."

"If you're not lucky," Cooper said, "you'll get a strap taken to your behind. Creels know how to behave around a lady, and don't you forget it."

Lauralee said, "I appreciate that, but remember, I'm just another cowhand on this cattle drive, like everybody else."

That was a nice sentiment, thought Bo, but it wasn't true. Lauralee was about as far from being just another cowhand as anybody could get.

Scratch said, "Here comes the fella who rode downstream to look for a ford."

Riley's memory turned out to be correct. The young Creel who had gone scouting reported that a little more than a mile downstream, the banks were gentle enough and the river shallow enough that the cattle could get across without too much trouble.

"We'll move the herd on down there and hold them overnight," Bo decided. "Make the crossing first thing in the morning."

"You think those sodbusters will come lookin' for any more trouble?" Scratch asked.

"After everything that's happened—and that almost happened—I hope not," Bo said. "But we'll have guards posted all night anyway. A herd on the move like this is always tempting trouble."

Alonzo Hammersmith reached into the back of his chuck wagon, picked up a sawed-off shotgun, and placed it on the seat beside him. He said, "I'd like to see those high-handed varmints try anything else. They took me by surprise the first time. Next time I'll say howdy with a face full o' buckshot."

"Let's hope it doesn't come to that," Bo told the irascible old cook. He waved a hand over his head and called to the members of the crew, "Move 'em out!"

They camped beside the river, which was a peaceful stream only a few feet wide and not any more than that deep.

Bo knew that tranquil appearance could be deceptive. He had seen the Guadalupe when it was up, when heavy rains in the hill country west of Austin caused raging floods all the way to the coast. The Guadalupe and the San Antonio Rivers were notorious for bursting out of their banks and inundating all the bottom land through which they flowed.

There wasn't much danger of that at this time of year, especially after a fairly dry season that had left the river at a slightly lower level than usual. Bo was confident they wouldn't have to worry about flash floods unless a hurricane came in before they reached Rockport. This was the right season for such devastating storms.

Lauralee made the mistake of offering to help Alonzo Hammersmith prepare supper. Bo would have headed her off from that if he'd had the chance, but before he knew what was going on, Hammersmith was bellowing at the top of his lungs.

"If anybody thinks I need a dang she-wolf to help me rustle grub, maybe I better just pack up and light a shuck outta here!" he threatened. "I been feedin' cowboys for nigh on to thirty years, and the day I need some fancy female critter tellin' me what to do is the day I throw my pots and pans in the river and go off to sit on a cactus!"

"But . . . but . . ." Lauralee said, looking surprised and flustered. "I didn't mean to offend you, Mr. Hammersmith. I just thought—"

"Thought you was a better cook than me!"

"No, I swear I never thought that," Lauralee said as she held her hands up, palms out in an entreating gesture. "I would never try to usurp your authority—"

"Never try to what? Now you're not only a better cook than I am, you're smarter, too, with them highfalutin words, is that it?"

Lauralee stood there wide-eyed, clearly surprised by the hornets' nest she had stumbled into and unsure what to say next for fear of stoking the fire of the cook's rage even more.

Bo took pity on her and went over to put a hand on her shoulder.

"We'll go on now, Mr. Hammersmith, and let you get on about your business," he said as he turned Lauralee away from the chuck wagon.

Hammersmith snorted and said caustically, "Damn well about time. And if you think I'm gonna apologize for my language, you can go rassle a skunk!"

Trying not to laugh out loud, Bo steered Lauralee to the other side of the camp. As supremely self-confident as she was, it was good every now and then to see her run up against a situation where she didn't know what to do.

"Honestly, I didn't mean to cause any trouble," she began.

"I know that," Bo told her. "A range cook is sort of like the king of all he surveys, though. Most of them don't take kindly to anything they take as a challenge to their authority."

"That's not what I meant to do," Lauralee insisted. "I just wanted to give him a hand."

"Doesn't matter what you meant. It's the way Mr. Hammersmith took it that counts."

"Like the way you don't want me here, even though all I'm trying to do is help."

"It's not a matter of not wanting you here," Bo said. "I'm always glad for your company. I just don't want to see you get hurt, that's all."

"What if I promise I won't?"

"I don't see how you can do that. Nobody knows what the future is going to bring." Bo shook his head. "There are no guarantees in life."

Quietly, Lauralee asked, "Did you really believe there were, back when you got married and had kids?"

Bo stiffened and said, "I don't reckon I want to talk about that."

"Why not? That's what this is all about, isn't it? This thing between you and me."

Bo shook his head.

"There's nothing between you and me except friendship, Lauralee."

"But there could be," she insisted. "If you weren't afraid."

A frown creased Bo's forehead. He said, "You think that's what it is? That I'm afraid of getting involved with you? You think the fact that I'm more than twice your age doesn't have anything to do with it?"

"You're only a *little* more than twice my age," she pointed out. "And if that doesn't bother me, why should it bother you?"

"Because I've got a sense of what's right and proper, that's why."

"And I don't, because I'm just a saloon girl. A trollop."

"I never said that," Bo protested. "And you know

good and well I don't think that. You're a lot more than that, and everybody knows it."

"Then it comes back to the fact that you're scared."

The two of them were standing in the shadows under a live oak. The glow from the campfire didn't quite reach them. Bo could see well enough to know that she was looking intently at him, however. She had let her hair tumble loose around her face when she took her hat off earlier, and now he saw the blond curls stir slightly as a night breeze made the tree branches sway and tremble.

He put his hands on her shoulders. She lifted her head and tipped it back slightly. He knew she expected him to pull her to him and kiss her. And he was tempted to do exactly that.

Lord, was he tempted.

But he said, "Lauralee, there are some things we just have to accept in life, no matter how much we wish we could change them. If I was younger . . . if I had something to offer you besides pain and regret . . . well, things would be different between us, I can promise you that. But they aren't, and we have to live with it."

"Living with things . . . hurts," she whispered.

"Yes, it does," Bo agreed. "But pain—all sorts of pain—is the price we pay for being alive."

"Damn it, Bo . . ."

"If you want to turn around and go back to Bear Creek in the morning, I'll understand."

She pulled away from him and snapped, "I'm not a quitter. Never have been and never will be. I said I was going along on this cattle drive, and by God, that's what I'm going to do!"

Her answer didn't surprise him at all.

Over by the chuck wagon, Alonzo Hammersmith called out, "Coffee's hot and the biscuits are done! Come an' get 'em 'fore I throw 'em out, dang your ornery cowboy hides!"

CHAPTER 24

Samantha couldn't help but notice that Trace Holland didn't come back to the Rafter F with Nick. She didn't really care where the gunman had gotten off to, but his absence made her curious. If she hadn't seen him sneaking around with Nick, she never would have given it a second thought.

But were they really sneaking around? she asked herself that night. She had seen them ride away together, sure, but they had done so openly.

Maybe she was just trying to distract herself from the fact that Lee was gone and she wouldn't see him for the next couple of weeks. That weighed even more heavily on her mind than Trace Holland's disappearance.

A couple of days later, when she was passing by the open door of the ranch office and saw Nick sitting at the desk with some papers in front of him, she decided to indulge her curiosity and went in.

"Nick, can I ask you a question?"

He didn't glance up from the papers, which were covered with printing and numbers. Samantha didn't know anything about how the ranch was run and didn't really care to know, even though she didn't think it was fair that her father intended to leave the spread to Nick and Danny and cut her out of it.

"What is it?" Nick asked.

"I noticed that Trace Holland hasn't been around the past couple of days. What happened to him?"

That made Nick look up. In fact, his reaction was rather sharp, Samantha noticed.

But his tone was deliberately casual as he said, "What do you care about Trace Holland?"

"I didn't say I did. I'm just curious, that's all."

She started to add that she had seen Holland riding off with Nick but then decided not to reveal that.

Nick waved a hand and said, "He drew his time and left, that's all. I don't know where he went and don't care."

Again, Samantha thought her brother was acting a little too disinterested. Plenty of times, she had seen Nick's reaction when he really didn't care about something, and this was different.

"I was just curious," she said again.

Nick grunted and looked back down at the papers.

"A saddle tramp like Holland's not worth being curious about," he said. "Forget him."

"Of course." Samantha hesitated. "What's that you're looking at?"

A slightly annoyed expression appeared on his face.

He wasn't accustomed to her asking questions about ranch business.

"I was just figuring what it would take to expand our herd. How much money . . . and how much range."

"I didn't know you were planning to expand the herd. I haven't heard Pa say anything about it."

"I'm just considering the possibility. Haven't bothered him with it yet."

"Oh. Well, that makes sense, I guess."

He couldn't conceal his impatience as he asked, "Was there anything else, Samantha?"

"No, I guess not. I'm sorry I bothered you, Nick."

"No bother. I've just got things to do, that's all."

She left the office, but she was more puzzled now than she had been when she went in.

She didn't like the idea that Nick was trying to hide something, and she especially didn't care for a gunman like Trace Holland being mixed up in whatever it was.

Despite what she had told Nick, she was more determined than ever now to find out what was going on.

And while she was doing that, maybe she wouldn't be thinking about how much she missed Lee . . .

The bunkhouse had always been forbidden for Samantha to enter. Her father didn't want her becoming involved with any of the cowboys who worked for him. She could do much better for herself than that, he had declared, and he would see to it that she did.

Once his feud with the Creels had heated up and he began hiring men of unsavory character for their gun-handling skills, Ned Fontaine was even more determined that his daughter wouldn't associate with any of them. She was allowed to be around the barn and the corrals during the day, but that was all.

So she couldn't try to find out from any of the hands if they knew where Trace Holland had gone. They would profess ignorance or just refuse to answer her, and then there was a good chance they would go to Nick or her father and tell them that she was asking questions about things that were none of her business.

That left her with only one option.

Spying.

She spent a lot of time in the barn, ostensibly taking care of the horses she used for riding, but her real purpose was eavesdropping on the hands when they came in to get something from the tack room or tend to their own mounts.

The Rafter F had its own blacksmith shop, since several of the men were qualified to work as farriers, and Samantha made a point of being around there whenever some of the cowboys had gathered for one reason or another.

The members of the crew took their meals at a long table in a wing built onto the bunkhouse. The weather was still nice enough that the windows in that dining hall were usually open, so Samantha managed to linger just below one of them one evening while the hands had supper.

She hadn't heard anything worthwhile, though, just some bawdy jokes that made her ears burn with embarrassment, before Danny stepped out onto the porch of the main house and called, "Hey, sis, where are you? It's time for supper!"

Samantha scurried through the twilight shadows and circled around to make it look like she was coming from the barn.

She was glad she hadn't overheard the cowboys making any ribald comments about *her*. She was sure they did from time to time, but hearing them might have been too much to bear.

"Where you been?" Danny asked in a surly voice as she came up to the porch. "Pa says you're always off somewhere these days, instead of underfoot like you usually are."

She figured Danny had added that part about her being underfoot. It didn't sound like something her father would have said. But Danny, despite being younger than her, had always acted like he considered her a pest.

"I was just out in the barn brushing Sweetie Pie," she said, referring to the white horse she rode more than any of the others.

Danny snorted.

"Damn stupid name for a horse," he muttered. "Reckon you like those horses more'n you like people."

"More than *some* people," she said, not bothering to disguise the tart tone that sprang into her voice.

"Then why don't you just marry one of 'em? Seems to me you got a better chance of doin' that than you do of findin' a real husband."

"Oh!" Samantha suppressed the urge to slap him. That would just cause more trouble than it was worth. "You're terrible, Danny Fontaine."

"Just honest, that's all," he said with a smug, self-satisfied grin.

She couldn't tell him about Lee Creel and how she hoped that the two of them would be married someday. Instead she said, "I don't see you out looking for a wife. You're too busy dallying with painted saloon hussies to court a respectable young woman."

"I'll get around to it in time, don't you worry. Right now I still got wild oats to sow."

"Maybe that's how I feel."

He snorted again and said, "Girls don't have wild oats, stupid."

Ned Fontaine appeared in the doorway. He said, "What are you two wrangling about now? I sent you to find your sister, Danny, not argue with her."

"There she is," Danny said, pointing. "I found her."

"Well, come in and eat supper before it gets cold. Good Lord, I'm surrounded by barbarians."

That evening, after she had eaten, Samantha realized that her spying on the ranch hands was misdirected. It would just be a fluke if she happened to overhear a conversation between any of the men about Trace Holland's whereabouts. Most of them probably didn't have any idea where the gunman had gone.

But there was one person on the ranch who did know for sure, or at least she was convinced he did.

Her brother Nick.

From now on, she decided as she sat in her room on the second floor of the ranch house, she would keep an eye on him.

Even now, she smelled tobacco smoke and knew it came from the cigar Nick smoked every evening as he sat out on the porch. The aromatic smell drifted up and in through her open window.

Acting on impulse, she blew out the lamp in her room, went to the window, and pushed the curtain back so she could look out into the ranch yard.

She couldn't have said what made her think anything was going to happen, but if it did, she wanted to be where she would know about it.

Nothing happened, of course, except that nearly half an hour dragged by tediously. She was wasting her time, Samantha told herself. She might as well go to bed.

If she was lucky, she might dream about Lee.

Then she heard the faint crunch of footsteps coming across the yard from the direction of the bunkhouse. Samantha slid the window up farther and leaned out a little so she could see better.

At first she couldn't make out anything, but then a figure ambled into the faint glow that spread across the yard from lamps in the house. She heard spurs chinging and recognized the shape as that of Owen McNamara, one of the hands who had been hired more for his skill with a gun than with a rope or a branding iron.

The only reason McNamara would be approaching the house right now was if he wanted to talk to Nick.

Without pausing to think about what she was doing, Samantha rushed out of her room, down the rear stairs, and out a side door into the night. She slid along the wall toward the front of the house, where she could peek around the corner and see onto the front porch.

McNamara had a shoulder propped against one of the posts that supported the roof over the porch. He was rolling a quirley as he said, "—handful of men left over there, boss, just like you thought when you sent me to scout around. We could take the rest of the herd without any problem."

Nick stood at the top of the steps, looking out at the night in his usual pose with his hands tucked into his hip pockets. He had a fresh cigar in his mouth, clenched between his teeth.

He said around the cheroot, "If you did that, you'd have to kill all the hands the Creels left behind. It was different when it was Palmer's bunch hitting the Star C herd. Even if any of them got spotted, nobody knew they were working for me. I can't have Rafter F men identified as rustlers."

In the shadows at the corner of the house, Samantha's eyes got so big she felt like they might pop right out of her head. Her heart slugged painfully inside her chest.

She had worried in the past that maybe Nick was

cutting some corners he shouldn't have, but she'd never dreamed that he had become an outright criminal.

And yet he was talking about having a gang of rustlers working for him, led by someone named Palmer. There was no mistaking his meaning. He had just admitted that he was behind all the thefts from the Star C herd.

Owen McNamara had finished rolling his smoke. He put it between his lips, took a lucifer from his shirt pocket, snapped it to life with his thumbnail, and held the flame to the end of the quirley. The light from the match cast harsh shadows over his hard-planed face as he set fire to the gasper.

He shook the match out, flicked it away, and said, "You know it wouldn't be any problem takin' care of those Star C punchers, Nick. The rest of the boys and I knew it would probably come to that sooner or later."

"Sure," Nick said, "and it might yet. But we'll wait and see how Palmer's bunch does."

Samantha had to clench her jaw tightly to keep from moaning in despair. Nick and McNamara were talking about murder now, and their conversation was casually cold-blooded, too.

What had happened to Nick? He had always been distant, more like an uncle than an older brother to her, but she would have sworn that he was a decent, law-abiding man at heart, despite the hardness she sensed in him.

Had ambition and greed hardened him even more, to

the point that he was willing to work with outlaws . . . to become an outlaw himself?

The things she was hearing seemed to indicate that was the case.

Even though the world was spinning crazily around her and she felt like she might be sick, she forced herself to listen. Her brother and McNamara were still talking.

"When will you hear from Palmer?" the gunman asked.

"I told Holland to ride straight back here as soon as Palmer's bunch has the herd. He doesn't have to go all the way to Rockport with them. All I need to know is that the Creels won't be selling those cattle and ruining my plans."

McNamara chuckled.

"You reckon Palmer will leave any of those Creels alive? From what I've heard, he ain't the sort to be merciful."

"I don't care," Nick said with a note of savagery in his voice. "As far as I'm concerned, he can kill all of them, and good riddance. If all the old man's sons and grandsons are dead, he won't have anybody to back him up anymore. The Star C will be mine, and as far as anybody knows, it'll all be legal."

Grandsons . . . The word hammered inside Samantha's skull.

Lee was one of John Creel's grandsons. Lee was with the cattle drive. The drive that Nick had sent a gang of vicious rustlers and killers to raid.

She turned away, unable to listen to any more. She had already heard enough to shatter her world. Her brother an outlaw. The man she loved marked for death. It was all too much for her to bear.

She had taken only a couple of steps when everything came crashing down on her and the shadows around her grew even darker, black and hungry enough to swallow her whole as she collapsed silently.

CHAPTER 25

A dank coldness had settled over Samantha, chilling her to her very bones.

That was the first thing she was aware of as consciousness seeped back into her brain. She began to shiver.

That motion warmed her up slightly. Her sluggish blood began to course faster through her veins. She realized that the temperature wasn't really all that cold.

It was all the things she had heard her brother say that had turned her insides to ice.

She was lying on the ground, huddled near the wall of the house where she had collapsed when she fainted. That was what had happened to her. She was convinced of that, even though she had never fainted before in her life.

She had never heard Nick talking about murdering someone before, either.

Especially not Lee Creel.

Samantha pushed herself to a sitting position. Her hair was loose and tangled around her shoulders. She pushed her fingers through it as she tried to figure out what she should do.

How long had she been unconscious? She didn't know. The night was quiet, no one moving around as far as she could tell, so it might have been a while.

She could go to her father's room, wake him up, tell him what she had overheard Nick and Owen McNamara saying.

But would he believe her? She knew how stubborn Ned Fontaine was. He had faith in Nick; otherwise he wouldn't have entrusted so many details of running the ranch to his oldest son in recent months. He wouldn't want to accept that Nick had allied himself with a gang of murderous rustlers and intended to destroy the Creels any way he had to.

No, Samantha realized, even if she told her father everything, his most likely reaction would be to tell her that she was imagining things, or that she had fallen asleep and dreamed the incriminating conversation.

At best, he would call Nick in and ask him about it, and Nick would lie. Samantha was sure of that.

And then Nick would know that she was aware of his plans. Such a possibility shouldn't have frightened her . . .

But as she felt a stab of cold fear in her heart, she knew it did.

Maybe she should ride into town and tell Marshal Jonas Haltom about it.

Haltom didn't have any jurisdiction outside the settlement of Bear Creek, though.

The county sheriff was all the way up in Hallettsville.

The idea that hit her next was so far-fetched for a moment she couldn't bring herself to grasp it.

The cattle drive had left for the coast several days earlier. Lee and the other men from the Star C were dozens of miles away by now. But a herd like that could only go so far.

A lone rider on a good horse could travel a lot faster.

A day, maybe two, and she could catch up to the drive, Samantha thought. She could take Sweetie Pie and another horse, maybe the big paint called Scudder, and by switching back and forth between them she could keep up a fast pace. She knew she was a good rider, even though she had never attempted anything like what she was thinking about now.

Nick and McNamara hadn't said anything about when the Palmer gang was going to hit the herd, only that Holland would return to the ranch when the deed was done.

Holland wasn't back yet. That didn't mean the rustlers hadn't already struck, but at least it was possible they hadn't. There was a chance Samantha could carry a warning to Lee and the rest of the Creels in time.

In doing that, she asked herself, would she be betraying her own family?

No. The answer rang hard and flat in her brain. Once Nick crossed the line into lawlessness, he wasn't family anymore. He was just an outlaw to be stopped.

Deep down, Samantha knew she didn't fully believe that was true. But if she kept telling herself that, she could use it to justify her actions.

Besides, there was Lee to consider. Wild idea or not, what she did next might be the best chance of saving his life.

She pushed herself to her feet, went to the side door she had used earlier, and tried it. Thank goodness no one had come along and locked it. The door opened, and she slipped inside.

Once she was back in her room, she practically ripped her dress off and pulled on one of her riding outfits. She would be in the saddle for long hours, so she needed to be comfortable.

She wouldn't take any extra clothes. She didn't want to weigh the horses down with anything that wasn't necessary.

Food was necessary, though. She knew that quite a few biscuits had been left over at supper. Being careful on the stairs so that the treads didn't creak underneath her, she went down to the kitchen and put all the biscuits in a canvas sack. If she ate them sparingly, they would last her until she caught up with the Star C cattle drive.

She wished she could say good-bye to her father and even to Danny. If she woke either of them, though, they would want to know what she was doing. They would stop her from leaving. She couldn't take that chance.

Still moving as stealthily as possible, she went into her father's study where the gun rack was and took down the Winchester '73 carbine she usually carried when she rode out on the range. She took a box of .44-40 cartridges, as well, stuffing it in the sack with the biscuits.

That wasn't much, but it would have to do.

Using the side door again, she left the house and headed for the barn. Everything was quiet and still around the place. Peaceful, as far as anybody could tell by looking and listening.

They wouldn't be able to see the evil underneath. Samantha didn't want to, either, but the knowledge of it had been thrust upon her.

It was better this way, she told herself. Better for her to be heartsick and disillusioned than for Lee to die at the hands of those rustlers.

Sweetie Pie bobbed his head and whickered softly in greeting as Samantha began getting her saddle on him. She put halter and reins on Scudder, too. She tied the sack of food and ammunition on the saddle, slid the carbine into the boot. She got a couple of canteens she could fill at the creek and slung them on the saddle, as well. Then she led both horses out of the barn.

She worried that someone in the bunkhouse would hear her and come out to see what was going on. The cowboys must have all been sleeping soundly, though, because no one raised an alarm. She walked and led the horses for a couple of hundred yards before she swung up into the saddle on Sweetie Pie's back.

Then she took a deep breath, told herself that she was doing the right thing, and rode away from her father's ranch, heading southwest into the night.

When everyone got up in the morning and found that she was gone, would they guess where she had gone? She didn't see how they could. Nick believed that his plan was still a secret.

They could try to track her, but there were so many hoofprints around the barn and the ranch yard that she didn't think anyone would be able to.

No, she decided, her only real enemy was time.

And every minute that ticked past might be a minute closer to death for Lee Creel.

The next morning, Nick was roused from sleep by an angry bellow from his father.

"Nick! Nick, get up! Your sister's gone, damn it."

Nick sat up in bed and cursed. He had consumed nearly an entire bottle of whiskey the previous night, after talking to Owen McNamara on the porch. He was drinking more and more these days.

That seemed to be the only way he could get his brain to slow down enough for sleep to overtake him. Otherwise he tended to lie awake in bed at night thinking about all the things he would do once the Rafter F was the largest, richest, most successful ranch in this part of Texas.

There was no reason he couldn't use that success as the basis to expand even more. Why settle for being the biggest in this area? Why not the biggest in the entire state?

That level of power and influence would open doors for him he never would have dreamed of otherwise. Why not Senator Fontaine, maybe? Or even Governor Fontaine?

Right now, though, he was just sleepy and hung over and irritated by his father standing just inside the door of his room, yapping at him like an annoying little dog and causing any pleasant thoughts to evaporate.

Nick raked his fingers through his tangled hair and said, "What the hell are you yammering about, Pa? What's that you're saying about Samantha?"

"She's gone," Ned Fontaine snapped as he advanced a couple of steps into the room. "I can't find her anywhere."

Nick glanced at the window. He could tell by the quality of the dim light coming through the gap between the curtains that the hour was fairly early. The old man had always been one to get up at the crack of dawn.

Nick had never minded his father being an early riser and insisting that everybody else should be, too, unlike Danny who preferred to carouse until all hours and then sleep until noon. There were always plenty of chores to do around a ranch.

Today, though, Nick didn't feel like it, so there was a snarl on his face as he threw the covers back and swung his legs out of bed.

"Samantha's bound to be around somewhere," he said as he stood up and reached for his trousers. "Did you check the barn? She's always fussing over those horses of hers."

"I looked out there," Fontaine said. "Sweetie Pie and Scudder are gone."

"Sweetie— What?" For a second, Nick had trouble wrapping his foggy brain around what his father had just said. "Wait a minute. Those are her horses. Aren't they?"

"Sweetie Pie is the white, Scudder is the paint," Fontaine confirmed. "They're both gone. And Jed Clemons said they were gone when he first went out there this morning."

Jed Clemons was the old cowboy who served as the Rafter F's main horse wrangler. Nick knew he was always in the barn well before the sun came up each morning.

"She's gone riding," he said with a bleary-eyed frown.

"In the middle of the night? Taking an extra horse with her?"

Son of a bitch, Nick thought. Something definitely was odd here. Maybe the old man was right to be worried about Samantha after all.

This mystery couldn't have anything to do with his

own plans, though, Nick assured himself. His sister didn't know anything about those.

Hurriedly, he pulled his clothes on. As he stomped into his boots, he asked his father, "Have you talked to Danny?"

Ned Fontaine made a disgusted noise and said, "Danny never knows anything about what's going on unless it has to do with whiskey and shameless women."

"Yeah, most of the time. Samantha probably talks to him more than she does to either of us, though."

Fontaine didn't argue with that. They weren't a close, demonstrative family by any stretch of the imagination.

Nick led the way down the hall to his brother's room. He pounded a fist on the door and called, "Danny! Wake up in there!"

There was no response.

Nick shouted through the panel again, then disgustedly gripped the doorknob and twisted it. The door wasn't locked. He threw it open and stalked into the spacious, well-appointed room that somehow still managed to look and smell like a pigsty because of Danny's filthy habits.

It wasn't unheard of for Danny to pass out in some whore's crib or spend the night playing poker in Bear Creek, then come dragging back to the ranch in the middle of the day. Nick halfway expected to find him gone, too.

But there was an ungainly lump of tangled sheets in the middle of the bed, and raucous snores came from it. Muttering a curse, Nick stepped over to the bed, grabbed one end of the sheet, and heaved.

As the bedclothes unfurled, Danny came flying out of them. He landed on the floor with a heavy *thump* and let out a howl of surprise and anger.

"What the hell are you doing?" he demanded as he glared up at Nick. If anything, his eyes were even more bleary and red-rimmed than those of his brother.

"Getting your lazy behind out of bed," Nick replied. "Do you know where Samantha is?"

That question made Danny look more confused than angry. He said, "What are you talking about? She's in her room, I reckon, or maybe out at the barn."

Nick shook his head. His father had followed him into the room and was sucking at his teeth, making worried sounds that grated on Nick's nerves.

"She's not either place," he told Danny. "And two of her horses are gone. The white and that big paint. She rides them more than any of the others."

"Well, there you go," Danny said with a wave of his hand. "She's out ridin'." Then he frowned and went on, "Wait a minute. You said *two* of her horses are gone?"

"Yeah. That doesn't sound like she's just gone for a short ride, does it?"

Danny grabbed hold of the bed to steady himself as he climbed to his feet. He wore only the bottom half of a pair of long underwear, and Nick's nose wrinkled at the smell coming off him. It was a mixture of whiskey, vomit, and the sort of cheap toilet water soiled doves drenched themselves in to cover up the fact they hadn't had a bath in a while.

If sin and degradation had a smell, Danny Fontaine's current aroma was it.

But that didn't matter now, and it wouldn't matter in the future, either, Nick thought. Once he was governor, he would make sure to keep Danny out of the public eye. The kid could do whatever he wanted, as long as he was discreet about it.

"Did you talk to your sister after supper last night?" Ned Fontaine asked.

"Naw," Danny said. "I went into town—"

"I reckon we know that," Nick said dryly.

"And I didn't see her before I left," Danny snapped. "Or after I got back, for that matter."

Something occurred to Nick. He turned to his father and asked, "Had her bed been slept in?"

"I . . . I don't remember," Fontaine said. "I didn't really look that close . . ."

"Let's go look now," Nick suggested.

The three of them went down the hall to Samantha's room. Nick opened the door, and it took him only a second to see that the covers hadn't been pulled back on the bed. They looked like maybe Samantha had sat on the bed for a while, but it didn't appear that she had slept in it.

With a curse, he turned away from the door. His father caught at his arm and said, "What are you going to do?"

"I'm gonna go find her, of course," Nick said.

He questioned every man on the ranch. None of them would admit to having seen Samantha since the previous day, and Nick figured they were all too afraid of him to lie. He sent the hands to look for her, ordering them to spread out all over Rafter F range.

The best tracker on the ranch was a middle-aged Mexican named Gomez. Nick thought he was part-Indian, which would account for his skill at following a trail. Gomez found some tracks he thought might belong to Samantha's horses. He and Nick followed them to Bear Creek.

Nick reined to a halt on the bank and stared across the stream at the Star C range. Why in blazes would Samantha go over there? He couldn't come up with a good reason.

For that matter, it was impossible to be sure that the tracks he and Gomez had followed actually were those of Samantha's horses.

Gomez nodded toward the Creel ranch and asked, "You want me to go over there and take a look around, boss?"

Nick pondered the question while mentally cursing his sister. Whatever Samantha was trying to pull, why had she had to go and do it right now? Nick had too much on his plate to worry about this. And if Gomez crossed the creek and ran into any of the Creel punchers and got into a fight with them, it would just stir up trouble that Nick didn't need.

"No," he said. "We'll go back and see if any of the others find her."

Gomez nodded, as stolid as ever. He and Nick turned their horses away from the creek.

When Samantha came back—and Nick was sure that she would, sooner or later—she needed to have a strap taken to her, he thought. There was a time when their father would have done exactly that.

These days, Nick wasn't sure that Ned Fontaine cared enough to do such a thing. If that turned out to be the case, then he'd have to take care of it himself, he mused.

He was the head of this family now, and by God, the sooner the others understood and accepted that, the better!

CHAPTER 26

Bo, Scratch, and the others pushed the herd across the Guadalupe River without incident the next morning after the near-disastrous encounter with the farmers. They continued southwest the rest of the day without running into any more trouble.

As they got ready to make camp late that afternoon at a spot Alonzo Hammersmith had selected, Lauralee rode up to Bo. She was covered from head to toe with a thick layer of grayish-brown dust and looked miserable.

"I hope you're satisfied with yourself," she said. "You told me to ride drag just so I'd get filthy, didn't you?"

"That never crossed my mind," Bo said, which was stretching the truth a mite. "It's just a job that has to be done. Somebody's got to push those stragglers back to the herd."

"You didn't give me the dirtiest job there is so I'd change my mind and go back to Bear Creek?"

"Nope."

As a matter of fact, he had thought that she would be

less appealing with trail dust all over her, and therefore it would be easier for him to resist the temptation she represented.

Turned out the idea wasn't totally successful. Even filthy, Lauralee Parker was a beautiful woman. No amount of trail dust could hide that completely.

She took off her hat, revealing a distinct line across her forehead above which the dust hadn't settled.

"I look ridiculous," she said.

"Not really," Bo said, and this time he was telling the truth.

"You stuck me back there with a bunch of teenage boys."

Bo shrugged and said, "The less experienced hands usually ride drag. That's just the way it is on a cattle drive."

Lauralee clapped her hat back on and muttered, "All right, all right, I'll quit bellyaching. I don't want to prove your point for you."

"What point is that?"

"That I shouldn't be on this drive in the first place."

With that, she hauled her horse around and rode off toward the herd, which some of the hands were gathering in a big meadow between stands of cottonwoods.

Scratch rode up beside Bo and said with a smile, "Stubborn gal, ain't she?"

"In more ways than one," Bo agreed.

The next day they crossed Coleto Creek, again without incident. It was not far from here, Bo reflected, where James Fannin and a force of Texas volunteers had engaged the Mexican army in battle during the revolution. Facing overwhelming odds—and plagued by Fannin's own indecisiveness, to be honest, Bo recalled from those days—the Texans had been defeated and the survivors taken prisoner and marched into the town of Goliad.

It was near there where those prisoners had been herded together and massacred by their Mexican captors, with only a few escaping to carry word of the bloody atrocity.

That massacre had come back to haunt the Mexicans a few weeks later when the Texan army under Sam Houston charged across a grassy field near the San Jacinto River screaming the battle cry, "Remember the Alamo! Remember Goliad!"

Bo Creel and Scratch Morton had been among them.

The Texans had carried the day and won their independence. And a lifelong bond of friendship had been forged.

Scratch rode up beside Bo as he sat watching the cattle cross the creek.

"Rememberin' back to the Runaway Scrape days?" Scratch asked.

"Yeah, and San Jacinto."

"A mighty long time ago."

"In some ways it seems like yesterday," Bo said. "But it wasn't. Texas has changed a lot since then."

"So have we," Scratch said. "My knees and my back

tell me about it every mornin' when I crawl out of my bedroll and stand up."

It would take several days now for the herd to reach the San Antonio River. That would be the last major ford the cattle would have to make, although there would be a number of little streams to be crossed as they came closer to the coast. There was a bay northeast of Rockport they would have to circle, too, before they reached the seacoast settlement.

The next two days were uneventful. Cattle drives were a little like war, Bo thought—long stretches of utter tedium, punctuated by occasional outbursts of heart-stopping danger.

He hoped the stampede they'd had to cope with back on the other side of the Guadalupe was going to be the only instance of the latter on this drive.

In camp that night, Bo sat down next to his nephew Lee, one of Cooper's boys, who was perched on a log near the fire. Lee had proven to be a good solid hand, one of the best in the bunch, in fact. The young man wore a pensive look on his face tonight, though.

Bo took a sip of the coffee in the tin cup he held and asked, "Something bothering you, Lee?"

"No, not really, Uncle Bo. Just, uh . . . missin' somebody, I guess you'd say."

Bo grinned and thumbed his hat back.

"That somebody being a girl, I reckon," he said.

"Yes, sir. A mighty special girl."

"Been courting her for a while, have you?"

Lee hesitated, then said, "In a manner of speakin', I guess."

"Are you thinking you might marry her?"

A bit of a grim cast came over Lee's face in the firelight as he said, "I'd like nothin' better . . . but I don't know if it'll ever happen."

"Why not?"

"Well . . . her pa . . . Ah, there ain't no use talkin' about it."

Bo nodded sagely and said, "Yeah, if the girl's pa doesn't like you, that can make it harder. But it doesn't mean it'll never happen."

"You think so?" Lee looked and sounded like he didn't want to let himself hope as he asked that question.

"Sure. If a couple of people want to be together bad enough, they'll find a way to make it happen. You just keep that in mind, son."

"Thanks, Uncle Bo. I will." Lee tossed the dregs of his coffee in the fire and stood up. "My turn to ride nighthawk, so I reckon I better get at it. 'Night."

"Good night," Bo said.

Lee walked off to saddle a horse. Bo sat there sipping his coffee for a couple of minutes before Lauralee came up and sat down on the log beside him. She wasn't quite as filthy tonight because Bo had taken pity on her and moved her from drag to one of the flanks.

"I heard what you told Lee," Lauralee said. "About two people finding a way to get together if they want to bad enough. You really believe that, Bo?"

Well, he had set a nice little trap for himself, he

thought. But he wasn't going to lie this time, so he said, "Yes, I do."

"No matter what the obstacles between them, eh?"

"That's right." He paused. "But both of them have to want it, not just one."

"You'll never make me believe you don't want me, Bo Creel. You're just too damn stubborn to admit it."

Bo looked down into his coffee cup and muttered, "I reckon I'm not the only one around here who's stubborn."

Lauralee laughed and leaned closer to him. Lowering her voice so that only he could hear her, she asked, "You know what I'm going to do when we get to the San Antonio River, Bo?"

He figured she would tell him whether he answered or not, so he didn't say anything.

"I'm going to take a bath," she went on, so close to him now he felt the warmth of her breath against his ear. "I'm going to find me a nice swimming hole and take off all my clothes and climb in. I'm going to scrub all this trail dust off every inch of my skin. Every single . . . little . . . inch of me."

Lord, have mercy, Bo thought.

It wasn't really a prayer, but even if it had been, the Almighty would have picked a pretty odd way to answer it.

Because the next instant, gunshots roared from the direction of the herd's bedground, and their echoes rolled like thunder across the prairie.

CHAPTER 27

Bo and Lauralee leaped up from the log as the gunfire continued. Confused, angry shouts rang out. The men here in camp raced for their horses.

"Stay here!" Bo told Lauralee. "Must be rustlers hitting the herd."

"The hell with that!" she responded. "I can shoot!"

Alonzo Hammersmith came around the end of the chuck wagon holding the big wooden spoon he'd been using to stir a pot of mulligan stew. Bo grabbed Lauralee's arm and practically threw her at Hammersmith. The grizzled old cook had no choice but to catch hold of her.

"Hang on to her, Alonzo!" Bo shouted as he ran toward his still-saddled horse. "Whatever you do, don't let her go!"

Lauralee screeched angrily as she tried to writhe out of Hammersmith's grip. The cook's arms were heavily muscled from wrestling around barrels of flour and sugar and salt, though, so she couldn't pull free.

Scratch came running up as Bo swung into the saddle.

"Rustlers?" the silver-haired Texan asked as he hit the leather right after Bo.

"Must be," Bo replied.

He lifted his reins, kicked his horse into a run, and headed for the herd. Scratch was right beside him.

Up ahead, Colt flame bloomed redly in the darkness, deadly crimson flowers that split the night for an instant and then disappeared.

There was no way to tell who was doing the shooting around the herd. Swift hoofbeats and furious yells competed with the booming gunshots and added to the confusion.

Bo headed in the direction he had seen his nephew Lee ride off a short time earlier. He shouted, "Lee! Lee Creel!"

"Over here, Uncle Bo!"

Gunfire almost drowned out Lee's response, but Bo heard it and veered his horse toward his nephew. He spotted a large dark shape on the ground and realized a second later that it was the body of a horse.

Flame spouted from the muzzle of a gun as someone fired over the top of the dead animal. That had to be Lee, thought Bo. The young man's horse had been shot out from under him, but he was using it for cover as he fought back against the attackers.

Bo and Scratch galloped toward him. So Lee

wouldn't think he was being jumped from behind and start shooting at them, Bo called, "Hang on, son!"

Riders charged out of the shadows, their guns blaring as they threw lead at Lee. Bo opened fire from horse-back and Scratch did likewise. Both men knew the back of a running horse was no place for accuracy, but they wanted to take some of the heat off Lee.

Besides, a shot that found its target through blind luck could be just as deadly as one that was aimed.

The diversion worked—in a manner of speaking. Several riders peeled off from the group of attackers and came at Bo and Scratch with their guns blasting. Bo felt the hot breath of a slug passing close to his cheek and knew that blind luck could work both ways.

With the instincts they had developed over years of fighting side by side, Bo and Scratch split up, Bo going left and Scratch angling right. The maneuver was well-timed. The men who had charged them wound up going between them, unable to stop in time.

Lead from the Texans' guns raked through the raiders in a lethal crossfire. Now the range was close enough for a degree of accuracy, even in bad light, especially when the men doing the shooting were experienced gun-handlers.

A couple of men tumbled out of their saddles. The others wheeled around, though, and returned slug for slug. The air around Bo buzzed with bullets like a swarm of angry hornets was after him.

The sharp cracks of a rifle began to sound. Bo looked around and saw that Lee had gotten his Winchester in action. The young man was up on one knee now, firing as fast as he could work the rifle's lever.

Bo heard something else over the chaos around him. It was a rumble like the sound of distant drums, accompanied by a hellish clacking as if Satan's imps were playing castinets. The rumble came from hooves, the clacking from horns banging together.

The cattle were on the move.

Bo wasn't surprised. With all the shooting and yelling going on, it would have been shocking if the herd *hadn't* stampeded. As long as the cattle bolted in the right direction, they were doing the rustlers' work for them.

Bo had no doubt it was rustlers hitting the herd. He had worried that the drive would draw too much attention, and so it had.

A choking cloud of dust rose from the stampede and rolled across the landscape to mix with the acrid billows of powdersmoke. Bo called for Scratch to follow him and headed for the last place he had seen Lee, as best he could determine where it was. The dust and smoke blotted out the moon and stars now.

"Lee!" Bo called to his nephew, knowing that by doing so he might attract some bullets. "Lee, are you there?"

"Here, Uncle Bo," the reply came through the murk.

A lot of the shooting had died away quickly once the cattle stampeded. The rustlers would be busy keeping the spooked beasts headed generally in the direction they wanted them to go.

Bo knew he had to round up his brothers and nephews as quickly as possible and light a shuck after the thieves.

He couldn't let them get away with that herd. The future of the Star C depended on it.

"Uncle Bo!" Lee said as he stumbled out of the clouds of dust and smoke carrying his rifle.

Bo hauled back on his reins and brought his horse to a stop.

"Did they get you?" he asked.

"No, but they came close enough I can still hear the angels singin'. The varmints came out of nowhere—"

There was no time for explanations now. Bo holstered his Colt, took the reins in his right hand, and held his left down to Lee while he took that foot out of the stirrup.

"Come on," he said. "We've got to get after them."

"I'll just slow you down," Lee protested.

"We'll find a horse for you. There are bound to be some running loose."

Bo knew that because he had seen at least two of the rustlers fall. And although he hated to think it, with all that lead flying around there was a good chance some of his family members had been hit, too. Maybe even killed.

If that turned out to be the case, the Creels would have an even bigger score to settle with those rustlers.

Lee clasped wrists with Bo, stuck his foot in the stirrup, and swung up behind his uncle. He had just settled down on the horse's back behind Bo's saddle when a fresh fusillade of gunfire racketed through the night.

These shots came from a different direction. Bo's head jerked around as he peered toward them and spotted muzzle flashes winking in the darkness.

These sounds of battle came from the camp . . .

Where he had left Lauralee.

CHAPTER 28

Bo and Scratch hauled their horses around and galloped toward the chuck wagon. Bo was already worried sick about Riley, Cooper, and his other nephews besides Lee, and now fear lanced into him as he thought that Lauralee might be in danger. He wished she had gone on back to Bear Creek a few days earlier like he wanted.

Wishing was a waste of time, though. He had known that for more than forty years.

The dust was a lot thinner around the campsite. Bo could see the bedrolls scattered around, all of them empty now, as well as the chuck wagon and the rope corral where Alonzo Hammersmith's team of mules and the extra horses of the remuda were kept.

Some of those horses were down, probably shot deliberately by the attackers. That would make it more difficult for Bo and his relatives to go after the rustlers.

This new attack was designed to slow down pursuit, too. Whoever was in charge of the gang was crafty and cunning. He had held some of his force in reserve to strike the trail drivers' camp after the main thrust to steal the cattle had been made.

Now instead of going after the herd, Bo, Scratch, and Lee were rushing back to help those at the campsite fight off this new attack. Bo figured some of the others were doing the same thing.

The campfire was still burning. By its garish light, Bo spotted several figures crouched behind the chuck wagon, returning the fire of raiders farther out in the darkness. He hoped one of those defenders was Lauralee, but when he searched for the bright flash of her blond curls, he didn't see it.

A shotgun boomed, sending out twin tongues of flame a foot long from its muzzles. That would be Alonzo Hammersmith. Pistols roared and rifles cracked. Somebody was stretched out under the wagon, shooting at the rustlers.

As Bo reined in, Lee jumped off the horse and landed running. Bo and Scratch weren't far behind him.

Hammersmith's white spade beard jutted out belligerently as he waved them to the cover of the wagon. The three men fired on the run. Scratch's pair of Remingtons kept up a deadly tattoo as he triggered each revolver in turn.

They darted behind the wagon and were safe for the moment, or at least safer. The chuck wagon was constructed of thick, sturdy boards that would stop most bullets.

"If those bastards shoot up my foodstuffs, I'll skin

'em and nail their hides to the wall!" Hammersmith bellowed.

Bo ignored that and asked, "Where's Lauralee?"

To his great relief, he heard her call from under the wagon, "I'm here!"

When he looked down, she stuck her head out and grinned at him. Her hat hung behind her neck by its chin strap, and she had a rifle in her hands. As she worked the repeater's lever, she went on, "Are you all right, Bo?"

"I'm fine," he assured her. "How about you?"

"Don't worry about me. I think I've winged a couple of the sons of bitches."

Bo was glad to hear that but even gladder to know that she hadn't been hit so far.

The fight wasn't over yet, though.

The rustlers were still out there, hammering the chuck wagon and the rest of the camp with bullets.

Lauralee squirmed back around to start shooting again. Lee knelt at the rear corner of the wagon and opened up with his Winchester, which he had just re-loaded. Hammersmith stood behind him and fired over his head with the shotgun. Lee winced from the scatter-gun's deafening roar.

"Try not shootin' that thing so close to a fella's ears, why don't you?" he called to Hammersmith.

"Try shootin' and not bellyachin' so dang much!" the old cook responded. "Your ears'll stop ringin' in a week or so!"

Bo and Scratch used the driver's box and the wagon

tongue for scanty cover as they blazed away at the rustlers. All they had to aim at were muzzle flashes, so Bo couldn't tell if they were doing any good or not. It seemed to him the rustlers were shooting just as much as they had been to start with.

Then a swift rataplan of hoofbeats welled up, and more riders rushed to the defense of the camp. Bo heard Riley shouting his name and called to his brother, "Over here!"

Half a dozen men rode up, leaped out of their saddles, and started throwing lead at the attackers. That was enough to turn the tide. Bo saw fewer and fewer muzzle flashes from the enemy position.

"They're pulling back!" he said.

Not all of the rustlers fled, however. For long minutes, the shooting back and forth continued.

The knowledge that he and his companions were doing exactly what the rustlers wanted them to do gnawed at Bo. With every minute that went by, the stolen herd was getting farther away. But he and the others couldn't go after it as long as they were pinned down here defending the camp.

"Look out!" Riley yelled as brightly blazing torches suddenly flew through the air. Some of the rustlers had crawled close enough to light the torches and fling them at the camp. A couple of the burning brands landed on top of the chuck wagon and immediately set its canvas cover on fire.

"My wagon!" Alonzo Hammersmith howled. The air

seemed to sizzle with the curses that spewed from his mouth.

"Lauralee, get out from under there!" Bo called to her. He bent down and held out a hand to her as she crawled clear of the wagon. He clasped her hand and pulled her upright. She stumbled and fell against him, but he caught her and managed to stay on his feet.

"Bo," she said. The burning wagon behind her cast a nightmarish halo around her mass of blond hair and struck red highlights from it.

"Are you all right?" he asked.

"Yeah, I . . . I think so. What about you?"

"So far," he said.

Then the crackle of flames made him look around.

The dry summer had left a lot of the grass around the campsite dead, and now it was on fire, blazing up like tinder. Smoke stung the eyes and made it hard to see. Bo knew they had to get out of here or risk being caught in the conflagration.

A while back he and Scratch had come too blasted close to burning up in a wildfire in northern Texas. Bo didn't want to have to go through that again.

He should have known that the rustlers weren't through yet. Scratch shouted a warning.

"Here they come!"

Mounted now, the attackers charged through the camp, firing right and left as they leaned forward over the necks of their horses. Lee had to throw himself desperately to one side to avoid being trampled. Bo swung around with Lauralee in his arms and dived out of the way, taking her with him.

He rolled and came up with his gun in his hand. For a split second, he found himself looking up into the face of one of the rustlers, a man with craggy, rough-hewn features and a mustache.

Flame geysered from the muzzle of the revolver in the man's hand. Bo heard the bullet whip past his ear. He triggered a shot of his own, but the rustler kept riding and Bo figured he had missed.

Then the riders were gone, galloping off into the darkness. There was a chance they might come back, but Bo didn't think that was very likely.

They had done what they set out to do. They had stolen the herd and crippled the crew.

"Clear out!" Scratch bellowed. "Grab whatever you can and get clear of the fire!"

Men snatched up bedrolls and saddles and stumbled away from the flames. Other men helped wounded companions. The horses, panicked by the smoke and flames, had already broken free of the rope corral and scattered, so at least they escaped the blaze.

"My wagon!" Alonzo Hammersmith wailed. He started toward the chuck wagon, which was a mass of flames by now.

Scratch grabbed the cook's suspenders and hauled him back.

"You gotta let it go, old-timer!" Scratch said. "Nothin' you can do about it now!"

"I'll kill those—"

Hammersmith's threat dissolved into another river of lurid profanity.

For the next quarter-hour, everyone who was still on their feet was busy trying to salvage as much as they could from the fire. Several of the younger Creels grabbed blankets and starting beating out the flames. Gradually, they brought the blaze under control, but not before a wide swath of prairie had been scorched.

Bo and Lauralee looked for men who had been hurt. They found three dead rustlers, and then Bo stopped short at the sight of another huddled shape on the ground.

"Oh no," he said, his voice hollow.

"Who is it?" Lauralee asked.

Bo dropped to a knee next to the fallen man. He rolled the body onto its back, revealing a young face in the glare from the still-burning chuck wagon.

"My nephew Tim," he said. "One of Hank's boys."

Tim Creel had a large, dark stain on the front of his shirt where he'd caught a bullet. Bo checked for a pulse, knowing he wouldn't find one. He didn't.

A short time later they found Cooper sitting with his back propped against a rock. At first Bo feared that his brother was dead, too, but then Cooper opened his eyes and lifted his head.

"Bo," he said in a weak voice.

Bo knelt beside him and asked, "How bad are you hit?"

"They knocked my . . . leg out from under me. Don't

reckon . . . the bone's broke . . . but I lost a heap of blood."

Bo squeezed his shoulder and said, "We'll take care of you, Coop, don't worry."

"What about . . . Davy . . . and Jason . . . and Lee?"

"All of them were all right the last time I saw them."

Bo took out his Barlow knife, used it to cut a strip of cloth off Cooper's shirt, and tied it tightly around his brother's leg above the wound. That would slow down the bleeding.

He folded another piece of cloth into a pad and pressed it to the bullet hole in Cooper's thigh.

"Hold this here," he told Lauralee. "Press down hard on it."

"I've dealt with bullet wounds before," she said as she moved to do what he told her. Her face was pale in the firelight, but composed. Bo knew she wouldn't lose her nerve.

For the next several hours, that was how things went: tending to the wounded, salvaging what could be salvaged, assessing the damage. Bo ached to get started after the rustlers, but he knew that taking care of his family came first.

By the time the gray light of dawn stole over the ruined campsite, the extent of their predicament was apparent. Tim Creel was the only one who had been killed, but three of his cousins were badly wounded, along with his uncle Cooper. The chuck wagon was a pile of ashes, with only the iron tires from its wheels and some of its metal fittings remaining intact. The remuda was scattered to hell and gone, although a few of the saddled horses had remained nearby, including Bo and Scratch's mounts.

Riley looked around, took his hat off, and wearily scrubbed a hand over his face.

"What are we gonna do now?" he muttered.

Bo stood nearby with Scratch and Lauralee. He said, "We need to see if we can round up some of those horses that ran off. Tim's body has to be taken back home, and the wounded need medical attention, too. The closest town is Victoria. The ones going back will head there first."

"The ones going back," Riley repeated. "Not everybody is?"

"Scratch and I are going after those rustlers," Bo said. He hadn't asked his friend about that, but on the other hand, he didn't have to. He knew Scratch would be just as eager as he was to get after the killers.

"I'm comin' along with you, Uncle Bo," Lee declared.

"So am I," Davy said. He had a bullet burn across his cheek but was otherwise unharmed. His brother Jason nodded grimly.

Several more of the Creels spoke up and said they were going with Bo and Scratch, too.

Riley said, "One way or another, we've got to get that herd back. Count me in."

Bo looked into his brother's eyes and nodded. Whatever came next, they would fight that battle together.

Lauralee opened her mouth to say something, but before she could, the sound of hoofbeats drifted to them through the early morning air that stunk with the smell of ashes.

Somebody was coming, and Bo didn't even want to think about what fresh trouble this might be.

CHAPTER 29

Lee had never been more surprised in his life than when Samantha Fontaine appeared in the dawn light spreading over the Texas landscape, riding a white horse and leading a paint. He couldn't stop himself from exclaiming, "Samantha!"

She reined in, threw herself down from the saddle, and ran toward him.

"Lee!" she cried. "Lee, you're alive!"

"Darn right I am," he said as she ran up to him. He put his arms around her and crushed her tightly to him, drawing strength from the warm feel of her body in his embrace.

"What the hell!"

That angry bellow came from his uncle Riley.

Lee realized belatedly that he was standing there in the middle of his uncles, brothers, and cousins while he hugged one of the hated Fontaines.

But he didn't really give a damn anymore. He realized that, too. He was tired of having to skulk around and hide his feelings for Samantha.

"That's the Fontaine girl," Riley went on. "Damn it, Lee, let go of her!"

Lee stepped back and turned toward his uncles, but as he did so he slid his arm around Samantha's shoulders and kept her close beside him.

"Take it easy, Uncle Riley," he said. "I can explain—"

"Explain what you're doin' carryin' on like that with Ned Fontaine's daughter?" Riley snorted disgustedly. "I don't think so!"

Bo looked surprised by Samantha's arrival at the ruined camp, but not angry and upset about it like Riley. He said, "What are you doing here, Miss Fontaine?"

"She probably came to see if her pa's hired guns wiped us out," Riley said before Samantha could reply.

"My father didn't have anything to do with me being here," Samantha said, "or with . . . what happened."

She looked around at the burned ground, the destroyed chuck wagon, and the grim, blanket-covered shapes lying to the side. Lee saw horror and despair in her eyes as she went on, "I swear, he doesn't know a thing about it."

"He didn't hire the rustlers who attacked us last night?" Bo asked.

"No." Samantha drew in a deep breath as if she were gathering her courage to perform an unpleasant task. "But my brother Nick did."

"What!" Riley roared. "I knew it. I knew the Fontaines were behind this!"

Samantha shook her head and said, "No, it was all Nick's idea. My father didn't know about it, and neither did Danny and me. Pa and Danny, they still don't. But when I found out, I . . . I came after you. I thought maybe I could catch up . . . and warn you . . ."

Riley snorted again and shook his head.

"A likely story," he said coldly. "I don't believe it for a second. And I'd still like to know why you're so damned cozy with this girl, Lee!"

With a faint smile, Bo said, "I reckon that ought to be pretty obvious, Riley." To Samantha, he went on, "Maybe you'd better start at the beginning and tell us everything you know about this, Miss Fontaine."

For the next ten minutes she did so, and Lee was astounded at hearing how she had trailed her brother and Trace Holland, then spied on Nick until she found out what he was planning.

"I didn't want anybody to get hurt," Samantha concluded. She looked at Lee as she said that, and he knew she was talking mostly about him. "All I could think of to do was to come after you and try to warn you. But . . . I didn't get here in time. I'm sorry. I was camped a couple of miles back up the trail last night. If I had known how close you were . . ."

Her voice trailed off into a sigh.

Bo said, "If you were that close, you must have heard all the shooting during the night."

"I did," Samantha said with a nod. "I knew then that I was too late. I started to mount up and come on down here, but I . . . I was afraid."

"You did the right thing," Lee told her. "It wouldn't have done any good for you to come blunderin' into the middle of that ruckus. You would've just gotten yourself killed for no good reason."

"Like poor Tim got killed?" Riley asked. His voice was still harsh with anger.

"I'm sorry . . ." Samantha moaned.

"You're not to blame for this, Miss Fontaine," Bo said. "And no one holds it against you that you didn't want to get caught in the middle of a gun battle."

"Speak for yourself," Riley snapped. "I'm not sure I believe any of that wild story."

Lauralee spoke up, saying, "I believe it. If Miss Fontaine isn't telling the truth, what reason would she have for following us like she did?"

"Maybe the old man sent her to spy on us."

"That don't make any sense, Uncle Riley," Lee said. "You heard her. Ned Fontaine don't even know what his boy Nick's been up to."

Riley's glare made it clear that he still didn't accept Samantha's story, but for the moment he didn't say anything else.

Bo asked, "Did Nick say anything about why he sent those rustlers after us?"

"He didn't want you taking the herd to the coast and selling it. Something about the money you'd get for the cattle." Samantha shook her head. "That's all I know."

Bo rubbed his chin and frowned in thought. After a moment he said, "Nick must have something to do with Gilbert Ambrose calling in that note. I've suspected that all along, and what Samantha just told us makes that even more likely."

"All this is a waste of time," Riley said. "We've got to get after those rustlers, and our wounded need help. Let's figure out who's going on and who's headed back."

"I'm going with you after the rustlers," Lauralee said. "That's what I was about to say when Miss Fontaine rode up."

Bo blew out an exasperated breath.

"After everything that's happened so far—" he began.

"You mean the stampede and the fight with the rustlers?" Lauralee broke in. "Seems to me like I handled myself all right both of those times. Actually came in pretty handy, to be honest."

Scratch said, "She's got a point there, Bo."

Bo frowned at his old friend and asked, "Whose side are you on?"

"The side of doin' what's right, as usual. Lauralee's got more grit than a lot of *hombres* I've known. Pretty good hand with a shootin' iron, too. I don't mind havin' her along."

Several of the other men muttered their agreement with Scratch's position.

"Anyway," Lauralee said, "you're going to have to split up because some of the men have to go back with the wounded. You'll be shorthanded when you go after those rustlers. You don't want to make the odds against you even worse, do you, Bo?"

"You're the stubbornest woman I ever met, you know that?"

She smiled and said, "I never claimed to be otherwise, now did I?"

"I'd like to come along, too," Samantha said.

Lee was shaking his head before the last words were out of her mouth, but it was Riley who exclaimed, "Hell, no!"

"My brother is the one responsible for this," Samantha said. "For all the damage and the men who were wounded and . . . and the poor boy who was killed. I can't atone for what my family has done, but if I can help even a little, it'll be a start—"

"Forget it," Lee said. "It's too dangerous."

"Miss Parker's going along."

"We haven't settled that yet," Bo said.

"Yes, we have," Lauralee said.

Riley said, "If your pa hadn't already passed out from gettin' shot, Lee, the idea of you being mixed up with a Fontaine probably would have done it. How long have the two of you been carryin' on?"

"There hasn't been any carryin' on," Lee said. "Well, nothin' improper, anyway. Samantha and I have been . . . friends . . . for several months now."

"Seems like more than friends to me," Riley said contemptuously.

"That can be hashed out later," Bo said. "Not that it's really anybody else's business."

Lee felt grateful to his uncle for expressing that sentiment.

Bo went on, "Miss Fontaine, I believe what you've told us, and I don't think you came here to spy on us. But it's still not a good idea for you to come with us, any more than it is for Lauralee."

He held up a hand to forestall the argument Lauralee opened her mouth to make.

"The important thing is, we don't have any more time to waste wrangling about this. This fella Palmer you told us about already has too big a lead with our herd. I think we can catch him before he gets to Rockport with the cattle, though . . . if we get started after him right away."

Riley jerked his head in a curt nod and said, "Now you're talkin'. You women do whatever you want. But if you can't keep up, don't expect us to slow down for you."

"You really think I can't keep up, Riley Creel?" Lauralee demanded.

"I won't hold you back," Samantha promised.

Lee still thought it was a terrible idea . . . but now that his involvement with Samantha wasn't a secret anymore, he had to admit that he sort of liked the idea of being able to spend more time with her. He had already missed her a lot during the drive.

Surely he could come up with some way to keep her out of the line of fire when they caught up to the rustlers.

Bo shook his head and muttered something about

a bad idea, but he didn't argue any more with the two women. Instead he began splitting up the group, picking the men who would be responsible for taking the wounded to Victoria and returning Tim's body to the Star C. He chose mostly the younger hands, the Creel grandsons with the exception of Lee, Jason, and Davy, for that task.

Predictably, the youngsters complained. They wanted to come along and hit back at the rustlers, wanted to help recover the herd and avenge Tim's death.

Bo overruled their arguments, though, and as trail boss, his word was law when it came to things like this.

Every minute of delay chafed at Lee, and he was sure the others felt the same way. Certain things had to be done before they could set out in pursuit of the killers, though. They had to round up as many horses as they could. Some of the young men heading back would have to ride double, but that couldn't be helped.

Alonzo Hammersmith was going with the group to Victoria. Bo told the old cook, "I'm counting on you to look after those youngsters, Mr. Hammersmith."

"I'll get 'em there," Hammersmith promised. "Shouldn't take more'n a day, day and a half. That's gonna be a hard ride for your brother, though, with a bullet hole in his leg. If we still had a damn wagon to put him in . . ."

"I know," Bo said. "Cooper's tough, though. Keep the leg bandaged up good and tight. He'll make it."

Hammersmith nodded.

By mid-morning, they had found enough horses

for everyone in the group going after the rustlers to be well-mounted. The few supplies they'd been able to salvage had been split up. Both bunches were grim-faced as they separated, some of the riders going east toward Victoria, the others headed southwest toward the coast.

Lee rode alongside Samantha, who was now mounted on the white horse she called Sweetie Pie. She had given the paint to one of the other men. Without enough horses to be able to switch out fresh mounts, the chase was going to be hard on the animals. They had to make do with what they had, though.

Quietly, Samantha asked, "You do believe me, don't you, Lee? I swear I didn't know what Nick was planning until a couple of days ago."

"Sure I believe you," he told her without hesitation. "Never entered my mind to doubt you. You wouldn't think your own brother would do something like that."

"No," she said with a hollow note in her voice. "I never would have believed it if I hadn't heard it with my own ears. I mean . . . he's my brother."

"Yeah," Lee said. He tried not to sigh.

He didn't want to think about how she would feel when justice caught up to Nick.

Because the Creels weren't going to let him get away with what he had done.

Sooner or later there would be a reckoning, and Nick Fontaine was going to die.

CHAPTER 30

Trace Holland lowered the field glasses. Sitting his horse on a slight rise half a mile away, he had watched as the group of survivors from the cattle drive divided and went their separate ways.

He was glad now that he hadn't headed for home the night before, as soon as Palmer succeeded in stealing the herd from the Creels. Nick had told him to come right back, but he'd figured that it wouldn't hurt to camp nearby and let his horse rest before he started the return trip to the Rafter F.

If he hadn't done that, he couldn't have given in to the impulse to spy on the survivors this morning. Nick might want to know what they were doing.

And if he hadn't been watching the ruined camp from a distance, he never would have seen Samantha Fontaine ride in.

He knew she'd been fooling around with Lee Creel, of course. He had seen them together several times. But he'd never expected her to follow the cattle drive. She had to have a pretty good reason for doing something like that, but damned if Holland could figure out what it was.

The way she'd been hugging the Creel boy, though, she sure wasn't trying to keep their romance a secret anymore.

Now she had ridden off to the southwest with Lee and the rest of the Creels who were going after the stolen herd. It was obvious to Holland that was what they had in mind and equally obvious that Samantha had thrown in with them.

Nick would want to know about that. Holland was certain of it.

There wouldn't have been a problem if Palmer had gone ahead and killed all the Creels like he was supposed to. Palmer had taken the easy way out, though. Once he had the cattle and his payoff from selling the herd was assured, he hadn't cared about anything else. He and his men had lit out, leaving Holland behind.

No way Holland was taking on the Creels by himself, then or now.

Instead he let them go and turned his horse north, toward the Rafter F and whatever gun-job Nick Fontaine had for him next.

Bo kept the group moving at a fast pace, but he knew he had to be careful. If they pushed their mounts too hard, the horses would break down. That would ruin any chance of catching up to the rustlers before they reached Rockport.

He rode at the head of the group with Scratch and Lauralee, who asked, "Do you really think we have a chance to catch them? They have more than twelve hours' lead on us."

"We can make that up," Bo said. "They still have to cross the San Antonio River. That'll slow them down a little. And even though we have to be careful with our horses, we can still move faster than that herd can."

Scratch said, "Yeah, but that fella Palmer won't care how much beef he runs off of 'em, as long as he keeps you from sellin' 'em and takin' the money back to your pa."

"I don't follow all of this," Lauralee said with a slight shake of her head.

"There's only one explanation that makes any sense," Bo said. "You know how Gilbert Ambrose at the bank plans to call in my father's note. Nick Fontaine has to be behind that somehow. Ambrose would have given Pa an extension, but Nick forced his hand. Now Nick's sent those rustlers after us to keep us from coming up with the cash Pa needs to save the Star C."

Lauralee nodded slowly and said, "I guess that makes sense, all right. You don't have a bit of proof, though."

"We'll worry about proof later—*after* we've gotten those cattle back."

"Yeah," Scratch added, "I reckon ol' Gil Ambrose will be eager to talk once we've had a word with him."

"You mean you'll scare the truth out of him," Laura-lee said.

Bo shrugged.

"I'll do whatever I have to to keep Nick Fontaine from stealing the Star C," he said.

Farther back in the group, Samantha rode beside Lee. She didn't want to get too far from his side. She felt like she was surrounded by enemies, even though Bo, Scratch, and Lauralee had been sympathetic to her.

All the others still regarded her with suspicion— except Lee, of course.

"When we catch up with those rustlers tomorrow or the next day, you're gonna stay back so you ain't in any danger," he told her.

"But you'll be right in the middle of any fight," she said.

Lee nodded and said, "Yep, I sure will. That's where I belong. You don't."

"I told you, I need to do something—"

"Look, Samantha," he broke in, "I'll be honest with you. If you're anywhere around when the shootin' starts, you'll just be a distraction to me. That'll make it more likely that one or both of us will get ourselves shot."

She tried to tell herself that he was just being practical, but she couldn't keep from being a little offended by his blunt tone.

"Well, I certainly never meant to be a problem—"

Again he didn't let her finish. He said, "If you really want to help, there are a couple of things you can do."

"Tell me," she urged.

"Like I said, stay out of the way when the showdown comes . . . and when we get back to Bear Creek, tell the law about what your brother did."

Her breath caught in her throat. For a moment she couldn't say anything, then she managed, "You want me to testify in court against Nick?"

"If it comes to that. Nick may not have pulled the trigger, but you know he's responsible for my cousin Tim bein' dead, don't you, Samantha?"

She knew Lee was looking over at her, but she kept her eyes on her saddlehorn, unable to meet his gaze.

"I know," she said quietly. "I just never thought . . . He's my brother, Lee. I know he's done terrible things, but I can't just forget all the good times. I can't forget how he took care of me when I was a little girl. He wasn't always . . . evil."

"I reckon not many people start out that way. And I sure don't know why some of 'em wind up on that trail. But I know we all got to pay for what we do, good and bad."

"Yes," she whispered as she nodded. "I understand that. And I'll do the right thing, Lee. I promise."

"That's all anybody can ask of you."

She hoped it wasn't more than she could ask of herself.

By nightfall, they were approaching the San Antonio River. Bo and Scratch scouted ahead to make sure the rustlers hadn't bedded down the herd on this side of the river.

That would have been a lucky break, but luck wasn't with them. They found the ford where the cattle had crossed. Judging by the tracks and the droppings they found, the herd had come through here several hours earlier.

"We cut into their lead, but they're still ahead of us," Scratch said as he rested his hands on his saddlehorn and leaned forward to ease muscles aching from a long day in the saddle.

Bo nodded and said, "Yes, and there's not much left between here and Rockport to slow them down. All the creeks are so small the cattle will be able to go right across them without any trouble, and the terrain's as flat as a table."

"Wouldn't surprise me if that varmint Palmer keeps 'em movin' until after dark, too," Scratch commented. "We got to make camp and let these horses rest for a while, though, or they won't be worth anything."

"I know," Bo said, trying not to let despair creep into his voice. He was not the sort of man to give up and never had been, but the deck seemed to have been stacked against his family from the start in this matter.

He went on, "We'll make camp here at the river. Why don't you ride back and show them the way? I'll get started building a fire."

Scratch lifted a hand in acknowledgment and turned

his horse. He rode away as Bo sat his saddle in the fading red light of the sunset.

After a couple of minutes, Bo shook off the gloomy mood and dismounted. He started gathering wood for a campfire.

This area along the river was the last bit of rugged countryside between there and the coast. The banks were about twenty feet high in most places, and the streambed was choked with brush and deadfalls that had washed down during times of flooding and gotten hung up.

The ford was located where a gully with gently sloping sides crossed the river. That gully had acted as a funnel to keep the herd moving in the right direction.

In the years right after the war, when driving cattle to the coastal markets had been about the only thing cash-poor ranchers in this area could do to make any money, enough herds had moved through here to beat down the brush. It had grown back to a certain extent since the cattle trails to the railhead in Kansas had opened and the drives didn't come this way anymore, but the vegetation still wasn't as thick here at the ford as it was in other places.

Bo didn't have any trouble finding an armful of dead branches from the cottonwood trees that grew in profusion along the banks and beside the river. He was carrying them toward a spot that he thought would be a good place for a campfire when he heard a horse whinny somewhere nearby.

The sound put a frown on Bo's face. It was too soon for Scratch to be back with the others. Not only that, but it sounded like the horse was on the other side of the river.

That didn't have to mean anything—there were plenty of innocent reasons a rider could be traveling through here—but Bo hadn't lived as long as he had by being careless. He set the armload of firewood on the ground, grabbed his horse's reins, and slid silently into a thick clump of trees where he and the animal would be out of sight.

The ground on the western side of the river sloped up in a small rise of the sort that passed for high ground around here. Bo watched the top of it as he listened to the growing sound of hoofbeats.

Half a dozen riders came into view. Positioned against the red glare of the sunset the way they were, he couldn't make out any details about them. They were just tall, mounted silhouettes.

As the men started down toward the ford, Bo drew his gun. Instincts forged over years of finding himself and his friend Scratch in trouble warned him that these strangers weren't to be trusted.

The men rode all the way down to the river and stopped there to let their horses drink. What Bo overheard them saying confirmed his hunch that they were up to no good.

"Looks like we beat that Creel bunch here, Walton," one of them commented.

"That's a good thing," the man called Walton said.

"Now we got a chance to get ready for 'em, instead of havin' to jump 'em after they've made camp." He waved a hand at the vegetation along the stream. "We'll hide the horses and spread out in the brush. We'll let 'em ride right into our gunsights before we open up."

The callous words made Bo's blood run cold. He had no doubt that Palmer had sent these men. The vicious ambush they were planning was intended to wipe out any pursuit.

"Judd's payin' us extra for this, right, Walton?" another man asked. "We're runnin' more of a risk than the fellas who are just pushin' those cows down to Rockport."

Walton let out a cold laugh.

"We're not runnin' any risk. You wait and see. They'll all be dead before they know what hit 'em."

CHAPTER 31

Bo's pulse hammered in his head. He wanted to step out into the open, challenge those cold-blooded killers, and open fire on them. He was confident that with the element of surprise on his side, he could bring down several of them.

But the odds against him would be too high. They would get him, too, and once he was dead, he had no chance of warning Scratch and the others about the trap that was being set for them.

What he needed to do was fade back downstream a ways without Palmer's men noticing him, then circle around and get back to the others before they rode right into that ambush.

It would be difficult, though, to get through the brush without making enough noise to give himself away.

That wasn't the only problem facing him, he realized a second later when one of the men said, "Look at that pile of branches over there. Danged if it don't look like somebody's been gatherin' firewood."

Bo bit back a curse. He must be getting careless in his old age, he thought. When he'd dropped the armload of branches on the ground, it hadn't occurred to him that someone might notice something odd about it.

Walton reacted instantly, reaching for his gun as he barked, "Spread out! Somebody's been here in the last few minutes. Could've been one of the bunch we're after!"

There was no point in stealth now, Bo thought as he grabbed his saddlehorn and swung up onto his horse. Now he had to get back to the others and warn them as quickly as possible.

Unfortunately, the six gunmen blocked the easiest way out of the big, twisting *arroyo* where the river flowed. The banks were too steep to climb where Bo was, so he had no choice except to turn downstream and send his horse crashing through the undergrowth as he weaved around the cottonwoods.

"There he goes!" Walton yelled as the noise alerted him to Bo's presence. "Get after him! But no shooting! The rest of that outfit might hear!"

That was a good point. Scratch would hear gunshots and know that something was wrong. He wouldn't let the others waltz right into danger. Bo's Colt was already in his hand, so he figured he might as well discourage the pursuit by loosing a few rounds at them.

He twisted in the saddle, which was another mistake. Something slammed into his left shoulder with stunning force. He felt himself coming out of the saddle and managed to kick his feet free of the stirrups. If he was dragged in this thicket, the brush would rip him to shreds.

He lost his gun when he hit the ground. Rolling over from the momentum of his fall, he saw that a low-hanging branch had swept him out of the saddle. In the thick growth, he hadn't seen it coming in time.

The impact of his collision with the ground had knocked the air out of his lungs. Gasping for breath, he scrambled upright as the riders closed in on him. He reached his feet just in time to get knocked down again as one of the rustlers dived from the saddle and tackled him.

Bo went over backward and landed with the man on top of him, slugging away at him. He blunted the ferocity of the attack by lifting his knee into the outlaw's belly and driving it into his guts. With that opening, Bo looped a punch to the rustler's jaw and knocked him to the side.

Hoofbeats thundered around him as he rolled over and tried to get up. One of the other men whooped as he drew back a booted foot and kicked Bo in the back. That drove Bo to his knees. He reached up, grabbed hold of a stirrup, and pulled himself to his feet again, trying to ignore the pain he felt shooting through him as he made a lunge for a holstered gun. He hadn't given up on the idea of firing some shots that would alert Scratch to the trouble.

Instead another man leaned over in the saddle and clipped Bo on the head with a gun butt. Stars exploded behind Bo's eyes. His legs turned to rubber underneath him, and when he fell he landed in a thorny bush that felt like a thousand tiny knives stabbing him. Even that jabbing agony wasn't enough to keep him from losing consciousness.

Just before the world faded away around him, he heard one of the men say, "You want me to go ahead and cut this bastard's throat, Walton?"

When the leader of the bushwhackers answered, his voice sounded like it came from a thousand miles away.

"No, we'll keep him alive for now. If he's one of the bunch we're after, he might come in handy. If he's not . . . well, we can kill him just as dead later on!"

The sun had dipped completely below the horizon by the time Scratch got back to the rest of the group, leaving only a fan-shaped, reddish-golden glow in the western sky.

"Where's Bo?" Lauralee asked him immediately.

Before Scratch could answer, Riley said, "It'll be dark soon. I reckon we'd better make camp."

Scratch thumbed his hat back and said, "That's what Bo sent me to tell you. The San Antonio River ain't far ahead, only a couple of miles. We were hopin' the cattle'd be there and the rustlers would be waitin' until mornin' to cross, but they're already over the river and gone. Be a good place for us to camp, though. Bo stayed behind to gather some wood and get a fire goin'."

"All right, I guess we'll keep moving, then," Riley said. "Ought to be enough light left for that."

As Scratch fell in alongside them, Lee asked, "Could you tell how far ahead of us the rustlers are?"

"A few hours, I'd say. They've made good time. That fella Palmer is really pushin' 'em."

"No reason not to," Riley said with a disgusted snort. "He doesn't care about running any fat off them. He just doesn't want us to have them."

Lee said, "If they're only a few hours ahead, we ought to be able to catch up to them tomorrow."

"Maybe," Scratch said. "Bo was worried that Palmer would keep on drivin' 'em into the night, since there's really nothin' but open ground in front of them now, all the way to the coast."

"Then we shouldn't be stopping to make camp," Riley said. "We need to keep going, too, if there's a chance that's what the rustlers are going to do."

"Problem with that is, these horses need a night's rest," Scratch pointed out. "We've already asked a lot of 'em."

No one could argue with that. They were all experienced enough riders, even Lauralee and Samantha, to know that their mounts were worn out.

They continued over the gently rolling hills as they approached the river. The bright glow of the departed sun faded to rose. Behind them, blue sky began to turn purple. Another day was done and the timeless rhythm of the universe continued, paying no heed to the doings of the puny humans who populated this world.

There was still enough light for them to see the line of trees that marked the river's course. The hills sloped inward, forming the gully that provided a good place to ford the stream.

Scratch expected to see the leaping orange flames of a campfire up ahead. Bo had had time to get a blaze going. The ford was still dark, though, and the river's high banks, along with the rise on the other side, made it even gloomier than the surrounding countryside.

A frown creased Scratch's forehead. This wasn't really anything to worry about, he told himself. Bo could have gotten busy with something else and just hadn't built the fire yet.

That didn't stop him from slowing his horse and saying to the others, "Hold on a minute. Best let me go take a look around up there before you ride in."

"I thought you said Bo was waiting for us," Riley said.

"He's supposed to be, but I don't see him."

"Maybe he found an even better place to camp," Lauralee suggested.

"Yeah, maybe," Scratch said, but that idea didn't make the prickling on the back of his neck go away. He was going to follow his instincts, even if they turned out to be wrong. "Just stay here. I'll be back in a minute."

"I'm coming with you," Lauralee said. Scratch wondered if she was worried about Bo just because he was.

"Get your rifle out," he told her as he urged his horse forward.

Lauralee drew her Winchester from the saddle boot and worked the lever to throw a .44-40 shell into the chamber. Scratch rode with the reins in his left hand and his right hand resting on his thigh where it was close to the ivory-handled butt of the Remington revolver on that side.

"You think something's happened to him, don't you?" Lauralee asked quietly.

"Nope, not really. But he said he'd get a fire started, and I don't see one up yonder. Whenever Bo says he's gonna do something, he usually does it. It takes a mighty good reason for him not to. I'll rest easier when I know what that reason is."

"He had better not have gone and gotten himself hurt—or worse," Lauralee said. "Slowly but surely, I'm wearing him down."

Even in this tense situation, Scratch couldn't help but chuckle at the confidence he heard in the beautiful young woman's voice.

"You reckon so, do you?" he asked.

"He can't keep saying no to me forever."

"I ain't so sure about that. Bo's got his own special brand of stubbornness." Scratch's grin disappeared as he grew more solemn. "The grievin' came on him more than forty years ago, and it's never let loose of him. Or he's never let loose of it. Works out the same either way."

"But I've heard him laugh. I've seen him smile. I've seen pure joy in him, Scratch."

"Yep, because he's too stubborn not to go on livin'. But now and then you catch him when he don't know anybody's lookin' at him, and you can see it in his eyes, the way he looks off and sees things nobody else sees.

The hurtin' is buried deep, but it's still there." Scratch paused. "I reckon it always will be."

"That's no way to be," Lauralee said.

"Maybe not . . . but those are the cards he was dealt."

They were close to the river now. In the still twilight air Scratch heard the faint whisper of the water as it flowed over the streambed that was a mixture of sandy soil and rocks. He reined in and looked around, hoping to see Bo or at least his old friend's horse. Instead he saw only shadows . . .

Shadows torn apart suddenly by the orange flame spurting from a gun muzzle as a shot blasted.

CHAPTER 32

Bo wasn't too surprised to wake up and find that he was still alive. He had heard Walton tell the others not to cut his throat.

But he expected to regain consciousness to the sound of guns going off, and instead a hush surrounded him. He listened for a minute or so, and the silence was broken only by an occasional rustle as somebody shifted in the brush.

His wrists were tied behind his back. Somebody had looped a cord around them and drawn it tight. His feet and legs were loose, though. A sour-tasting bandanna had been shoved in his mouth as a gag and tied in place with another bandanna.

He remembered the fight with the men Judd Palmer had sent back to bushwhack the pursuers. Did the quiet mean that the ambush hadn't taken place yet?

Or was it the stillness of death? Had Scratch and all the others been wiped out already?

That couldn't be, Bo told himself. If the others were dead, the rustlers would have killed him, too.

The fact that he was still alive meant Scratch was, too. The faint noises he heard came from the gunmen who had hidden in the brush to carry out their deadly chore.

Somebody shifted close beside Bo. He sensed the movement as much as heard it. Cracking his eyes open to mere slits and staying absolutely still so as not to give away the fact that he had regained consciousness, he looked around as much as he could to take stock of his situation.

He couldn't see very well because most of the sun's light had faded from the sky, leaving the area along the creek even deeper in dusky shadows. He could tell that trees surrounded him. After a moment his eyes picked out a shape that didn't belong, a human shape crouched behind a bush.

That had to be one of the rustlers, thought Bo. It was obvious from the man's tense stance that he was waiting for something.

Bo heard the steady thud of hoofbeats as two horses approached the ford.

Only two horses. That meant the whole group wasn't about to ride into the trap and Bo was grateful for that.

But two of them were, and Bo strongly suspected that one of them would be Scratch. His old friend wanted to take another look around before bringing the others in.

Someone was with him, though. Riley? Lee?

A murmur of voices drifted through the twilight.

Bo recognized Scratch's familiar bass rumble. Then, replying to it, a woman's voice . . .

Lauralee.

Bo didn't have any doubt of that. It was just like her to insist that she was coming along, no matter where or when or why. Knowing that she was about to come under the guns of those ruthless killers made desperation course through Bo's veins.

He heard a quiet metallic sound close by. The man with him had just pulled back the hammer on his revolver . . .

Bo acted on instinct, not planning what he was going to do. He had to warn Scratch and Lauralee somehow, even though he couldn't yell. He twisted around sharply, drew his knees up, and kicked the man in front of him in the rear end.

Bo put every bit of strength he could into that double-legged kick. The heels of his boots landed solidly, and the impact drove the man forward into the bush that he had been using for cover. The unexpected attack made him jerk his finger on the trigger, too, and the gun in his hand roared.

Bo could only hope that the weapon wasn't pointed at Scratch or Lauralee when it went off.

Scratch reacted to the shot with swift deadliness. The Remington seemed to leap into his hand, and flame spouted from the muzzle as he fired at the flash he had just seen.

At the same time, he shouted, "Get back!" at Lauralee.

Somewhere in the gloom along the river, a man yelled, "Get 'em!" More shots blasted.

Scratch didn't know where Bo was, but finding out his friend's fate would have to wait. He had his other gun out now, and both Remingtons roared as he twisted in the saddle and sent slugs screaming through the trees and bushes where the bushwhackers were hidden.

Beside him, Lauralee's Winchester began to crack wickedly. He should have known that she wouldn't cut and run, he thought fleetingly. She was one gal who just didn't have any backup in her.

Scratch didn't want to turn his back on the bush-whackers and give them a better target, so he did the un-expected. He kicked his horse into a run and charged straight across the river. Water splashed up around the animal's hocks. Lauralee was right behind him.

That took them out of the crossfire the ambushers had set up. Scratch whirled his mount. The man who had yelled the order to get them was still making a racket. Scratch aimed at the voice and triggered.

The yelling stopped.

But only for a second. Another man shouted, "Let's get out of here!"

Scratch wasn't surprised. Varmints like that didn't want to fight unless all the odds were on their side.

Riders appeared on the far side of the river, thunder-ing down the gully toward the ford. That would be Riley and the rest of the boys, Scratch thought. He called, "Bushwhackers in the trees!" and started firing again.

The trap had backfired on the would-be killers. Now they were the ones caught in a crossfire as the Creels charged them and drove them straight toward Scratch and Lauralee. The light made shooting tricky, but the two of them had pretty good shots as the bushwhackers tried to flee.

As Scratch's guns roared and bucked in his hands, he offered a silent prayer for his friend's safety. He had no idea where Bo was, and there was a heck of a lot of lead flying around down there.

As soon as the man Bo had kicked accidentally fired his gun, all hell broke loose along the river, just as Bo expected.

One thing you could always count on was Scratch Morton putting up a good fight!

Bo heard a heavy *thud* and a dark, looming shape fell backward on him. That was the bushwhacker Bo had kicked. He figured the man had been struck by one of the slugs Scratch or Lauralee fired.

However, the bullet hadn't killed the man. He tried to scramble to his feet.

Bo flung his legs up, threw them around the man's neck, and caught him in a scissors hold. Growing up, Bo and his brothers had wrestled frequently, as most boys will, and he still remembered how to grapple.

The bushwhacker must have dropped his gun when he was hit. Bo felt both of the man's hands tearing at his legs, trying to pull them loose. Bo just tightened his grip and hung on with grim determination, squeezing hard on the man's neck to cut off his air.

The bushwhacker bucked and thrashed, and his increasing panic told Bo that he couldn't get his breath. That was just what Bo wanted. Eventually the man would pass out from lack of air.

Suddenly Bo felt pain in his leg. The man had gotten out a knife and slashed at him. The thick leather of Bo's high-topped boot had turned aside the blade without it doing any damage other than what felt like a minor cut, but if the man sank the knife in Bo's leg, he'd have no choice but to let go.

Bo's muscles bunched as he rolled over and heaved harder with his legs. He twisted with all his strength and heard a sharp, sudden snap.

The bushwhacker went limp.

Bo knew he had broken the man's neck.

That was a shame in a way—he wouldn't have minded questioning the man about Judd Palmer's plans—but then Bo thought about his nephew Tim and how the young man's dead face had looked, and he didn't mind so much that he'd just killed this son of a bitch. He would never know if this man was the one who shot Tim, but he had been there, been part of it.

Around the ford, pistols boomed and rifles cracked. Hoofbeats and shouts filled the twilight air. It was a full-fledged battle now. Bo heard bullets whipping through the branches not far from him, so he squirmed over next to the body of the man he had just killed and hunkered as low behind the corpse as he could, using it for cover.

The shooting went on for several more minutes, then died away fairly quickly. As the echoes of the gun-thunder rolled away, Scratch called, "Bo! Bo, are you around here?"

Scratch sounded like he was all right. That made relief surge through Bo. He raised his head and made the loudest noises he could through the gag.

"Scratch, I think I hear something!"

That was Lauralee, and she didn't sound like she was hurt, either. Bo closed his eyes and offered up a prayer of thanks for that. He prayed that the rest of the Creels were unharmed, too.

Crashing in the brush sounded nearby. Bo kept making noise, and suddenly some branches parted and Scratch was beside him, followed closely by Lauralee.

Gun in hand, Scratch toed the corpse over just to make sure the *hombre* was dead. While he was doing that, Lauralee dropped to her knees beside Bo and started working to remove the gag from his mouth.

"Bo, are you all right?" she asked anxiously.

The gag came loose. Bo turned his head to the side and spat a couple of times to get the bad taste out of his mouth. Then he said, "Yeah, I'm fine. A scratch on my leg, but that's all. If you could get my hands loose . . . ?"

"Roll onto your side," she told him. She worked at the knots for a minute, then said, "Scratch, I think you're going to have to cut this cord off of him."

"Let me strike a match so I can see what I'm doin'," the silver-haired Texan said. "After all this, I'd hate to cut the old fella's wrists."

"Old fella?" Bo repeated. "You're a month older than me."

"Yeah, but you were born old," Scratch said with a chuckle.

He fired up a lucifer and held it in his left hand while he used his right to slide the blade of his Bowie knife under the bonds around Bo's wrists. A few moments of sawing with the razor-sharp blade had Bo free.

He sat up, rubbing his wrists and hands to get the feeling back into them, and asked, "What about the others? Was anybody hurt?"

"Don't know yet," Scratch said, sounding more serious now. "I wanted to find you first before I checked on them."

"Help me to my feet and let's go see."

It didn't take long to establish that a crease on Jason's upper arm was the only injury any of the Creels had suffered. Samantha Fontaine was already binding it up with a strip of cloth ripped from the bottom of her shirt.

"Thanks," Jason told her with grudging gratitude.

"It's the least I can do," Samantha said.

No one argued with her about that.

Riley, Lee, and Davy checked the bodies sprawled along the riverbank. When Riley saw his brother approaching with Scratch and Lauralee, he grunted and asked, "Do you know how many of the bastards there were?"

"Six," Bo replied. Riley hadn't asked how he was doing, but that came as no surprise. Riley had eyes. He could see that Bo wasn't hurt bad.

"We got five of 'em. Reckon the other one got away."

Bo shook his head and jerked a thumb over his shoulder at the trees behind him.

"The sixth man's back there."

Lee said, "You killed him, Uncle Bo?"

"Seemed like the thing to do at the time."

Riley rubbed his chin and said, "The important thing is that none of them got away to warn the rest of the bunch that we're still alive. I assume they were part of the gang that stole our herd?"

"That's right," Bo said. "The leader's a man named Judd Palmer. The more I think about it, the more familiar that name is. I think I've heard of him somewhere before. Maybe saw a Wanted poster on him one of the times that Scratch and I were working as deputies."

"Palmer sent these men back to ambush us?"

"Yeah. So we've still got a chance to take him by surprise."

"If we can catch up to him before he makes it to Rockport," Riley said.

"We've got a better chance than we did before," Bo said. "We've got some extra horses now." He looked at the bodies of the slain rustlers and added, "These fellas don't have any use for them anymore."

CHAPTER 33

Lee had to give Samantha credit. When the shooting started and he told her to stay put, she stayed put. She hadn't ventured closer to the river until the roar of gunfire ceased.

Later, after the bodies of the dead rustlers had been disposed of—there was a handy ravine a couple of hundred yards downstream—Lee carried a cup of coffee to her where she sat on a cottonwood deadfall not far from the fire. He had a cup for himself, too.

"Here you go," he said as he handed the coffee to her.

"Thank you," she said. Her voice had a hollow note to it. She took the cup and sipped the hot, black brew.

"Are you all right?" he asked.

"Why wouldn't I be? Six more men are dead, and the man I love was almost killed, too."

"Now hold on a minute," Lee told her. "Don't waste any sympathy on those *hombres*. They were owlhoots, plain and simple, and there's a good chance they done plenty of bad things in their lives. They would've killed every one of us and never blinked. They got what was comin' to 'em, and that's the God's honest truth." He took a sip of his coffee. "As for me almost gettin' killed . . . Well, none of those bullets that were flyin' around came close enough for me to hear 'em, so I reckon I wasn't really in that much danger."

"And that was just pure luck, too."

Lee shrugged and said, "A man's got to have luck on his side sometimes. Like that day when your horse ran away with you, and you found yourself on the wrong side of Bear Creek. I figure that was just about the luckiest day of my life."

She looked at him for a long moment, then smiled and shook her head.

"You have an answer for everything, don't you, Lee Creel?"

"Yes, ma'am. And most of 'em have to do with me lovin' you and you lovin' me."

She leaned closer to him and rested her head on his shoulder.

"When we get back," she said quietly, "we have to do something about this."

"About you and me, you mean?"

"Yes, but what I was really talking about is that silly feud between my father and your grandfather. We have to put a stop to all this trouble."

"Oh, I've got that figured out already," Lee said.

Samantha lifted her head and frowned at him.

"You do?"

"Yep," he said with a nod. "It seems to me that once

the two of us are married, those two ol' goats won't have any choice but to stop fussin' with each other."

Samantha licked her lips, said in a half whisper, "Married?"

"That's right. If you'll have me, that is."

She looked around at the primitive camp on the bank of the San Antonio River and said, "This isn't exactly the most romantic place for a proposal, but . . . Yes. I'll marry you."

A couple of minutes later, when Lee finally broke the kiss he had planted on her, Samantha said, "Your brothers are glaring at you."

"Let 'em," Lee said. "They'll get over it. They might as well start gettin' used to the idea that the Creel-Fontaine feud is over."

It was the middle of the day when Trace Holland rode into the yard in front of the Rafter F ranch house. He had pushed his mount fairly hard, riding until well after dark the previous night before making camp. Then he had come on the rest of the way today. The horse's head hung down in weariness as Holland dismounted.

The screen door banged as Nick Fontaine stepped out onto the porch. He said, "I thought I heard the dogs barking. Figured somebody was riding in." He paused, then asked bluntly, "Is it done?"

"It's done," Holland said. He knew what Nick meant, and neither of them had to put it into words. He went on,

"There's something else I reckon you'd like to know about, though."

"What's that?"

"It's about your sister."

Nick's breath hissed between his teeth. For a second he looked like he was about to come down off the porch and attack Holland with his bare hands, and the gunman wondered if he had made a mistake by being cryptic.

But then Nick regained control of himself, jerked his head toward the door, and said, "Come on inside. I'm not having this conversation out here."

"I ought to take care of my horse—"

"Jed!" Nick bellowed. The old wrangler hurried out of the barn and came toward them. Nick went on, "Jed will see to your horse."

Holland nodded and dismounted. He handed the reins to Jed Clemons and then followed Nick into the house.

They went to the study. Nick didn't offer Holland a drink or anything, just fixed him with an intense gaze and waited.

"Where's your pa?" Holland asked.

"In his room. He's been under the weather lately. It hasn't helped that he's worrying himself sick about Samantha. You said you know something about her? About where she is?"

Holland drew in a deep breath and said, "She's with the Creels, headed for the coast."

Nick's face darkened until it looked like he was about

ready to pop a blood vessel. In a low, dangerous tone, he said, "What? What's she doing with the Creels?"

"Best I can figure it, she took off after that cattle drive and caught up to it yesterday morning, after Palmer's bunch ran off the herd the night before."

"Palmer left some of them alive?"

"He left most of them alive," Holland said. "That fella's not to be trusted, boss. I think once he had the herd, he didn't care any more about doing the rest of the job." The gunman shrugged. "Maybe he had something else in mind, though. I don't really know. He's not in the habit of letting anybody else in on his plans."

Nick cursed bitterly, then said, "What about Samantha?"

"The Creels split up. Looked like some of them were bringing the wounded back. The others headed south, after the herd." Holland paused. "Your sister went with that bunch. I was watching from a hill close by when they rode off."

Nick sank down in the chair behind the desk. His hands clenched into fists. Without looking at Holland, as if he were talking to himself, he said, "What the hell made her go after the Creels like that?"

"Only thing I can figure out is that she found out somehow about what Palmer was gonna do and went after them to warn them."

One of Nick's fists slammed down on the desk.

"But why?"

Holland knew he had to tell the rest of it, even though it would only enrage Nick that much more. He said,

"When she rode up, she started hugging and kissing one of those Creel boys. The one called Lee, I think. From the looks of it, they're sweet on each other and have been for a while."

He didn't mention that he had known about the romance between Samantha and Lee Creel for several weeks. Nick didn't need to know that.

Nick stared at the gunman in disbelief. He said, "She . . . she wouldn't dare . . . with one of the Creels!"

Holland shrugged and shook his head.

"I'm sorry to have to be the one to tell you, boss," he said. "That's what I saw, though, and when you think about everything else that's happened, it's the only thing that makes sense."

Nick's jaw clenched firmly in anger, so hard that a little muscle jumped in his cheek. He said, "That little bitch. That treacherous little bitch."

Holland didn't want to intrude on that anger anymore, in case Nick decided to turn it on him. He was familiar with the old saying about shooting the messenger.

"I've had a long ride," he said. "I need to go clean up, maybe get some coffee and something to eat . . ."

"Wait a minute," Nick said sharply. "You said some of the Creels went after Palmer?"

"That's right."

"Then they could still cause trouble for me. Ruin all my plans."

"There were only about half a dozen of them," Holland said. "And they'd really have to hustle to catch up to Palmer before he gets to Rockport and sells that herd."

"But it's possible."

Holland couldn't deny that, and his silence was just as good as if he had answered.

"Go ahead and get something to eat," Nick went on, "but then you need to saddle a fresh horse."

"You're sendin' me back out?" Holland didn't like that idea, but if Nick had made up his mind there wasn't much he could do about it.

"Not by yourself. You'll be taking McNamara and some of the other men. Was Bo Creel one of the bunch that went after Palmer?"

The abrupt question took Holland a little by surprise. He said, "Yeah, and that friend of his, too, Scratch Morton."

Nick nodded and said, "The most dangerous pair in the bunch. I have to be ready if they try to turn the tables on me, Trace. If they take the herd back from Palmer, I can't afford to let them come back here with the money they'll get for it."

"So you're sending me and McNamara and the rest of the boys to meet them on the way?"

"That's the idea," Nick said. "But you won't be going alone."

Nick reached down to shake his brother awake. As usual, Danny was asleep. He hadn't let his sister being missing interfere too much with his degenerate habits, so he'd headed for town the night before for an evening of drinking and whoring.

At least he wasn't tangled up in the sheets this time. Nick grabbed his shoulder and bounced him up and down a couple of times.

Danny came awake with a startled yell and grabbed for the Colt that lay on the nightstand next to his bed. Nick caught his wrist before he could get hold of the gun and start shooting blindly.

"Settle down, you damned fool," Nick snapped. "It's me."

"Nick? What the hell?" Danny groaned and sank back against the pillows. "Leave me alone. My head feels like a big ol' Longhorn bull stepped on it a few times."

"You've got to get up, Danny. I found out what happened to Samantha."

That got through to the younger man. Whatever his faults—and they were numerous—Danny loved his sister. He sat up, raked his fingers through his tangled hair, and said, "What's that about Samantha?"

"She was kidnapped," Nick said. "By Lee Creel."

Danny's eyes widened. His hangover was forgotten now. After a moment while Nick's words sunk in on his whiskey-numbed brain, he lunged for the gun again.

This time Nick let him have it.

"I'll kill the son of a bitch!" Danny raged as he waved the Colt around. "Where are they? Where can I find him, Nick?"

"Lee went with the rest of the Creels on that cattle

drive to the coast. They'll be on their way back in a few days."

Danny swung his legs out of bed and stood up. He looked a little shaky, but he didn't fall down.

"I'm not waitin' that long," he declared. "Let's get some of the boys and go after 'em."

Nick shook his head and said, "I can't leave the ranch right now, not with Pa sick. But you can handle this job, Danny. You can take Holland and McNamara and the others and ride out to meet that bunch of no-good scum." He stuck another needle in. "There's no telling what Lee's done to poor little Samantha by now. We can't change that, but we can even the score for her."

"I'll kill him," Danny promised as he brandished the Colt. Nick moved the gun barrel aside, just in case. "I won't give him a chance to lie or make excuses, Nick. I'll just blow holes in the son of a bitch as soon as I lay eyes on him!"

"I knew I could count on you, Danny," Nick said, and somehow he managed to remain solemn and not allow the smile of satisfaction he felt to appear on his face. Danny was reacting just as Nick had known he would.

The only problem Nick could see with this plan was that once the bullets started to fly, his brother and sister would both be in danger. It was possible that neither of them would make it back to the Rafter F alive.

It would be a real shame if things turned out like that, but it was more important that the Creels not get back with the money in time to pay off that note. Of course it might not come to that. They might not recover the herd. They might try to and be killed by Judd Palmer and his men, as they should have been to start with.

Any of those possibilities would be all right in the long run, Nick realized . . . as long as they ended with him in control of both the Rafter F and the Star C.

"Are you sure you can't come along, Nick?" Danny asked.

Nick squeezed his shoulder and said, "That's all right, little brother. I know you'll uphold the honor of the Fontaine name."

CHAPTER 34

Copano Bay lay to the left, stretching blue, flat, and tranquil to the horizon. A day and a half of hard riding had brought Bo, Scratch, and the others to this point. Rockport was only a few miles away now.

For the past several hours, Bo's mood had darkened as it became obvious that they weren't going to catch up to the herd before it reached the coast. Judd Palmer and his men must have driven the cattle night and day to cover so much ground so quickly.

If Palmer had already sold the herd and taken off, there wouldn't be anything Bo could do about it. He could prove that Palmer hadn't had the right to sell the cattle, but that would be just one more charge against the outlaw. Whoever had bought the herd in good faith couldn't be forced to make good the loss, at least not right away. That would take lawyers and courts and a lot of time.

Time that John Creel and the Star C didn't have.

"I've never been down here before," Lauralee said as

she rode beside Bo and Scratch. "The water is beautiful. So peaceful."

"Not so much whenever a hurricane comes in," Bo said, "but yeah, right now it's nice."

Lauralee licked her lips.

"I can taste the salt in the air," she said with a smile.

"You should see the Pacific Ocean," Scratch told her. "It's a whole heap bigger. Although when you're standin' on shore and all you can see in front of you is water, it's sort of hard to tell much difference, I reckon."

"Maybe I'll see it someday. Bear Creek's a nice place, but I never said I intended to spend my whole life there. I think maybe I'm a little fiddlefooted, like the two of you."

Bo wondered briefly if she was building up to asking if she could come along when he and Scratch went on the drift again. That would never work.

He had plenty of other things to worry about at the moment, though.

"We'll head straight for the cattle pens at the south end of town," Bo said. "That's the most likely place to find the herd. Lauralee, you and Miss Fontaine go on into town. I seem to recall there's a hotel right across the street from the harbor. You can wait for us there."

"Wait a minute," Lauralee said. "I planned to go with you."

"And I want to stay, too," Samantha added.

"No, ma'am," Lee told her. "I told you, the only way you could come along is if you agreed to stay out of the line of fire."

"And you agreed that you'd take orders just like any other hand," Bo said to Lauralee.

She tossed her head defiantly and said, "If I was just any other hand, you wouldn't be sending me off. You'd expect me to ride for the brand like the rest of you."

"We're not going to argue about this," Bo said.

"Fine," Lauralee snapped. "But this isn't fair and you know it, Bo."

"I never said I was fair."

She glared at him but didn't say anything else.

As they approached the town, the countryside was flat as a table and dotted with clumps of oaks twisted into unusually gnarled shapes by the nearly constant wind off the gulf. The air was so damp that the least effort made sweat pop out on a man's face.

The steeples on the local churches came into view first, then a few minutes later Bo spotted roofs. He pointed out the direction Lauralee and Samantha needed to go, and the two young women rode off toward the settlement while Bo, Scratch, Riley, Lee, Davy, and Jason continued toward the cattle pens. The breeze carried the smell of the pens to them before the enclosures ever came in sight. As the riders drew nearer they heard the cattle bellowing, too.

"Those are our cows, damn it," Riley said.

"Recognize their voices, do you?" Scratch asked dryly.

"You know it has to be them."

"More than likely," Bo agreed. "Palmer couldn't have

beaten us here by more than an hour or so. Maybe he hasn't had time to make a deal with a buyer yet."

Scratch said, "Are we gonna hunt up the local law?"

"We'll deal with the law later," Bo replied grimly. "Right now we have to find out where we stand."

Once thousands of cattle had been herded into these pens, he thought as he and the others rode past the sturdy enclosures. Most of those cows had been bound for the rendering plant. Then shipping magnates had discovered that there was money to be made by loading the cattle on boats here in Rockport and taking them to markets in New Orleans and on around Florida and up the East Coast. It had been a brisk trade for a while.

Now, with the development of trail towns like Abilene and Dodge City in Kansas and even talk of expanding the railroads into Texas soon, only a fraction of the cattle went through here that once had. Some of the pens stood empty.

But some were full of bawling beeves, and as the riders passed those pens, Riley pointed and said excitedly, "Look! There's the Star C brand!"

He was right. Bo saw the familiar C-for-Creel with a star around it, too. These were the cattle that Judd Palmer and his men had rustled.

Bo spotted several cowboys standing by the fence up ahead, talking to a man in a suit and a cream-colored Stetson. He heeled his horse into a trot and headed for the little group.

The well-dressed man looked a little nervous when he saw six hard-faced cowboys bearing down on him.

He didn't appear to be armed. He faced the riders as they reined in.

"Are you the cattle buyer around here, mister?" Bo asked.

"That's right. Name's Lloyd Fuller. What can I do for you fellas?"

Riley pointed at the cattle in the pens and said, "Did you buy those cows?"

"As a matter of fact, I did," Fuller said.

"The men who sold 'em are rustlers!" Riley shouted. "Those cows belong to John Creel of the Star C!"

"And that's who I bought them from," Fuller said coolly. "Or from Mr. Creel's representative, at least."

Riley looked like he wanted to dive off his horse and tackle the buyer. Bo held out a hand and motioned for his brother to calm down. He said, "Mr. Fuller, if the man who sold you those cows claimed to represent John Creel, he lied to you. My name is Bo Creel, and this is my brother Riley. We're John Creel's sons, and we were bringing this herd down here before it was stolen from us."

Fuller's mouth was a taut, angry line now as he said, "I have a letter from John Creel authorizing the bearer to sell those cattle."

"A damn forgery!" Riley broke in.

Fuller ignored him and went on, "That letter absolves me of any responsibility in the matter. As far as I'm concerned, it was a legal transaction, and if you feel differently, you'll have to take the matter up in court."

"We don't have time for that," Bo said. "How much did you pay?"

"I'm not sure that's any of your business—"

"Mister, you might be wise to answer the question," Bo said quietly.

Faced with half a dozen angry men, Fuller must have decided he didn't want to argue anymore. He said, "Fourteen thousand five hundred dollars. I would have gone sixteen thousand if the animals had been in better shape. Someone's been running them . . ."

His voice trailed off as a look of comprehension appeared on his face.

"That's right," Bo said. "The rustlers ran them to get here ahead of us. How long ago did you pay them off?"

"Well, that's just it. I haven't actually paid them yet. I was just on my way to deliver the money."

Bo's heart leaped. If Palmer didn't have the cash yet, that meant there was a chance to save the Star C.

"Where are you supposed to meet Palmer?"

"I don't know if I should—"

"Just tell him, mister," Scratch advised. "Hell, come along with us and you can see for yourself that Bo's tellin' the truth."

"All right, I suppose that makes sense. I was supposed to meet the man I made the agreement with at the hotel down by the waterfront. My cash is in the safe there."

The hotel, Bo thought.

Where he had sent Lauralee and Samantha.

* * *

The hotel was a whitewashed, two-story building with covered porches all around it, sitting in the middle of a green lawn that sloped down slightly to the water. Several small palm trees grew around it. The trees weren't native to this area, but they had been brought in and appeared to have taken to the climate.

People on the verandah stared as Lauralee and Samantha rode up and dismounted. There were buggies and carriages parked in front of the hotel, but no saddle horses. And the people who stayed here certainly weren't accustomed to seeing young women dressed in men's clothing, riding astride and carrying guns.

"We seem to be causing a bit of a scandal," Lauralee said. "You think I should tell 'em I own a saloon, too?"

"Surely that's not necessary," Samantha replied with a weak smile.

Lauralee chuckled and said, "I was just joshing. We might as well go in and see if we can get rooms for everybody."

They climbed the steps to the porch, and as they started toward the entrance, one of the double doors opened and a man stepped out. Like the two young women, his range clothes made him look a little out of place. His hat was tipped back on curly black hair above a brutal, rough-hewn face.

His eyes met Lauralee's and for some reason she felt a little shiver go through her.

Then the man moved past her, to her relief, and she and Samantha went on into the lobby.

The room had polished wooden floors and potted palms in the corners, along with fancy divans and wing chairs scattered around. It would be nice to dress up and have dinner in a place like this, Lauralee thought. Maybe she could convince Bo of that while they were here. *If* they stayed here. It was possible the chase after the rustlers could continue. Maybe it would be a better idea to wait for Bo and Scratch to get here before she rented any rooms.

A slick-haired clerk behind the desk asked, "Could I help you *ladies* with something?"

His tone of voice made Lauralee bristle. He seemed to be implying that she and Samantha actually weren't ladies, and just because they were covered with trail dust didn't make that true.

Before she could frame any sort of sharp retort, though, the clerk glanced over her shoulder and his eyes got big with surprise and fear. He exclaimed, "Sir, what—"

That was as far as he got before an arm looped around Lauralee's neck and jerked her backward against a man's hard-muscled frame. She felt something round and hard prod against her side and recognized it as a gun barrel.

"I knew I'd seen you somewhere before, honey," a harsh voice said in her ear. "You were with them damn Creels when we took the herd."

Lauralee twisted her head enough to see the ugly face

of the man who had passed them on the porch. She realized too late that he was one of the rustlers, maybe even their boss.

Samantha gasped and tried to turn and run, but the man stuck out a booted foot and tripped her. She stumbled and fell to the floor, and the man pinned her there with his foot.

"Hold still or I'll hurt you," he said. To Lauralee, he went on, "Where's the rest of your bunch?"

He eased his arm's pressure on her throat just enough for her to answer, and as he did she heard the swift rataplan of hoofbeats outside. Instinct told her who those new arrivals were.

"I reckon you're about to find out, you son of a bitch," she said.

CHAPTER 35

Lloyd Fuller had a buggy at the cattle pens. He drove hurriedly behind Bo, Scratch, and the other men as they headed at a gallop for the hotel that was the centerpiece of Rockport's waterfront.

As Bo reined in at the hitchracks in front of the hotel's big lawn, he saw a couple of familiar mounts tied there. He recognized the horses Lauralee and Samantha had been riding. So the two young women had made it here.

They would be all right, he told himself. There was no reason they would have run afoul of Judd Palmer . . .

He saw how wrong he was when someone kicked open the hotel's front door and emerged onto the porch. The well-dressed guests who had been sitting there in wicker chairs enjoying the gulf breezes scattered in fear as a tall, ugly man came onto the porch with one arm looped around Lauralee's neck and his other hand cruelly clasped around Samantha's arm. He forced the two women along in front of him.

Bo's recognized the man instantly, even though they had only traded a glance in the firelight during the fight at the trail camp. His instincts told him he was looking at Judd Palmer.

Somehow, the boss outlaw had known who Lauralee and Samantha were and realized that the pursuit had caught up to him before he got his hands on the money for the herd.

"Back off, Creel!" Palmer yelled. "Won't take but a second to snap this girl's neck if you try to prod me."

"Take it easy, Palmer," Bo said, keeping his voice steady and level. "You don't want to do anything that'll get you in more trouble than you're already in."

A harsh laugh came from Palmer's mouth. He said, "You really think I'm worried about the law? Hell, there's already enough paper out on me to get me hanged a dozen times over." He looked over at the buggy Lloyd Fuller had just brought to a stop next to Bo and the other riders. "Fuller, you get in here. I want that money you owe me. And while you're at it, you might as well give me whatever else is in the safe, too."

"Then you really *are* a thief, like these men said," Fuller responded coldly.

"Now you're catchin' on."

Fuller shook his head and said, "I won't give you a damned cent. And I'm sure someone's gone for the law by now. You might as well surrender."

Bo knew that wasn't going to happen. He had come up against hardened outlaws like Palmer plenty of times before. Men like that always believed they could shoot and fight their way out of anything—and most of the time they were right.

"My men are in Plummer's Saloon, right over there," Palmer said as he nodded toward a nearby building. "All I have to do is yell, and they'll come out of there shootin'. What's it gonna be, Creel? Do you play along with me, or do I kill these two gals?"

Before Bo could answer, Samantha said to Palmer, "Did my brother really hire you?"

Bo could tell that question took the outlaw by surprise. He turned his head to look at Samantha and asked, "You're the Fontaine girl?"

That was enough of an answer for Samantha. She lunged at Palmer and used her free hand to claw at his eyes. He yelled in pain and anger as her fingernails raked bloody furrows down his cheeks. Instinctively, he shoved her away.

That loosened his grip on Lauralee, who rammed an elbow back into his stomach and twisted free. She tackled Samantha and took them both off the verandah. As they landed on the green lawn, that left Judd Palmer standing there in the open in front of the hotel's doors.

He grabbed for the gun on his hip.

It hadn't even cleared leather when six slugs smashed into him. Bo, Scratch, and the others fired so closely together that the shots blended into one gigantic roar. The bullets pounded into Palmer's body with such force that he was lifted off his feet and thrown back against the doors. Blood spouted from the holes as he hung there for a second, then pitched forward, dead.

In the silence that filled the air after the gunfire, Riley turned to Lloyd Fuller and said, "I reckon you know now who you need to pay for those cattle, mister."

"Worry about that later," Bo snapped. "We've still got trouble!"

Just as Palmer had predicted, men rushed out of the nearby saloon, and when they saw their boss lying dead on the hotel verandah and the Creels with guns in their hands, they grabbed their own weapons and began blazing away.

Bo, Scratch, and the others dived from their saddles to take cover. The trunks of the palm trees weren't thick enough to provide much shelter, but they were better than nothing.

Lee sprinted across the lawn toward Samantha and Lauralee, firing as he ran.

"Stay down!" he shouted to the two young women. They crawled behind some shrubs planted along the front of the porch. Lee dropped to one knee beside the bushes and threw lead at the rustlers as they scattered and hunted cover themselves.

It was a fierce fight for the next few minutes. Davy fell as a bullet ripped through his leg, but he kept shooting as he lay there on his belly. A slug creased Riley's left arm, but he ignored the pain and kept fighting, too. One by one the rustlers fell, most to the deadly accurate shots of Bo and Scratch.

Finally, when only a couple of outlaws were left, one of them threw his gun out from behind the wagon where he had taken cover and thrust his hands high over his head.

"Hold your fire!" he yelled. "Don't shoot! I'm givin' up, damn it!"

"You yellow dog!" the other remaining rustler howled furiously. He swung his gun toward his companion, but in doing so he revealed himself at the corner of the building where he had taken cover.

That instant's glimpse was enough for Scratch, who drove a Remington round through the rustler's head, blowing a big chunk of it away in a grisly mess. As the corpse flopped to the ground, the lone survivor came out into the open, still with his arms up, and pleaded again, "Don't shoot!"

"Down on your knees, mister," Bo ordered. "And don't try anything funny."

The outlaw complied. Scratch kept him covered while Bo looked to the wounds that his brother and nephew had suffered. Riley and Davy would both be all right, Bo saw to his relief. Neither wound was serious.

Lee came over with Samantha and Lauralee. He had his arm around Samantha, who appeared to be shaken but unhurt.

So did Lauralee. She threw her arms around Bo, who patted her awkwardly on the back and asked, "Are you all right?"

"I am now," she told him.

Bo looked at Scratch and told him, "Get that *hombre* up and bring him over here." When Bo was facing the frightened rustler, he went on, "You're going to testify that Nick Fontaine hired you to rustle Star C cattle from the ranch and to steal that herd on the way down here."

"I sure will, mister, and it's the God's honest truth, too," the man said. "I never killed anybody, I swear, just stole cows. I hadn't ought to hang for that."

"That'll be up to a court to decide. But it won't hurt your chances if you help bring to justice the man who's really responsible for all this trouble." Bo looked at Samantha, whose face was pale and drawn, and added, "I'm sorry about that, Miss Fontaine."

"You don't have any choice, Mr. Creel," she said. "I know that. You have to save your father's ranch. I just . . . don't know what's going to happen to my father . . . when he finds out about Nick."

Lee led her away, talking softly to her as he tried to comfort her. Lauralee started binding up the wounds that Riley and Davy had suffered, to stop or at least slow down the bleeding until they could get some real medical attention.

And Lloyd Fuller came over to Bo and said, "I suppose I should pay you for those cattle, Mr. Creel."

"That's why we're here," Bo said. He was greatly relieved at how things had turned out, despite all the violence it had taken to reach this point.

But he knew the trouble might not be over yet.

They started for home the next morning. Riley's arm was in a sling, and Davy's leg was heavily bandaged. The doctor had advised them both to rest for a few days before traveling, but those words fell on deaf ears. All the Creels were ready to get back to the Star C.

They compromised by using some of the money from the sale of the herd to buy a buggy. Davy would be able to handle the team, and he and his uncle wouldn't have to spend long hours in the saddle.

Bo had the rest of the money—more than enough to pay off Gilbert Ambrose at the bank—in a money belt fastened around his waist. He didn't plan to take it off until he was ready to put it on the banker's desk.

"This has been quite an adventure," Lauralee commented as she rode between Bo and Scratch. "From the stories I've heard, you two get into scrapes like this all the time."

"Stories can be exaggerated," Bo pointed out.

"But we've been mixed up in our share of ruckuses," Scratch added. "It's been fun, too."

"If you call being shot at fun."

Scratch laughed and said, "We ain't never been in any danger of dyin' from boredom, now, have we?"

"That's true enough," Bo agreed with a chuckle of his own.

Maybe it was time to start thinking about giving up the wandering life, though, he mused. He was getting on in years. The family could probably use his help around the ranch, too.

Riley probably wouldn't like that. He was used to being in charge, and he would take Bo's continued presence as a threat to that. Bo knew he didn't really have any right to displace his brother, not after Riley had devoted decades to helping their father make a success out of the Star C.

Maybe he could stay in Bear Creek without living at the ranch. He could so something in town, maybe help Lauralee run the Southern Belle. She would like that . . .

"You're a million miles away from here, Bo Creel," she said, breaking into his thoughts.

"More like a hundred," he told her with a smile.

Luckily, he didn't have to make up his mind yet.

They still had a ways to go yet before they would be home.

CHAPTER 36

Late the next day they crossed the San Antonio River at the same ford where Judd Palmer's men had tried to ambush them. No one particularly wanted to stay in that place, so they pushed on since there was still a little daylight left. They made camp about halfway between the river and Coleto Creek.

There was plenty of time to return to Bear Creek and beat Gilbert Ambrose's deadline on the bank loan, so Bo didn't push the group too hard. That made the journey easier on the wounded Riley and Davy in the buggy.

He didn't want to delay too much, though, just in case something else happened. He certainly couldn't rule that out.

Any time a man got to feeling too confident, that was when trouble had a habit of sneaking up behind him and walloping him over the head.

That night as he sat next to Scratch, each of them sipping coffee, Bo said, "You know, I've been thinking—"

"You might as well stop right there," Scratch interrupted him. "I know what you're goin' to say."

Bo smiled and asked, "Oh, you do, do you?"

"Yep. You're gonna say we're gettin' too old for all this hell-raisin'. That it's time we stopped larrupin' around all over creation. That we might even start thinkin' about settlin' down. Puttin' our feet up. Puttin' our boots under some gal's bed."

"I'm sure Emmaline Ashley wouldn't mind that," Bo said.

Scratch nodded across the campfire toward Lauralee, who was talking to Samantha Fontaine. Lee was there, too, with his arm around Samantha's shoulders, and the two of them looked like they had been born to be next to each other.

"I reckon Emmaline, nice as she is, would be drove plumb crazy in a month if I was around all the time," Scratch said. "But you got maybe the best gal in the whole blamed state of Texas right over there, Bo, and she's in love with you. Think about that. A gal who looks like that, who can ride *and* shoot, *and* who owns a saloon, to boot! Good Lord, man! You couldn't draw it up on a piece of paper any better'n that."

"Only problem with that is she deserves better than some shiftless old codger."

"You really ought to let her make up her own mind about that."

Bo cradled his coffee cup between his hands and looked down into the black brew. He didn't see any answers floating there, no matter how hard he searched.

"Ten, fifteen years from now, I'll be gone," he said without looking up. "She'll still be a relatively young woman. What happens to her then?"

"I expect she'll cry her eyes out for a while, then she'll dry 'em and go on livin'. Don't you worry about that lady, Bo. She ain't got no quit in her. Not one damned bit."

That was true, Bo thought. He had seen evidence of it many times, including her dogged pursuit of him.

"It's just not right," he said stubbornly. "I'm old enough to be her—"

"Husband," Scratch said. "You're old enough to be her husband. Ain't nobody can argue with that."

Bo looked at his old friend and said, "Who's going to follow you around and get you out of trouble?"

Scratch snorted.

"You ain't been payin' attention. It's been me gettin' you out of trouble all these years."

"Is that so?"

"It dang sure is."

Bo laughed. He said, "Tell you what, Scratch. I'll think about it. Lauralee, I mean."

"I know what you mean," Scratch said with a nod. "You think about it, and then for once in your life, Bo Creel, you do what's best for you, not for everybody else in the whole dang world."

* * *

After breakfast the next morning, when everybody was getting ready to ride, Bo went over to Lauralee just as she picked up her saddle to put it on her horse.

"Let me take that for you," he said.

"I can do my own saddling," she said.

"I know that, but I'm old-fashioned. I was raised to be a gentleman."

She swung the saddle out of his reach and lifted it onto the horse's back.

"I tighten my own cinches," she said as she did exactly that.

"Sure, but I just thought . . ."

She turned her head, looked at him, and said, "Good Lord, Bo, are you trying to be nice?"

"Well, that's sort of what I had in mind—" he began.

The roar of a gunshot interrupted him. He heard someone cry out in pain and jerked around to see Lee collapsing with blood on his shirt. Samantha screamed, tried to grab him, and they both went down in a tangled sprawl.

"Don't hurt the women!" a man yelled. "But kill the Creels!"

Samantha must have recognized the voice, because she cried, "Danny, no!"

Then more gunshots drowned out her protest.

The group had stopped for the night at the base of a wooded knoll. The shots came from the trees that overlooked the camp. Ambushers, evidently led by Danny Fontaine, must have crept up there during the darkness and waited for dawn to launch their attack.

Riley and Davy were already in the buggy. Riley leaped out of the vehicle and crouched behind it to return the fire. Davy made it out, too, although with his wounded leg his exit amounted more to rolling off the seat and falling to the ground. He pulled himself up with one hand, braced himself, and started shooting with the other.

Bo, Scratch, Lauralee, and Jason scattered. Bo and Lauralee went to ground behind a log while Scratch and Jason took cover behind some brush. Neither of those places provided much shelter.

Samantha huddled over Lee, shielding him with her own body. Bo couldn't tell how badly his nephew was hit. Lee wasn't moving, though, so he was out of the fight at least for the moment.

Bo knew they were in a bad spot with the enemy holding the high ground. But if he could flank them somehow . . .

His horse and Lauralee's mount were close by, and both animals were already saddled. He said, "If Scratch and Jason cover us, we might be able to get on our horses and get around on the other side of that knoll."

"Sounds good to me," Lauralee said. "Let me fill up the empty chambers in my Colt."

A moment later she gave him a grim nod to indicate her gun was fully loaded and she was ready. This was *loco*, risking her life this way, Bo thought. And yet she would be in just as much danger if they stayed where they were.

"Scratch!" he called. "Cover us!"

The silver-haired Texan nodded to show that he understood. He and Jason started firing even faster, pouring lead toward the gunmen hidden at the top of the rise.

Bo and Lauralee leaped to their feet. They saved their bullets for the moment and concentrated on running. Their horses hadn't spooked—yet—but they needed to hit the saddle as quickly as they could.

A few bullets whipped around Bo's head, but the fusillade from Scratch and Jason had made the killers duck for a moment. That gave Bo and Lauralee just enough time to leap onto their horses. They kicked the animals into a run and leaned forward over the horses' necks to make themselves smaller targets as they raced toward the other side of the knoll.

As they rounded the rise, Bo saw flame spurt from a gun muzzle as the man who had been holding the horses opened fire on them. He leveled his Colt and triggered it, and Lauralee fired an instant later. The man dropped the reins and spun off his feet as both slugs ripped through him.

"Good shooting!" Bo yelled over the thunder of hoofbeats.

"You, too!" Lauralee replied.

They started up the far side of the rise, and as they did, several of the bushwhackers appeared to meet this new threat. Bo fired again and saw a man double over as the bullet punched into his guts.

Beside him, Lauralee had holstered her revolver and pulled the Winchester from its sheath. The rifle cracked again and again as she sprayed the hilltop with lead.

As usual, hired gunmen had no stomach for a fight when the odds turned against them. Bo saw men running through the trees, fleeing. At least one of them caught a horse, because a moment later Bo heard swift hoofbeats rattling away. He couldn't see where the man had gone.

He reined in and told Lauralee, "Hold up a minute."

She followed suit, hauling back on the reins and bringing her mount to a stop.

It sounded like only one gun firing from the hilltop now, and those shots seemed rather aimless. Bo shouted, "Hold your fire up there! You're surrounded, mister!"

"Go to hell, Creel!"

This time even Bo recognized Danny Fontaine's voice. He called back, "We don't want to kill you, Danny! Throw your gun down and come out of those trees!"

"I'll never surrender to a bunch of damned kidnappers!"

Lauralee repeated, "Kidnappers? What in the world is he talking about?"

"I don't know," Bo said. "But if his sister can't talk some sense into him, he's not coming off that knoll alive. I reckon we've knocked the other bushwhackers out of the fight, except for the ones that lit a shuck."

"Danny!" Samantha cried shrilly from the other side of the hill. "Danny, stop this, please!"

"Don't worry, sis!" he shouted back to her. "I'll get you away from them!"

"I'm not their prisoner! Please, Danny, don't be crazy! I'm with the Creels because I want to be!"

"The bastards're makin' you say that—"

"No!" Samantha insisted. "No, it's true. I swear, Danny! Please stop shooting!"

Bo and Lauralee had their guns trained on the growth where Danny Fontaine's voice came from. Bo figured that on the other side of the hill, Scratch and the other men had their sights on the same target. Danny's only chance now was to surrender.

A few moments of tense silence went by. Then Danny called, "You're not lyin'? Lee Creel didn't kidnap you?"

Bo heard a sob in Samantha's voice as she told her brother, "Of course not! Lee wouldn't have to kidnap me! I'm in love with him, and he's in love with me!"

"What!" Danny roared.

"It's true," Samantha insisted. "Please throw your gun out, Danny, and come down from there. Please. I don't want to lose you."

Several more heartbeats went by, stretching out painfully, before Danny finally said, "Hold your fire, damn it! I'm comin' out!"

Bo saw a revolver sail out from behind a tree, and a second later Danny stepped into sight with his hands raised. He started slowly down the hill toward the camp, and after a few steps Bo and Lauralee couldn't see him anymore.

"We'd better get back around there," Bo told her.

"What about the others?" she asked. "At least one of them got away."

"I don't reckon we have to worry about them. Once a hired gun knows he's not likely to get paid anymore, he's finished."

They rode back around the knoll, and Bo felt relief go through him when he spotted his nephew Lee sitting up with his back against one of the buggy wheels. There was a bloodstain on his shirt where he'd been wounded, but he didn't appear to have been hurt too badly.

Danny stood nearby with an angry but confused look on his face as his sister confronted him. Scratch and Jason had their guns pointed at the young man in case he tried to cause any more trouble.

"I don't understand any of this," Danny was saying to Samantha. "I thought Lee Creel had carried you off to . . . to molest you."

"Why in the world would you think that?" she asked him.

"Because . . . because Nick said . . ."

"Nick," Samantha said bitterly as her brother's voice trailed off. "Danny, there's a lot you don't know about our big brother."

"I know you shouldn't be here with these damned Creels," Danny snapped.

From horseback, Bo said in a flinty voice, "Shut up and listen to your sister, Danny. She's got a lot to tell you, and when she's finished you might see things a little differently."

CHAPTER 37

While Samantha was talking to her brother, Bo and Scratch checked the bodies of the other gunmen Danny had brought with him. Four of them were scattered around the top of the knoll, all dead. A couple of them looked vaguely familiar to Bo. He decided he had probably seen them with the Fontaines in Bear Creek.

"We leavin' 'em for the coyotes?" Scratch asked.

"It'd serve them right," Bo said. "But I reckon we've got time to bury them."

"Before somebody else workin' for Nick Fontaine tries to kill us, you mean."

Bo shook his head and said, "I think Nick may have shot his bolt when he tried to trick Danny into killing us. I'm not sure he has any hired guns left."

"Besides the one or two varmints who got away," Scratch reminded him.

"That's true," Bo said. "I guess we'll have to keep our eyes open."

"We'd be doin' that anyway."

They rounded up the horses that had belonged to the dead men and then slung the corpses over the saddles to take them back down the hill.

When they reached the camp, Danny Fontaine looked more confused than angry, as if he were having trouble grasping what Samantha had told him. He also appeared to be stone-cold sober, which was unusual for Danny.

"You understand now that nobody kidnapped your sister?" Bo asked the young man.

"Yeah, I reckon so," Danny said grudgingly. "That don't mean I like you Creels, though."

Riley said, "I don't care whether you like us, as long as you're not trying to kill us."

By now Lauralee had bandaged the bullet hole in Lee's shoulder. He came over to Danny and asked curtly, "Was it you who shot me, Fontaine?"

"Well . . . no," Danny admitted. "When I left the Rafter F to come after you, I was mad enough to shoot you on sight, but I guess I'd calmed down a mite by the time we got here. I saw you standin' there with Samantha and she didn't seem like she was upset or scared, so I was tryin' to figure things out when Trace Holland drilled you."

Bo said, "Holland started the ball, did he? That doesn't surprise me. He's been Nick's man right from the start."

"Yeah . . ." Danny said slowly. "I guess Nick gave him some orders before we left."

"Like making sure when you found us that it turned into a fight." Bo nodded. "That makes sense. He wanted all of us dead, and he didn't care if you and your sister got killed, too."

Samantha began, "Nick wouldn't—" but she stopped short before she finished. After a second she went on, "After everything we've found out, I don't suppose there's any point in saying Nick wouldn't do anything, is there?"

"He doesn't seem to draw the line, as long as he thinks it'll help him get what he wants," Bo said.

Danny said, "We have to go back. We have to talk to Pa and straighten all this out."

Bo had a feeling that it would take more than talking to settle this affair. He was afraid more powder would have to be burned.

But he nodded and said, "That's where we're headed."

Around the middle of the next afternoon, Trace Holland rode into the Rafter F on an exhausted horse. He was pretty worn out from the long, hard ride himself.

Seemed like he was making a habit of that, and he didn't much like it.

Jed Clemons came out of the barn and met him. The old wrangler asked, "Where's the rest of the bunch you left with?"

Holland didn't answer. It was none of Clemons's business. Instead he asked, "Is Nick in the house?"

"Far as I know. I ain't his keeper."

Holland curled his lip at the old-timer and gave him

a cold stare. Clemons took the reins and hurriedly led Holland's horse toward the barn.

Holland turned and went up onto the porch. He didn't knock, just opened the door and walked into the house. He was too tired and disgusted for niceties.

"Nick!" he called. "Nick, you around?"

Heavy footsteps sounded in the hall leading to the study. Nick Fontaine stalked toward Holland with an irritated frown on his face. He said, "Keep your voice down, damn it. My father's resting. Where's Danny? Did you stop the Creels?"

"Everything went to hell—again!" Holland snapped. "Those Creels are the luckiest bastards on the face of the earth." He added grudgingly, "It doesn't hurt that they're some of the best shots I've ever seen, too."

"Then they're not dead," Nick said in a hard, flat voice. "They still have the money to pay off that note."

"Yeah, I'm afraid so. I heard some of 'em talkin' about it before the ruckus started."

Nick's fists clenched. He made a visible effort to control himself and asked, "What about Danny and my sister?"

"They're all right, as far as I know. I'm pretty sure the Creels captured Danny."

"Where are the rest of the men?"

"Dead, most of them," Holland said grimly. "A couple of them took off for the tall and uncut rather than stay there to get killed."

"And you did the same thing," Nick said in an accusing tone.

Holland shrugged.

"I wasn't going to take on the whole bunch by myself. That'd be *loco*. Besides, I figured you needed to know what happened, so you could figure out your next move."

Nick laughed hollowly and said, "There is no next move. Bo Creel has beaten me at every turn. This scheme was my best chance to ruin the Star C and take it over, and now—"

"What?" The question came from the top of the stairs. "What are you talking about, Nick?"

Holland looked up, saw Ned Fontaine standing there. The old man's face was drawn taut with pain, and he seemed shocked by what he had just heard, too.

"Pa, you should go back to your room and rest," Nick said quickly. "I'll handle this—"

"Nick, what have you been doing?" Fontaine persisted. "What's this damned gunman talking about?"

"What have I been doing?" Nick repeated. Rage darkened his face. "I've been doing what you wanted. I've been trying to make the Rafter F the biggest ranch around here! The biggest in all of Texas, one of these days!"

"How are you doing that?" Fontaine demanded. "I won't abide anything illegal—"

Holland couldn't help himself. He laughed.

Fontaine started down the stairs. His face was flushed now, like Nick's. He said, "By God, Nick, what *have* you been doing? All that rustling over on the Star C . . . were you behind that?" He waved a hand at Holland.

"I thought you hired all those hardcases to protect our ranch, not to break the law and go after the Creels!"

Nick's lip curled in a snarl as he said, "I don't care what you thought. I did what was necessary. I did what you never would have had the guts to do!"

Fontaine stopped halfway down the stairs. A shudder went through him, and he gripped the banister tightly to brace himself. After a second he continued, "Your sister is mixed up in this somehow, isn't she? And your brother? Are they in danger, Nick? Have you done something that's going to get them killed?"

"They're fine," Nick snapped. "Nobody's going to get killed—except Bo Creel." He looked at Holland. "Get a fresh horse, and tell Clemons to saddle one for me, too."

"What are we doing, boss?" Holland asked softly.

"Creel will take that money straight to the bank. We're going to stop him."

Holland shook his head and said, "It's over, Nick. If they've got your sister and Danny, they can figure out you were behind the whole thing. They'll have the law on you." The gunman started to turn away. "Reckon it's time I pulled my freight."

"Damn you!" Nick shouted. "Whatever money Creel's got on him, it's yours if we stop them before they get to the bank, Trace. It's bound to be more than ten grand. You could go a long way on that. California, Mexico— hell, wherever you want to go! Just side me on this." He paused. "Unless you're afraid of Creel and Morton."

Holland had expected him to play that card. Being accused of cowardice didn't really matter to the gunman. He knew that wasn't true.

He was a lot more interested in the money, and he had a grudge to settle with Scratch Morton, too. It would be a big gamble . . .

But hell, life was a gamble, wasn't it?

"All right," Holland said. "I'll go to Bear Creek with you."

"Fine," Nick said with a curt nod. "Let me get my gun."

Holland supposed he would finally get to see if those stories about Nick being fast on the draw were true.

"Stop," Ned Fontaine said from the stairs. "Nick, you can't do this. I don't understand all this talk about money, but if you kill Bo Creel you'll be an outlaw."

"Yeah—but the ranch will be bigger and more successful than ever when the Star C goes under and the Rafter F takes over. That's what you always wanted, isn't it, Pa?"

"Not by breaking the law! I never wanted my son to go insane and—"

Fontaine's face twisted as his words broke off. All the color washed out of it. He started to double over, and as he did, he lost his balance.

"Pa!" Nick yelled as his father fell forward and toppled the rest of the way down the stairs.

Fontaine came to a stop almost at Holland's feet. The gunman muttered, "What the hell—" and stepped back.

Nick's momentary concern had evaporated. He said

again, "Let me get my gun belt," and started toward the study.

"What about—"

"We'll tell Jed to come see about the old man on our way out. Maybe we can still beat Bo Creel to the bank."

CHAPTER 38

It was a bloodied and battered bunch that paused on the banks of Bear Creek late that afternoon.

"Reckon this is where we split up," Bo said. "Scratch and I will take the money on into town and give it to Ambrose. The rest of you go on to the ranch. We'll see you there later."

"Damn it," Riley said. "After all we've been through, we ought to get to see you hand that money over, Bo."

Samantha said, "Lee's too weak after being shot."

"I never said that," Lee put in. "I'm fine."

"No, you're not," she told him. "You need rest and some proper medical attention. So do your uncle and your brother."

Bo said, "We'll send Doc Perkins out from town right away." He paused. "Right after we've delivered the money."

"All right," Riley said, but he still didn't sound happy about it. "You be careful, though. Nick Fontaine's still around somewhere, and he can't be trusted."

Samantha looked pained at that blunt statement, but

she didn't argue the point. She knew as well as anyone that her older brother had turned bad.

"Am I free to go?" Danny asked.

"Go ahead," Bo told him. "But remember, you know the truth now. Don't let Nick talk you into doing anything foolish."

"He's not going to talk me into anything," Danny promised. "I don't like you Creels and I never will, but hell, I'm not an outlaw. Nick tried to turn me into a killer. We're gonna have some words about that." He lifted his reins. "Come on, Samantha."

She shook her head and said, "I'm going to the Star C with Lee. I'm going to stay with him until the doctor has taken care of him."

"They're still our enemies—" Danny started to bluster.

"No, they're not. If you'll just give them a chance, they can be the best friends we've ever had."

From the look on Danny's face, Bo didn't expect that to ever happen. The young man jerked his horse around and galloped away, splashing across the creek as he headed for the Rafter F.

"I'm sorry, Samantha," Lee said. "He's just a hot-headed *hombre*. I know somethin' about that. He'll come around."

"He'll have to," she said, "if he wants me to still be his sister."

Jason spoke up, saying, "I can come with you and Scratch to town, Uncle Bo. Just in case there's any trouble."

"You're the only one who's not shot up, Jason," Bo

told him. "You get everybody else back to the ranch safely. That's the best thing you can do right now."

With obvious reluctance, Jason accepted that decision. With him and Samantha on horseback and the three wounded Creels crowded into the buggy, they started for the Star C.

That left Bo, Scratch, and Lauralee to ride on into town.

As they headed in that direction, Scratch asked Lauralee, "Was it as big an adventure as you thought it'd be?"

"It was pretty exciting," she said. "Pretty scary at times, too. I'm not sure I'd like to live like that after all, if that's the kind of trouble you two always find yourselves in."

Scratch chuckled and said, "Shootin' scrapes do seem to follow us around."

"Well, at least this one's over," Lauralee said.

Bo didn't say anything.

But his instincts told him she might be wrong about that.

A short time later they rode into Bear Creek. They passed the wooden bridge over the stream that divided the more respectable business district from the saloons and gambling halls on the other side of the creek. The bank was up ahead, one of the few brick buildings in the settlement.

There were no hitchracks directly in front of the bank, so Bo, Scratch, and Lauralee reined in and dismounted at the hardware store on the corner.

"You didn't have to come all the way with us," Bo

told Lauralee. "You could have gone across the creek, back to the Southern Belle."

"I'll be there soon enough," she said. She smiled. "I'm like Riley. I want to see this through to the end."

Bo returned her smile and leaned his head toward the bank.

"Let's go on and give Mr. Ambrose his money, then."

The three of them started to walk the short distance remaining on this journey, and as they did, two men stepped around the corner of the hardware store into their path.

Bo just had time to recognize them as Nick Fontaine and Trace Holland before he realized the men were drawing their guns.

"You'll never save that ranch, Creel!" Nick shouted. Insane hatred twisted the lines of his face.

As always when he was confronted with danger, Bo let his instincts and reflexes take over.

But instead of reaching for his own Colt, his arm shot out and swept Lauralee back and down, out of the line of fire. He heard a gun roar, felt the shock of a bullet. The impact rocked him back, but he managed to stay on his feet.

Beside him, Scratch had the twin Remingtons out, flame belching from their muzzles. Trace Holland's gun erupted, but the bullet went into the ground in front of him as Scratch's slugs tore into his body. Scratch fired both Remingtons again and Holland fell. The front of his shirt was already a bloody mess.

Nick Fontaine got off a second shot, but he hurried

this one and it whipped harmlessly past Bo's ear. Bo's Colt seemed to weigh a ton, and he thought he was slow as molasses getting it out of the holster.

But then the gun came up and bucked in his hand as he slammed out a shot, and he saw the black leather vest Nick wore jump a little as the slug went through it into Nick's chest. Nick staggered and fired a third time as blood welled from the corner of his mouth. The bullet kicked up dirt to Bo's right.

Bo fired again, but just as he squeezed the trigger his legs buckled under him. The bullet went high and chipped brick splinters from the wall of the bank. Bo hit his knees and caught himself with his left hand. His right thrust the Colt toward Nick and triggered it again.

This shot went home and knocked Nick halfway around. Bo was close enough to see the life go out of Nick's eyes. The gun slipped from his finger and thudded to the ground, and Nick followed it a second later, sprawling in death.

Bo dropped his own gun and toppled onto his side.

Lauralee had hold of him a second later, throwing her arms around him as she sobbed, "Bo! Bo!"

Scratch was on Bo's other side, grabbing hold of him, as well.

A great weakness filled Bo. But he knew he couldn't give in to it. Not yet. He still had something to do.

Two things to do.

"Help me . . . up," he breathed through teeth clenched against the pain.

"Bo, you need a doctor," Lauralee said.

"Help me . . . to the bank," he insisted.

"Reckon we better do it," Scratch said. "I think I know what he wants."

Together, they lifted him, and then, with Scratch and Lauralee flanking Bo and holding him up, the three of them made their halting way past the bodies of Nick Fontaine and Trace Holland toward the bank entrance. The shooting had drawn a lot of people out of the buildings, including Gilbert Ambrose. The banker stood there with a shocked expression on his face.

Bo, Scratch, and Lauralee stopped in front of him. Bo's hands fumbled awkwardly under his shirt for the money belt. It was slick with blood when he touched it. He found the buckle, unfastened it, and pulled the belt out.

"Paid in full," he said as he dropped it at Ambrose's feet.

Then he turned to look at Lauralee and did the other thing he had to do before it was too late.

"I . . . love . . . you," he said.

He saw the mingled grief and happiness on her face, her beautiful face with the tears streaming down her tanned cheeks, and as darkness washed over him he thought that if she was the last thing he ever saw in this world, that wouldn't be a bad memory to take with him across the divide.

Bo leaned on the cane as he walked out of the First Baptist Church in Bear Creek. Lauralee was beside him, her hand on his arm in case he needed her to help him, but Bo didn't expect that to happen. He was getting around pretty good these days.

The bullet from Nick Fontaine's gun had put him flat on his back for a month. Doc Perkins had expected him to die. The medico admitted that much, then added, "What I failed to take into account was that you have the constitution of a man twenty years younger than you really are, Bo."

"Plus he's too damn stubborn to die," Scratch had put in, prompting the doctor to nod and agree, "Yes, that, too."

As usual, Scratch wasn't far from Bo's side today. He and Emmaline Ashley had followed Bo and Lauralee out of the church. Now they all turned, along with everyone else in attendance, to watch Mr. and Mrs. Lee Creel emerge into the autumn sunlight.

Samantha was beautiful in her wedding gown, Bo thought. He was glad to see her happy again. She was a fine young woman and deserved to have some good things in her life after the death of her older brother and the illness that had laid her father low.

Ned Fontaine was strong enough to attend his daughter's wedding today, and there was that for the family to be thankful for. He and his remaining son followed Samantha and Lee out of the church. Fontaine was gaunt and wan, and he had to lean on Danny.

Fortunately, Danny had been sober for the past couple of months and seemed to be taking seriously the idea that he had to be responsible for running the Rafter F now.

Lee, completely healed from the wound he had suffered when Trace Holland shot him, helped his new bride up into the buggy that was waiting for them and climbed in beside her. He grinned and waved his hat at the crowd, then took up the reins and sent the buggy rolling away from the church as the wedding guests cheered and applauded.

The ones loudest in their approval were the Creels, from old John Creel down to the youngest grandchild.

Lauralee said to Bo, "Cooper looks happy to have a new daughter-in-law . . . even if she is a Fontaine."

"All that's over and done with," Bo said. "Pa even rode over to the Rafter F the other day with Riley. They had a talk with Ned and Danny and told them that if they ever needed any help with anything, the Star C was ready to pitch in." Bo chuckled. "From the sound of what Riley told me, those two old-timers were about as wary around each other as a couple of old dogs, but at least they didn't go to biting and snapping."

"That's good to know," Lauralee said. She hesitated, then went on, "How long does Mr. Fontaine have?"

"A few months, according to Doc Perkins," Bo said. "A year at the most. But from the way things are going, Danny might make a hand after all. Fontaine can go to his grave knowing that his ranch will be all right."

Scratch added with a grin, "And he might even have a new grandson by then. You can't ever tell."

"Don't be crude, Mr. Morton," Emmaline told him.

"Now come on with me. We're having dinner on the grounds, and I brought an apple pie you have to have a slice of."

Scratch's grin widened as he linked arms with the widow and said to Bo, "Can't argue with fresh apple pie, now, can I, partner?"

"You sure can't," Bo told him.

As they watched Scratch and Emmaline walk away, Lauralee said, "You think they'll be the next ones getting married, Bo?"

"Scratch?" Bo shook his head. "He thinks the world and all of Emmaline, but one of these mornings he's going to lift his head like an old bull scenting something on the air, and he'll have to go charging off to find out what it is. Scratch Morton will never change, the old sidewinder."

"What about you, Bo Creel?" Lauralee asked.

"I don't know," he told her honestly. "I reckon time will tell." He linked his arm with hers and went on, "Right now, why don't we go try some of that pie Emmaline brought?"

Lauralee nodded, and together they walked toward the tables set up in the shade of the trees next to the church where the people of Bear Creek were gathering. An autumn breeze moved across the Texas plains, rustling the leaves and carrying the call of distant places.

J. A. Johnstone on William W. Johnstone
"When the Truth Becomes Legend"

William W. Johnstone was born in southern Missouri, the youngest of four children. He was raised with strong moral and family values by his minister father, and tutored by his schoolteacher mother. Despite this, he quit school at age fifteen.

"I have the highest respect for education," he says, "but such is the folly of youth, and wanting to see the world beyond the four walls and the blackboard."

True to this vow, Bill attempted to enlist in the French Foreign Legion ("I saw Gary Cooper in *Beau Geste* when I was a kid and I thought the French Foreign Legion would be fun") but was rejected, thankfully, for being underage. Instead, he joined a traveling carnival and did all kinds of odd jobs. It was listening to the veteran carny folk, some of whom had been on the circuit since the late 1800s, telling amazing tales about their experiences, that planted the storytelling seed in Bill's imagination.

"They were mostly honest people, despite the bad reputation traveling carny shows had back then," Bill remembers. "Of course, there were exceptions. There was one guy named Picky, who got that name because he was a master pickpocket. He could steal a man's socks right off his feet without him knowing. Believe me, Picky got us chased out of more than a few towns."

After a few months of this grueling existence, Bill returned home and finished high school. Next came stints as a deputy sheriff in the Tallulah, Louisiana, Sheriff's Department, followed by a hitch in the U.S. Army. Then he began a career in radio broadcasting at KTLD in Tallulah, which would last sixteen years. It was there that he fine-tuned his storytelling skills. He turned to writing in 1970, but it wouldn't be until 1979 that his first novel, *The Devil's Kiss,* was published. Thus began the full-time writing career of William W. Johnstone. He wrote horror (*The Uninvited*), thrillers (*The Last of the Dog Team*), even a romance novel or two. Then, in February 1983, *Out of the Ashes* was published. Searching for his missing family in a postapocalyptic America, rebel mercenary and patriot Ben Raines is united with the civilians of the Resistance forces and moves to the forefront of a revolution for the nation's future.

Out of the Ashes was a smash. The series would continue for the next twenty years, winning Bill three generations of fans all over the world. The series was often imitated but never duplicated. "We all tried to copy the Ashes series," said one publishing executive, "but Bill's uncanny ability, both then and now, to predict in which direction the political winds were blowing brought a certain immediacy to the table no one else could capture." The Ashes series would end its run with more than thirty-four books and twenty million copies in print, making it one of the most successful men's action series in American book publishing. (The Ashes series also, Bill notes with a touch of pride, got him on the FBI's Watch List for its less than flattering portrayal of spineless politicians and the growing power of big government over our lives, among other things. In that respect, I often find myself saying, "Bill was years ahead of his time.")

Always steps ahead of the political curve, Bill's recent thrillers, written with myself, include *Vengeance Is Mine, Invasion USA, Border War, Jackknife, Remember the Alamo, Home Invasion, Phoenix Rising, The Blood of Patriots, The Bleeding Edge,* and the upcoming *Suicide Mission.*

It is with the western, though, that Bill found his greatest success. His westerns propelled him onto both the *USA Today* and the *New York Times* bestseller lists.

Bill's western series include *The Mountain Man, Matt Jensen, the Last Mountain Man, Preacher, The Family Jensen, Luke Jensen, Bounty Hunter, Eagles, MacCallister* (an Eagles spin-off), *Sidewinders, The Brothers O'Brien, Sixkiller, Blood Bond, The Last Gunfighter,* and the upcoming new series *Flintlock* and *The Trail West.* May 2013 saw the hardcover western *Butch Cassidy, The Lost Years.*

"The Western," Bill says, "is one of the few true art forms that is one hundred percent American. I liken the Western as America's version of England's Arthurian legends, like the Knights of the Round Table, or

Robin Hood and his Merry Men. Starting with the 1902 publication of *The Virginian* by Owen Wister, and followed by the greats like Zane Grey, Max Brand, Ernest Haycox, and of course Louis L'Amour, the Western has helped to shape the cultural landscape of America.

"I'm no goggle-eyed college academic, so when my fans ask me why the Western is as popular now as it was a century ago, I don't offer a 200-page thesis. Instead, I can only offer this: The Western is honest. In this great country, which is suffering under the yoke of political correctness, the Western harks back to an era when justice was sure and swift. Steal a man's horse, rustle his cattle, rob a bank, a stagecoach, or a train, you were hunted down and fitted with a hangman's noose. One size fit all.

"Sure, we westerners are prone to a little embellishment and exaggeration and, I admit it, occasionally play a little fast and loose with the facts. But we do so for a very good reason—to enhance the enjoyment of readers.

"It was Owen Wister, in *The Virginian* who first coined the phrase *'When you call me that, smile.'* Legend has it that Wister actually heard those words spoken by a deputy sheriff in Medicine Bow, Wyoming, when another poker player called him a son of a bitch.

"Did it really happen, or is it one of those myths that have passed down from one generation to the next? I honestly don't know. But there's a line in one of my favorite Westerns of all time, *The Man Who Shot Liberty Valance,* where the newspaper editor tells the young reporter, 'When the truth becomes legend, print the legend.'

"These are the words I live by."

Turn the page for an exciting preview!

BAD MEN OF THE WEST . . .

William Johnstone and J. A. Johnstone are the
USA Today bestselling authors whose Western sagas
have won a legion of devoted fans. Now they take up
the tale of a legendary outlaw who tore up Texas,
and left behind a legacy of terror.

LIVE WILD, DRAW FAST, DIE HARD . . .

Born and bred in the Texas Panhandle town of
Comanche Crossing, William "Wild Bill" Longley
gunned down a dozen of its men in cold blood before
he got around to the sheriff and deputy—so he could
take over the job himself. Then he found the perfect
sidekick in a vicious career criminal named
Booker Tate. With his remorseless heart set on
a beautiful young woman, Wild Bill and Booker
take the whole town hostage until the young lady
agrees to a marriage to a man she despises.

That's when a cold-eyed stranger comes to town with
a dead man strapped to his saddle. In a town where
violence and murder rule the day . . . a terrifying
battle is about to explode—between ruthless Wild Bill
Longley and a bounty hunter named Tam Sullivan,
who's done a whole lot of killing of his own . . .

A DANGEROUS MAN
A Novel of William "Wild Bill" Longley

By *USA Today* Bestselling Author
WILLIAM W. JOHNSTONE
with J. A. Johnstone

On sale now, wherever Pinnacle Books are sold!

CHAPTER 1
Scar of the Noose

Two men rode through the freezing night, revolvers in their holsters and evil on their minds. Behind them lay a dead man, murdered for the few dollars in his pocket, his gun, horse, and new boots.

Wild Bill Longley had not known who the man was, nor did he care.

He needed boots, the man had them, so he shot him. Gut shot him, just to watch him die slowly and in agony, as was Longley's way in such matters.

As snow flurried in the icy wind and settled among the pines like streaks of wan moonlight, Longley drew rein and kicked away the dead man's ten-dollar horse as it pulled alongside him. "Damn it, Booker, you sure there's a town at the end of this trail? I'm freezing my nuts off here."

Booker Tate nodded. An uncurried, dangerous brute,

his red beard spread to the middle button of his mackinaw and long hair fell over his shoulders in greasy tangles. "Comanche Crossing is there all right, Bill, and it's ours for the taking. Man, I've been there afore, and it's prime."

"What about the town sheriff?" Longley asked. "Is he a gun?"

"Hell no. The sheriff is elected, Bill. Fat feller by the name of Frank Harm. We can take him, real easy."

"Maybe so, but I don't want no slipups on this venture, Booker. I mean, I don't want to come up against no big name draw-fighting lawman aiming to mess things up."

"Hell, Bill, there ain't a named draw fighter within two hundred miles of the Crossing," Tate said, grinning. "The only one I can think of is Con Collins and he never leaves the San Juan River country. Like I said, the town is there for them as wants it. Come the spring melt, we can ride out rich men."

"A hick town in the middle of nowhere ain't going to make us rich. And that's a natural fact."

"Yeah, maybe so, but we'll have enough to keep us in whiskey and women fer a year," Tate said.

"Well, that's always something, ain't it?"

"Damn right it is."

Longley lifted a whiskey flask from the pocket of his sheepskin and took a swig, then a second. He passed the flask to Tate.

Unlike his squat, simian companion, Bill Longley was a tall, dark and handsome man. He sported a trimmed imperial that set female hearts aflutter and usually affected the dress and languid, Southern manner of the riverboat gambler, though he possessed none of those gentlemanly traits.

The eyes he turned to Tate were a spectacular blue, but cold as floe ice, tinged with a lurking insanity.

"I say Bill, that time you was hung when you ran with Tom Johnson an' them, how did it feel?" Tate said. "I was always meaning to ask."

"Why do you ask me such a question, at this place and time? And you a man who has been my acquaintance only for two weeks?" The gunman's voice was flat, toneless, like lead coins dropping onto the trunk of a dead tree.

Tate heard that dead voice, accepted its warning, and stepped carefully. He smiled, or tried to. "Well, I figure when it's time to finally turn up my toes I'll be shot or hung. I know what getting shot feels like, but I ain't never been hung afore."

Longley undid the top button of his sheepskin, pulled the collar away, and craned his neck. "Take a good look. This is what it's like." A dull red scar about an inch deep, banded with distorted white tissue, circled his neck.

The terrible scar still bore its scarlet anger, but the vertical bands were white as bone and looked like small, writhing snakes.

It took a great deal to shock Booker Tate, but the livid legacy of a hemp rope did. "My God, Bill, an' you was only half hung," he said, wonder in his small, black eyes.

Longley adjusted his collar. "The posse as done it didn't stay around. They should've lingered awhile and made sure the hanging took."

"What happened to Johnson?"

"His neck broke like a dry twig. I heard it snap."

"You was lucky, Bill, an' no mistake."

Longley shrugged, his hard face empty. "If the vigilantes hadn't bungled it, I would have swapped one hell for another just a tad before my time. Luck don't even come into it."

"You're a rum one, Bill," Tate said. "An' no mistake."

"No, I'm a man who should be dead on a hell-firing trail to nowhere."

Tate smiled. "Comanche Crossing ain't nowhere. It's somewhere. Any place you can sleep in a bed is somewhere."

"Every town is nowhere to me." Longley smirked. "And Comanche Crossing will be nowhere after I get through with it."

CHAPTER 2
The Man Hunter

Tam Sullivan sat across the table from a man he'd just met. The raging snow and wind had forced him to look for shelter and the rancher had graciously obliged.

"It's a dugout saloon and hog farm, owned by a man name of Rufus Brooks, and he's a real bad 'un," the rancher told him. "Hell, boy, you can't miss it. Well, you can, but follow my directions and they'll take you right to the front door."

The man raised a lascivious eyebrow and smiled.

"Huntin' fer a woman, are ye? Young buck like you."

"Nope," Sullivan said. "I'm hunting a man. Feller by the name of Crow Wallace. You heard tell of him?"

"Who ain't heard tell of him? He's another bad 'un like Brooks, maybe worse. Stranger passin' through tole me Crow killed a man in San Antone real recent, then badly cut up another in a saloon down El Paso way."

Sullivan nodded. "The stranger said it right. But two weeks ago Crow made the mistake of robbing a Butterfield stage. He shotgunned the guard and got away with ten thousand dollars and a passenger's gold watch."

The rancher pushed the bottle of whiskey across his kitchen table, closer to Sullivan. "Ye don't say?"

Sullivan was not, by inclination, a talking man, but the rancher was a widower and lonely. That, the whiskey, and a reluctance to again brace the wild weather outside, loosened his tongue a little. "Seems like the passenger set store by the watch and added five hundred dollars to Crow's bounty."

"How much is he worth?" the rancher asked, a gleam of avarice in his eyes.

"Right now, two thousand five hundred dollars and ten percent of all monies recovered."

"And you mean to collect?"

"Seems like."

"Well, I'd like to help you, but—"

"I don't need any help," Sullivan said. "I'm a man who works alone."

"You said you tracked Crow this far?"

"Yeah." Sullivan waved a hand in the direction of the window. "Then this winter weather cracked down hard and I lost him."

"Well, if'n he ain't already skipped out of the New Mexico Territory, Brooks' dugout is the only place he could be."

"No towns farther north?"

"One. A burg called Comanche Crossing maybe

twenty miles south of Grulla Ridge, but nobody goes there. It's a straitlaced town if you know what I mean. Well, except for Montana Maine, that is. She's the big attraction, but they say she's mighty choosy about who she keeps company with." The rancher leaned back in his chair, like a man ready to state an undeniable case.

"No, if a man's looking fer shelter an' a willing woman and whiskey to go along with it, he takes his life in his hands and heads fer Rufus Brooks' hog ranch."

Sullivan nodded again. "Crow Wallace isn't a man who's easy to kill. If he's at the Brooks place, he'll be the toughest, baddest *hombre* there." He smiled. "That is, until I arrive."

Through snow flurries that bladed horizontally in a keening wind, Sullivan made out the glow of oil lamps in the distant darkness. He reckoned that was the place, unless the rancher had no liking for bounty hunters and had steered him wrong.

Well, he'd soon find out.

He urged his tired horse in the direction of the lights, then picked up an eyebrow of trail that led to an undercut limestone shelf about as high as a tall pine.

Under the torn sky, the area seemed a bleak, lonely, and dark place for a saloon and cathouse, but as Sullivan drew rein and looked around him, he decided that its isolation was probably one of its attractions. To an outlaw on the scout, a man who avoided the settlements and johnny law, it would be a haven of rest and plenty indeed.

Sullivan let his mount pick its way through a stand of Ponderosa pine then crossed a brush flat where a few struggling Gambel oaks rustled in the raw north wind. He came upon a well-marked trail, a wagon road that ran parallel to the base of the ridge then followed a gradual ramp to a broad shelf of rock.

Across a hundred yards of flat, a second ridge ascended like a gigantic step, its top thick with pine.

Most of Rufus Brooks' place, a saloon, and adjoining structure had been cut out of the rise, but they were fronted by a mud brick façade that gave them a Spanish flair.

To the left of the saloon's timber door, where Sullivan dismounted, was a painted blue coyote tall as a man. Its howling head was turned to the moon represented by a chipped white platter fastened to the wall.

The effect was quite artistic and he wondered if it was Brooks' work or that of a bored saloon girl.

If he were a betting man, his money would be on the girl.

The door swung open just as he slid his Henry from the saddle boot. He let the muzzle drop when he saw that it was a boy, a small, underfed Mexican with a mop of black hair and huge eyes.

"Take care of your horse, mister?" the boy asked.

"Seems like you ain't tall enough to rub him down," Sullivan said.

"I stand on a box. Brush him good."

It was only then that the bounty hunter noticed a barn

set in a clump of oaks, most of its front obscured by a massive limestone rock that had tumbled from the ridge during some ancient earthshake. "You got hay and oats in there?"

His question was answered by a thin man who stood framed in the doorway. "Hay with a scoop of oats, seventy-five cents."

Sullivan frowned. "A shade high, ain't it?"

As though he hadn't heard, the man continued. "Beer, ten cents. Whiskey, a dollar. The stew in the pot is a dollar a bowl if you provide your own eatin' iron."

Then, like a man who'd recited it many times before, "One hour, two dollars. All-nighter with bed, six dollars, and the young lady will expect champagne at ten dollars a bottle."

"What do you call this place?" Sullivan asked.

"Call it what you want to call it," the thin man said.

"Judging by your prices, I'd call it the Savoy."

"Take it or leave it,"

Sullivan tossed the reins of his sorrel to the Mexican boy. "Brush him down good and feed him hay and oats, and don't skimp on the oats."

"Nice looking hoss," the thin man said as the boy led the sorrel away. "How much you pay for a big American stud like that."

"Too much." Sullivan unbuttoned his sourdough, a tan-colored canvas coat with a heavy blanket lining that reached to his lean hips. His .44 Army Colt was holstered high in the horseman fashion.

He had killed four men with the graceful revolver, all

of them fugitives with dead or alive bounties on their heads. His conscience didn't keep him awake nights.

"I'm looking for a man goes by the name of Crow Wallace. Is he inside?"

The thin man shook his head. "I never ask a man his name. If he don't give it out, then it ain't none of my business. But mine's Rufus Brooks. Well known in these parts for my sweet, generous nature." He had the quick eyes of a bird of prey and his tall, scrawniness did not suggest physical weakness, but rather a lean, latent force that could move fast when called on to do so. Like a rapier blade.

"I don't doubt it," Sullivan said. "Now if you'll give me the road."

The inside of the saloon was pretty much what he expected. From the Mexican border to the Missouri Breaks, he'd been in a hundred just like it—dark, dingy dens where the oil lamps cast shadows and men with closed mouths and careful eyes stood still in the gloom. Every dugout shared in common the same stink, a raw mix of whiskey, spilled beer, sweat, vomit, piss, and cheap perfume.

The bar was a couple timber boards laid across barrels, a few bottles displayed on an old bookshelf behind, and above the bottles an embroidered sign.

Have You Written to MOTHER?

"What will it be, stranger?" Brooks asked.

Sullivan had already taken stock. Two shaggy men in

bearskin coats sprawled on an overstuffed sofa that was spilling its guts. A young Mexican girl in a state of considerable undress sat between them. The dugout behind the bar, a half-dome cut out of living limestone rock, was wide enough to accommodate two tables and some chairs. Three men holding greasy cards sat at a table sharing a bottle of whiskey.

One of the men, a breed with lank, black hair that fell over his back and ended at the top of his gun belt, looked up from his cards and saw Sullivan. "The game is poker, mister. Table stakes."

Sullivan took time to order a rye, then said, "I reckon not."

"Then go to hell," the breed said.

Sullivan smiled and said to Brooks, "Friendly folks."

The man shrugged. "He gave you an invite. That's neighborly."

"Man shouldn't refuse an invite," one of the bearskin coats said. "I mean, it ain't genteel."

"True words as ever was spoke, Clyde," his companion said. "I wonder what he'd say if old Queen Vic offered him a chair at her poker game."

The Mexican girl giggled. "That is silly." Her naked breasts were brown and small.

Sullivan ignored the comments. There was no profit in doing otherwise. He took off his gloves and reached into the inside pocket of his coat. He produced two things, a slender, silver cigar case and a piece of paper folded into a rectangle.

He chose a cheroot, lit it, then unfolded the paper and

smoothed it out on the bar. "Another rye." He turned toward the table. "Crow, your likeness don't do you justice. Makes you look almost human." He held up the wanted dodger to the breed and the men sitting with him.

"Can you read, Crow?" Sullivan asked. "Them big words where my finger is say, 'Wanted Dead or Alive.'"

Crow Wallace rose slowly to his feet, the chair screeching away from him along the stone floor. His right hand clawed over the handle of his Colt. "That ain't a dodger, mister. It's your death warrant." He had a strange way of talking, a lisp so pronounced that *mister* came out "mithter."

Sullivan could see his thick tongue move.

Wallace was a skinny little runt with buckteeth and a fish-pale face covered in red spots with yellow centers that gave him the look of a malignant teenager—which he was.

According to the dodger, Wallace was nineteen years old that winter, one of the new breed of draw fighters Texas had spawned by the hundreds after the War Between the States.

But young though he was, Wallace was a killer, fast and dangerous as a striking rattler.

"Here's how I see it, Crow," Sullivan said. "Unbuckle and drop the iron and bring them saddlebags over to me. Then we both walk out of here alive. See, that word right there says *Alive*."

Wallace smiled, a twisted, vicious grimace. "Then read this, bounty hunter." He drew.

He was fast. Real fast. Smooth as silk.

Wallace fired, fired again. One shot tugged at Sullivan's sleeve, the second split the air less than an inch from his ear.

Tam Sullivan jerked his gun and then adopted the duelist position, revolver extended in front of him with a straight arm, the inside of his left foot against the heel of his right. He thumbed back the Colt's hammer and fired.

Wallace took that shot smack in the middle of his forehead.

Already a dead man, Crow triggered his Colt dry and .36 caliber balls ricocheted off the floor then *spaaanged!* from wall to wall, precipitating a hasty stampede from the card table.

Sullivan shifted aim and centered on the chest of one of Wallace's companions. "You in? State your intentions."

"Hell, no, I'm not in," the man said. "I was only playing poker."

The older man hurrying behind him yelled, "I'm out of it. Don't shoot."

A movement flickered at the corner of Sullivan's eye.

Rufus Brooks eared back the hammers of a scatter-gun and flung the butt to his shoulder.

Sullivan fired by instinct.

The big .44 ball struck the side plate of the Greener. Badly mangled, it ranged upward into Brooks' throat just under his chin. By some strange quirk of velocity and energy, the ball continued its upward momentum and exited in an exclamation point of blood, brain, and bone from the top of the man's head.

Brooks stumbled back and the shotgun fell from his hands. He crashed against the bookshelf that toppled over and the *Have you written to* MOTHER? sign fell across his chest.

Sullivan glanced at the dead man. "She must be mighty proud o' you."

Both bearskin coats were on their feet and the young Mexican girl had vanished.

"You taking a hand in this?" Sullivan asked.

As the sound of hooves receded outside, the man called Clyde, a tinpan by the cut of his jib, shook his bearded head. "No we ain't, mister. Just don't expect no po-lite invites from me an' Jules here."

"He means to a fiddle soiree and such," Jules said with a French-tinged accent.

"I take that real hard," Sullivan said. "You boys disappoint me."

"Nothing personal," Clyde said. "But you shouldn't be around folks."

The door to the adjoining quarters opened and a slim woman who looked a tired and worn age stepped inside. She glanced at Sullivan's leveled Colt, dismissed it, then moved to the wreckage of the bar. For a moment she stared in silence at Rufus Brooks' lifeless body then spat in his face.

Sullivan smirked. "Not one to hold a grudge, are you honey?"

CHAPTER 3
Death of a Yankee

Bill Longley stood at his room window of the Bon-Ton Hotel and stared out sullenly at the sluggish river of mud the good folks of Comanche Crossing, New Mexico Territory, were pleased to call Main Street. Snow flurries cartwheeled in the wind and a wooden sign hanging outside a general store banged back and forth with the sound of a muffled drum.

By times, he was a past-thinking man, especially when it came to reminiscing about women he'd enjoyed and kills he particularly relished.

A grandfather clock in the hallway chimed midnight. The mud outside reminded him of another road in another time and place. . . .

The Camino Real, the old Spanish royal highway between San Antonio and Nacogdoches, ran within a mile of the Longley farm. On a cold, early December day in 1867 sixteen-year-old Bill was warned by his father to stay close because mounted Yankees had been seen patrolling the road.

Campbell Longley, who'd been a close friend of General Sam Houston and had helped bury the American dead at Goliad, had passed on two traits to young Bill. One was a virtue—his skill with firearms. The other, a vice—a pathological hatred of Yankees and blacks.

As snow flurried and the Camino Real turned to mud, Bill took his father's Navy revolver. Never one to avoid the chance of a confrontation with Yankee soldiers, he sneaked out of the house and headed for the highway.

"There are Yankees on the road! Stay away!" a woman wrapped in a blanket yelled at him from the shelter of a wild oak, frantically waving her hands.

"Where are they?" Bill hollered.

The woman pointed back down the highway. "That way. Stay clear. They'll kill you and eat you."

He walked up a gentle rise that led to the road. Snow clung to the brush and salted the trunks of the bare trees. As he stepped closer, he saw that the woman was old. Her gray eyes had faded to the color of smoke and the hair that showed under her bonnet was white. She was thin and looked hungry.

She carried a wicker basket, as did all the old men and women who scavenged along the Camino Real. She'd already found an old horseshoe and what looked to be a dented can of meat.

"Go back, son," the woman said. "That Yankee up

*there will arrest you and then you'll get skun an' your
hide stretched on a frame."*

"Who, grandma? Who'll arrest me?"

*"Black man on a hoss, wearing a blue coat. He's got
stripes on his sleeves and a rifle."*

"Did he say anything to you?"

*The woman shivered, from cold or memory he
couldn't tell.*

*"He told me to get the hell off the road. Said there's
too much thievery going on along the highway."*

*Bill's dark, sudden anger flared. "A black man spoke
to you like that?"*

*"Son, since the war ended, a black man can speak to
a white woman any way he damn pleases. Or didn't you
know that?"*

*"Not in San Jacinto County, he can't. Where the hell
is he?"*

"That way. Down the road apiece."

*Bill nodded and laid his hand on the woman's skinny
shoulder. "You go home now. I'll take care of the black.
He'll never sass a white woman again." He opened his
coat and revealed the Navy in his waistband. "I got me
some uppity negro medicine right here."*

*He watched until the old lady vanished from sight
behind a hill, then followed her directions, avoiding the
worst of the mud puddles as he walked, head bowed
against the chill wind and slashing sleet.*

*He saw the soldier sitting his horse under the thin
cover of an oak. A Spencer carbine lay across the*

pommel of his McClellan saddle as he intently peeled a green apple with a folding knife.

The corporal spotted Bill and took account of his ragged coat, pale, underfed face, summing him up as local white trash. Taking a bite of the apple, the soldier made a face and tossed it away. He wiped his mouth with the back of his hand and kneed his horse into motion, approaching Bill at a leisurely walk. The Spencer was upright, the butt resting on his thigh.

When he was a few feet away, the corporal drew rein and again studied the lanky teenager, not liking what he saw. "You, Reb. Git off the damned highway. We've had enough of thieves and footpads preying on decent folks."

"And if I don't?" Bill said, his anger simmering.

The soldier leveled his rifle. "Then I'll damn well blow you off the road."

Bill whimpered a little. "Please, mister, don't. I didn't mean no harm."

"You look like dirty, thieving Reb spawn to me," the soldier said. "Now get off the highway and run home to your mama and ask her to dry your tears."

The soldier then made a mistake. He turned his back on Bill.

It was a gesture of contempt that cost Corporal Thetas Washington, age twenty-six, his life.

Bill drew from the waistband, aimed at a spot between the shoulder blades and pulled the trigger. The .36 caliber ball shattered the black man's spine as he cried out in pain and rage at the time and manner of his death.

The sixteen-year-old didn't fire a second time. Powder and ball cost money his father didn't have. He waited until the soldier toppled from his horse then stepped beside him.

A clean kill!

The man was as dead as he was ever going to be.

Working quickly for fear of being discovered, Bill searched the man's pockets. He took twenty-three Yankee dollars, a nickel watch and chain, and a whiskey flask. Made from pewter, the Bonnie Blue Flag was engraved on its side. Under that was another engraving. "Lieut. Joseph Herbert, 17th Georgia Infantry."

Longley uncorked the flask, fastidiously wiped it off, then took a swig. He gathered the reins of the dead man's horse, picked up the Spencer, and walked back to the farm.

He had his first kill, a black carpetbagger at that, and he was so elated that even the icy wind and spinning sleet could not chill him.

Bill Longley was pulled from his pleasant reverie by a shadow of movement on the street. A careful man, he turned down the oil lamp and stepped to the window again, one of his beautiful .44 Dance revolvers in his fist.

The night was so torn and dark it took his eyes a few moments to adjust to the gloom. When they did, he saw a tall man on a sorrel horse stop outside the town sheriff's darkened office.

After a few moments, the rider swung out of the saddle and stepped to what Longley at first thought was a packhorse. Only when the tall man dumped the horse's burden into the street did he see that it was a body.

While the tall man worked the kinks out of his back and looked around him, Longley quickly moved away from the window. Suddenly he felt an odd sense of unease . . . as though a goose had just flown over his grave.